IN TOO DEEP

by

ROXANE BEAUFORT

Published by **CHIMERA**
ISBN 9781780806860

Chapter 1

'So you want me to try and get photos of Theona Blue, preferably *flagrante delicto?*' said Will Denton, staring across the desk at his editor-in-chief. The leather upholstered swivel chair creaked at the slightest movement of his big-framed body and long legs.

'Not try, succeed,' Denise Spalding answered brusquely. Talented, confident and glamorous, she ruled supreme, an iron fist in a velvet glove.

Will pulled a wry face. 'She's a tough nut to crack,' he reminded, 'is allergic to the press, and surrounded by heavies.'

'I know all that. This is why it's essential that *Hi Life* get to her first. Our readers expect the latest low-down on the rich and famous. We must get her before any other magazine does. You can do it, Will.'

He glanced at her from under his strongly marked eyebrows, aware of his cock hardening as it always did when he was near her. Power was an irresistible aphrodisiac, and Denise was very powerful indeed. She was one of the sexiest ladies he had ever met and, while a confirmed bachelor, he was something of an expert. Concealed by her prestigious mahogany desk, he surreptitiously fondled his balls and caressed his prick through his trousers.

Denise had always been a great lay, and she was a genuine redhead, too. The foxy triangle at the apex of her thighs matched her fashionably short, flicked-back hair. Bill ached to see it. If he pleased her by promising to get the gen on the famous rock-singer, then maybe she'd let him fuck her again, perhaps right now. They'd had an on-off relationship from the beginning, when she first started working for the magazine. That had been five years ago. But she was capricious. He never knew where he stood with her. Now approaching forty, a craggily handsome man with unruly brown hair, he had already been an ace reporter when she started out as a rookie with a college degree in media studies.

It had hardly seemed just that because of this diploma she had been made editor instead of him. But, as he had philosophically concluded, who ever said life was going to be fair? The powers that be who owned the magazine wanted a young woman, a modern thinking woman, with a finger on the pulse of today's happenings. He, on the other hand, had worked his way up through the ranks of journalism. He'd seen it all, been there, done that, got the T-shirt, but she had netted the job.

He'd not resented it, and could have moved had the situation proved too irksome, but after a while he'd had to admit that she was the right choice - as modern as tomorrow with an eye for trends and attitudes, attuned to popular opinion.

'Okay, you shall have Miss Theona Blue served up on toast,' he vowed, giving her the full benefit of his wide smile.

Denise rose, tall and graceful in a tailored skirt and silk blouse. 'Good,' she said, and came over to him, leaning against his shoulder. 'I knew you'd agree.'

'Have I ever let you down?' he asked, breathing in that gorgeous aroma of French perfume mixed with her own personal essence. His nose twitched as he caught the hint of something else - that of female arousal. Undoubtedly her fiery bush would be dampening.

'Not since that furore about your exposé of the private life of country and western singer, Delia Eddy. It was an audacious piece of investigative journalism, but you fouled up, Will, and Delia sued *Hi Life* and won her case. It cost the magazine plenty and the bosses weren't amused. They wanted to fire you, but I put in a word.'

'Why?' he asked, slipping an arm round her pliant waist, male pride dented because it was she who had got him off the hook.

She looked down into his face and smiled. 'Because you're a good writer and a first-class fuck.'

'What I said about Delia was true,' he averred, reaching up to feel her breasts through the silk, testing their weight and fullness and if she was wearing a bra, letting his thumbs revolve over the hardened nipples.

She didn't resist, gasping with pleasure, then saying huskily, 'I know.'

Will started to work open the buttons, absorbed in his task, but continuing to state his case. 'There was Delia, pretending to be a homespun, girl-next-door type, and in reality shagging every manager and band member on the circuit. I didn't pull any punches.'

'You never have done,' she whispered as he unfastened her blouse and then fondled her breasts through the cream lace, underwired cups. They were within an inch of his lips.

'I can't help it,' he went on, blowing gently on her nipples, his erection tenting the front of his trousers. 'That's how I am; I hate bull-shit.'

'Did you have to be quite so sarcastic?'

Will slipped a finger into the top of her bra, finding one rosy teat and teasing it into an even more needful peak. 'Sarcastic? I'm that all right. We Brits have a warped sense of humour, haven't we? Something to do with the climate; how can we be other than ironic when we can have a heat wave in March and snow in April?'

'Keep it under control when you interview Theona,' she advised, but her voice was unsteady as one of his hands left her breasts and wormed its way up under her skirt, encountering stockings, and a smooth area of thigh between a garter belt and the edge of her panties.

He brushed it aside, thrilling at the feel of crisp pubic floss, then the delicate silkiness of her sex-lips. The copious juice betrayed her excitement, and the throbbing in his groin increased. He put a hand behind her, palming her rounded buttocks and wondering yet again what she would do if he put her across his knee and spanked her. The thought of seeing those round globes turning scarlet under his blows almost made him come in his pants.

Would she get off on it? He rather thought she might; a woman in control of her business life relinquishing her will to a masterful man. He had never spanked, whipped or caned anyone, though it was one of his fantasies and he

3

often masturbated while looking at photos of bound and gagged girls, naked and ready for beating.

She relaxed, parting her legs slightly to make his invasion of her secret female parts that much easier. Will lost his nerve, deciding not to attempt to chastise her - not this time. He didn't want anything to put her off, dipping a finger into her moist vulva and massaging her swollen clitoris. Feeling her shiver and wanting to delay her orgasm, he stood up, his hands at her waist now, bending his head and finding her mouth. His tongue entered its honeyed depth, and her own responded with fierce little jabs. She moaned, low in her throat, and he held her tight, pressing her pubis to the bulge straining behind his fly, letting her know how much he wanted her.

'I've told my secretary I'm not to be disturbed,' she said, dragging her mouth from his. 'There are condoms in the drawer.'

Spring sunlight streamed through the plate glass windows of her splendid office, with its view over London's Chelsea Harbour. It struck across the red velvet couch that was a part of the impressive equipment, like the state of the art computer, the fax machine, the drinks cabinet. Many a time that settee had provided them with a place on which to fornicate.

Denise lay back on it and closed her eyes and Will hovered over her, hearing the muffled sounds of traffic passing far below, and the distant buzz of the people, machines and organisation needed to produce a glossy magazine like theirs. But all was muted, sounding like the sea pounding on some far off shore.

He knelt by the couch almost reverently, as if he was before an altar. In his own way, he adored this woman, with her sharp mind and lithe body. Her face was fashionably made up, yet her beauty seemed timeless. There was a touch of wantonness about her that contrasted tantalisingly with the smart, strictly functional clothes she wore to work, giving a hint of the real woman within.

He lifted her skirt again, and then held her hips, raising her bottom so the material would not ruck and cause her discomfort. She opened her hazel eyes and stared at him raptly, as if waiting for him to touch her. He dipped down and tongued her thighs between the taut white suspenders. She spread her legs wider, gripping his head in her hands, guiding him. He nosed her panties aside, running his tongue over her cleft before taking them off. He brought them to his mouth, inhaling the fragrance of her sex that clung like incense. Then he stared at her, seeing the russet, neatly trimmed wedge, the plump mound displaying its darkly enticing slit.

Denise tossed her head from side to side and her hands clasped her breasts, scooping them from the bra cups and playing with the red-brown nipples, pulling them, rolling them between her fingers. Will leaned nearer and bent her legs at the knee so that her thighs fell apart, the avenue widening, pink labia unfurling, crowned by her engorged clit.

He controlled his lust, but relieved his cock by unzipping. It shot out, long and sturdy, it's naked helm shiny with jism. Denise grabbed at it, running her silver lacquered fingernails up and down the stalk, examining the purplish dome, tracing each ridge and prominent vein. Knowing he couldn't hold on much longer he slipped a digit into her snatch, wriggled it around and then smoothed her moisture across her labia and over the needy bud.

He massaged it firmly, but when her jerking hips and gasping breath told him she was on the edge he reduced the pressure, delaying orgasm.

She lay still now, her eyes glazed, her lips as wet and lustrous as her labial wings. She placed her hand over his, whispering, 'Make it last. Give me a johnny and I'll put it on for you.'

He found the packet, handed it to her, heard her tear it open, and watched as she rolled the flesh-coloured rubber over his dick, her touch magical, his climax just around the corner.

Prepared now, he wetted her slit with a dribble of saliva. He licked her and she cried out with pleasure, then his fingers took over again, trailing back and forth across her delta.

'My clit!' she muttered fiercely. 'Rub it now!'

He did just that, no longer gentle but subjecting it to strong friction. She moaned, her hips lifted, her head snapped back and he felt her throb against his finger. He held her, widened her quivering cunt and sank three fingers into her hot wetness. Not his prick. He wasn't about to distract her from her moment of bliss. But, as the tension released, he kissed her mouth and enclosed her sex in his hand. Then, as she moved to lie full-length on the couch, he eased himself into her welcoming sheath, pushing his phallus in deep.

She heaved against him and he felt her inner muscles clamping round his cock. He braced himself on straight arms, trousers tangling round his legs, his movements frantic as he spurted into the condom.

'I want you to take Julia Jones with you on the Theona Blue job,' was the first thing she said as they lay on the couch afterwards.

This roused him from the sleepy euphoria that follows sex. 'Julia? Why her? She's green as grass and hopelessly naive. A pain in the arse, to be exact.'

'She needs experience. She's bright and enthusiastic and has that special quality about her which is so attractive to men and women alike. Don't tell me you haven't wanted to shag her.'

'She's a blonde bimbo,' he grumbled, taking off the rubber, knotting it and dropping it into the wastepaper basket. 'More of a liability than anything else. She's always losing things; notebooks, cameras, items of clothing. I can't see it working out.'

Denise shot him a cool glance, once more in charge. 'You'll take her with you. It's not up for debate,' she said decisively.

Julia was surprised when she was summoned to Denise Spalding's sanctum next morning. She had just come into work, expecting to cope with the usual tedium of being a junior reporter where nothing much exciting happened.

She could hardly believe her ears when she and Will were given their brief. Denise was everything Julia aspired to be: worldly, glamorous, knowing the trade inside out, captain of the good ship *Hi Life*. Julia was flabbergasted to learn she'd been considered worthy of going on an assignment with Will, a senior newshound of renown.

They'd left at noon, heading west in Will's Peugeot. He'd been conversational on the way, but once they had booked in at a hotel near Penzance he had been decidedly abrupt. She wondered if it was because she had misdirected them several times, finding map reading confusing. Then she thought it might be because they had separate rooms. Will had been trying to seduce her ever since she joined the team. Maybe he imagined this would be an ideal opportunity, but though she respected his skills, and was flattered by his attentions, she wasn't about to jump into bed with him. Her career was of paramount importance.

The five-star hotel was old and picturesque. It had once been a coaching inn and gleamed with antique brass, panelling, low-beamed ceilings and open fireplaces. Denise had booked them in there because it was not far from the palatial cliff-top retreat where their prey was allegedly staying. Julia was overawed. She could never have afforded such a place, but the magazine was paying.

On arrival in her room she spent some time simply prowling around, admiring the carpets and fittings and the en suite bathroom with its little tablets of lavender-scented soap and sachets of shampoo, provided for the guests and completely free. There was a phone, a television, a small fridge containing miniature bottles of alcohol and cartons of fresh milk, and a breakfast bar with a kettle and tea, coffee and drinking chocolate. The curtains were chintz, the leaded windows affording a view of the sea. The double bed had brass posts and a canopy draped in lace, and the secretaire was provided with writing paper, envelopes and pens bearing the hotel's logo, and a *What's on in Cornwall* guide, complete with a roadmap.

'Wow!' she exclaimed, bouncing on the springy mattress. 'I wish Arlene were here. She'd go mental over all this!'

She and Arlene went back a long way, one-time college students and now house sharing in London. Julia had chosen to go into journalism and Arlene was an up and coming dress designer. They were as different as chalk and cheese; Arlene vivacious and beautiful, with a stream of lovers; Julia pretty, keen, gauche, and a virgin.

Much as she was curious about sex, she was an incurable romantic, had been hurt by boyfriends several times, dumped because she refused to go the whole hog with them, and was looking for Mr Right. Arlene voiced the opinion that she was barking. No such creature existed. She had added cynically that all men really wanted was to get into a girl's knickers, and it was up to women to use them and abuse them in return.

Julia had watched a succession of personable men pass through the house, pausing in Arlene's bedroom for a spell, then given the elbow by that forthright young lady. Julia wished she had her insouciance, embarrassed to bump into one or other of them on her way to the lavatory. Sometimes they were naked or had a bathrobe on, or had stopped to don boxer shorts. She peeked at them, seen well-developed chests, pecs and legs, looked at rumpled dark hair, or fair or even ginger. Occasionally she'd been given a flash of a semi-erect penis surmounting a pair of balls, swinging in their hairy sac. She'd always blushed, stammered and passed on.

'Don't be daft,' Arlene had chided. 'You're fine. The chaps fancy you rotten, but you always scurry away like a frightened mouse. What's wrong with you? Don't you like any of them? Are you a lesbian?'

Julia wasn't and said as much, but she was unsure of herself, still experimenting with her naturally blonde, wavy hair, and trying out various styles of clothes. Arlene used her as a model, and encouraged her to show off her curvaceous figure, praising her pert breasts, slender waist and shapely bottom. Julia wished she was taller, perching herself on high heels or thick-soled trainers to add a few inches.

She stared at her reflection in the pier-glass, wondering what to wear for the evening's adventure. Will had told her he intended to reconnoitre as soon as they'd had dinner. He'd obtained a map of the area and knew precisely where Theona Blue was hiding, and the layout of the house and grounds. But Denise had ordered them to look inconspicuous, as if they were a couple of tourists.

Julia rooted through her grip-bag, pulling out her one good dress (a present from Arlene). It was a flimsy slip, with a short flaring skirt and camisole bodice brief to the point of immodesty. Blush-pink and resembling silk, it added colour to her cheeks as she held it up against herself. This would do for dinner, and she'd take along the matching bolero jacket for later.

Thrilled by her surroundings, she couldn't wait to take off her jeans and vest top, white bra and panties. Then, naked and feeling somehow wanton and hedonistic, she headed for the shower stall. The tiles had a floral pattern, the chromium shone, and she found a tube of chestnut smelling gel, spun the tap and warm water jetted over her. In these movie-star conditions her thoughts turned to sex; disturbing thoughts that made her nipples peak with more than contact with the spray. She stood with her legs apart a little, massaging the gel over her breasts, seeing the small avalanche of foam gliding into her dimpled navel and out again. It mingled with her golden pubes and disappeared into her cleft. Her hand drifted down to part the wet, silky hair and press on her clitoris.

Virgin she might be, but had discovered the joys of self-gratification long ago. At first she hadn't realised what it was, thinking that when she played with her pussy at night it was merely a bedtime ritual associated with sleep. It wasn't till later that a friend told her all about it and advised her how to use her fingers to best effect. Julia had never looked back. She was interested in men, longing to fall in love and experience intercourse, but sometimes wondered if anything could be as beautifully satisfying as fingering her own genitals.

She sighed, tensed, waited for the magic to begin. The gel was deliciously slippery, her finger coasting over her clit. She watched herself, wiping the mirror clear of steam, seeing that naughty blonde frigging herself, one hand holding the labial folds apart, the middle finger of the other slightly crooked as it teased her little organ into full stiffness. The water was reduced to a trickle, falling over her shoulder and running down to her feet. She worked her clit, stroked it carefully, her nipples becoming redder, hardening in response.

7

The temptation to bring herself off was too strong to resist. She wanted to make it last forever, but her clit decided otherwise and she couldn't stop rubbing it. She felt the sensation gathering in her loins and at the base of her spine, was rising from peak to peak, borne on ever increasing waves. The feeling reached her toes, clenched on the wet shower tray, and then roared back up her thighs, culminating in such a sweet burst of ecstasy that she whimpered, shuddering at each successive spasm.

With a deep sigh she came down from the heights, feeling guilty, but loving it too much to ever give it up. She finished washing and reached for the shampoo, dunking her head under the jets. Arlene told her she was lucky to have such curls. She never had to bother with hairdressers, apart from a trim now and again, but mostly she let it do as it pleased, tousled and shining. Yet she sometimes became bored with it, wishing it could be trained into a sophisticated coiffure, making her appear more mature.

As Arlene was fond of saying, 'No one's ever satisfied with their looks. My nose is too big. So are my tits. You'd like to be taller and change your hair. Stop fretting. You're okay as you are.'

Julia remembered this as she towelled herself dry, then blow-dried her hair and moisturised her skin with body lotion. She chose a new pair of ivory panties, hip-high and fastened with ribbons, and a matching bra. She didn't have much money to spend on clothes. Living in London cost a bomb and there wasn't a lot over for fripperies, but she had decided to pack her best underwear. One never knew what might happen and she intended to be prepared. The nights were still cool, so she added pale hold-up stockings, slipped her feet into her shoes, and dropped her dress over her head. A light application of make-up, a dash of perfume, and she was ready.

In a fit of bravado and extravagance she left all the lights on, let herself out and locked the door, slipping the key into her handbag.

'Shush! Keep the noise down,' Will hissed.

Julia had been doing her best to be quiet, though it was difficult in the dark. She kept tripping over things. Her thigh muscles ached from crouching. Bushes scratched her. Whenever they paused for breath, as now, she was terribly afraid they'd be spotted.

Once dinner was over Will had been ready to go, sensibly dressed in a black polo sweater and black trousers. He carried a shoulder bag containing his camera with the telephoto lens and a torch, and Julia trotted along behind him to where the car was parked. A short drive and he had made her get out, leaving the vehicle in a pitch-black, leafy lane and heading off on foot.

She'd almost had to run to keep up with his long stride, and had nearly cannoned into him when he stopped suddenly. That was when he cautioned her. As far as she could see in the gloom, they were standing by a high stone wall that seemed to stretch into infinity, and when Will shone the torch upwards the light was reflected off broken glass set in the copings.

'Bugger,' he muttered. 'The place is like a bloody fortress.'

8

'Is this it? Where Theona Blue is staying?'

He switched off the torch but she managed to catch his nod. 'It sure is,' he said.

'But we'll never get inside, will we?' It looked impregnable to her.

'Leave it to me, my dear Watson,' he replied mysteriously. 'We'll go for Plan B.'

He melted into the darkness and Julia hurried behind him. They seemed to be miles from civilisation. The way became rougher and undergrowth had to be pushed through. She heard Will cursing just ahead of her, then he whispered triumphantly, 'I've found it.'

'What?' she faltered.

'A way in,' and he flashed the torch over a low arched doorway set in the wall. It was half concealed by ivy and looked as if it hadn't budged for centuries. 'Denise was right. She told me she used to come here on holiday when she was a kid, and knew the former owners. She spent a lot of time here, friendly with their children, and she gave me a layout, including this secret door. Come on, let's get it open - but quietly does it.'

'Supposing it's locked?' Julia ventured.

'Supposing it isn't?' he chided, tearing at the ivy and clearing the door. 'Lend a hand, oh ye of little faith.'

In for a penny, in for a pound, Julia thought, and added her weight to his as he heaved against it with his shoulder. It resisted, creaking. He was wrong, she concluded. It was locked and probably bolted on the other side. No one would leave such an entrance free for intruders.

'It's giving, I can feel it,' Will grunted, redoubling his efforts.

The rusted hinges groaned, the thick oak juddered, the bottom of the door scraped on stone as it yielded inch by tortuous inch.

'I shouldn't think it's been opened for years,' Julia gasped, curiosity taking over. She never could resist a challenge.

Will squeezed through the narrow gap, taking the light with him. Julia didn't hesitate, scrambling in after him. She almost shrieked when cobwebs trailed stickily over her face, but remembered in time that silence was essential. Blackness, the smell of dank earth, the sharp odour of trampled vegetation surrounded her.

'Will, where are you?' she squeaked, and then jumped at the feel of his hand on her arm.

'It's all right. We're behind some bushes in a neglected part of the garden. Follow me.'

She didn't need telling. There was no way she was going to stay there alone. It was definitely creepy. She almost expected to come across Count Dracula's tomb, and she didn't have a wooden stake or a crucifix anywhere about her person. Arlene, she whimpered inside, I wish you were here. I don't think I want to be a reporter after all.

Will was ahead and she kept her eye on him. He parted the last screen of tangled greenery. A bramble whipped back, catching in Julia's skirt. She tugged.

It resisted. She heard the material tear.

'I've just ruined my new dress,' she grumbled, feeling the ripped fabric fall away from her right thigh and trying to hold it together with one hand.

'Shut up,' he growled. 'We've been lucky so far. Keep your eyes skinned for the bodyguards.'

All was quiet and they tiptoed from their hiding place. Will skirted the overgrown kitchen garden, getting ever nearer to the house. It was illumined by a great sweep of arc lights. They could hear noises now from the terrace at the rear, laughter, splashing, and the heady beat of the salsa.

Will was like a bloodhound on the scent. Julia could feel the tension in him and her own excitement escalated. She could do it, after all. She had the instincts of a sleuth that would make her into a top-grade journalist. She saw that Will had his camera at the ready, holding it like a weapon. She got hers out, priming it. It was smaller than Will's, but powerful. If he didn't get pictures, then she certainly would.

They crept past a large greenhouse, and reached a hedge which separated them from the main terrace. A kidney-shaped swimming pool lit up from inside, lay there like a blue lagoon. There was a paved area with tubs of flowers, sun-loungers, ironwork chairs and round tables. Julia could see figures by the pool - a naked woman sprawled on her back on the tiles, and a muscular black man with a shaven head, also naked.

Fascinated by what they were doing, Julia edged closer, forgetting Will and their mission. Now a rhododendron in full bloom concealed her. 'It's her,' Will's voice grated in her ear. 'That's Theona, and he's her trainer.'

He had his camera aimed in their direction. Julia heard the whirr as he took picture after picture. She could hardly think, every nerve and sense concentrated on Theona and her lover. His cock was huge, rising from a tangle of black hair, long, thick and skyward pointing. She envied Theona, who fastened her hand around this monumental object, her fingers unable to circle the girth. It looked deep purple in colour from that distance, and the mushroom-like dome shone.

Julia slipped a hand down to her quim, unable to resist pressing her gusset against her wet and aching clit. It throbbed through the delicate material and she passed her finger over it. She couldn't stop looking at the man's weapon, wondering how a thing that size could possibly be inserted in a woman's tender channel. Theona chuckled, pulled back his foreskin even further and slowly moved her head towards his crotch. Julia saw her tongue gliding round it, her lips kissing, and then she gradually took it into her mouth, sinking down till her nose was pressed against his wiry pubes.

She'd surely choke, Julia thought. But no, Theona's capacity seemed to be endless, her throat accustomed to such an activity. And Julia passed her tongue over her own lips, imagining what it would feel like to have her mouth plugged by such a big cock.

The man laughed, deep in his chest, and raising one broad hand, slapped Theona on her bare buttocks. His baritone voice boomed across the terrace, 'You dirty bitch. You need to be punished. What are you?'

'I'm a dirty bitch, Gus - a bad girl,' Theona retorted gleefully, and leapt up. With a hand pressed into the small of her back he propelled her across the terrace and they disappeared inside the house.

Beside herself with frustrated lust and curiosity, Julia broke cover, dodging from one patch of shadow to the next, eager to press her nose against the window that now sprang into light. She had the impression that Will was somewhere behind her, but couldn't be sure. At that moment it didn't seem to matter. All she wanted to do was watch the couple, see what they would do next, satisfy the burning desire to learn all she could about sex. Her nipples felt sore, chafed by her dress, and her panties were damp between her legs.

The window was slightly above eye-level, but she climbed onto a stone flower-filled urn, laddering her stockings in the process. This didn't matter. Nothing did, save the astonishing spectacle presenting itself to her.

She was staring into what she at first took to be a gymnasium. This must be where Theona did her training, keeping that marvellous body in perfect shape. But now the singer was bent over a vaulting horse, her tawny ringlets streaming down on one side of it, breasts pressed against the padding, her nubile body arched, her generous buttocks bare. The man she'd called Gus, a veritable giant in height and strength, was drawing her arms down and fastening cuffs on her wrists, attached to the contraption by chains. He did the same to her legs, forcing them apart, each ankle strapped to rings.

From her vantage point, Julia looked straight into the dark crease that divided Theona's bottom cheeks. She could see the tight rosebud of her anus, the hairy outer labia, the wet pink inner pair and the engorged clitoris poking out between. A quick glance around showed Julia that the padded horse was not the only piece of furniture in the room. There was a wooden crosspiece, a table with holes at strategic points in its length, also fitted with rings and chains. A rack ran along one wall from which hung whips and canes, flails and rods, bundles of leather harnesses, and articles that looked like gags and blindfolds.

Julia grasped the windowsill, camera forgotten in her excitement. What on earth was this place and why did it contain such weird and alarming objects? Yet the frightening aspect of it was making her adrenaline flow, and she was aware that her panties were damper than ever. Then her eyes nearly popped out of her head as Gus paced over to the rack and carefully selected a long-handled, flexible paddle covered in white leather. He swished it, then pressed his thumb against it and let go. The paddle twanged.

He took up a stance at Theona's hindquarters, his muscles rippling under that shiny dark skin, his haunches tight, his spread thighs supporting his trunk, his erection huge, though only partly roused. Julia held her breath. Gus raised one mighty, muscle-knotted arm and the paddle thwacked down on Theona's right buttock. She yelped, jerked, strained at her bonds. Gus threw back his arm again and the paddle walloped across her left cheek. The right one was already reddening. Julia's heart thundered, her clit demanding that she rub it. She saw Theona writhing, heard her cries, but now they held a new note, a keening wail like a cat on heat. With a jarring shock, Julia realised the singer was actually enjoying it!

Now Gus stood between her legs, smoothed his hands over the flaming red blotches embroidered on her rump, then took his massive prick and introduced the helm to her wet cunt. Theona moaned and lifted her hips as far as her restraints would allow. He reached underneath her, massaging her clit, and she shrieked her pleasure. Gus's powerful hips propelled his cock at a rapid rate. He thrust in and out of her, every inch of rippling back, neat waist and taunt bum proclaiming his athleticism. Poetry in motion, Julia thought, while thought was still possible. He tensed, flung back his head and cried out, then slumped over Theona, emptied of spunk.

At that moment, when Julia was just about to join them in their coming, she was toppled from her perch. She struggled against the hands that held her, shouting up at her assailant, a bald-headed, broken-nosed bruiser. 'What the hell are you doing? Let me go at once!'

'You ain't going nowhere, deary,' the man proclaimed. 'We have ways of dealing with nasty little trespassers like you.'

This galvanised her into action. She clawed, spat and kicked at him, trying to bring her knee up and jab him in the balls, but he simply laughed and squeezed her tightly in his iron-hard arms. She could hear another commotion, and a glance told her that Will, too, had been apprehended. One thickset man was grappling with him, while another had snatched his camera.

'Come on, you!' he shouted. 'And Roy, bring that nosy tart. We'll see what Miss Blue has to say about you. She don't take kindly to intruders. You'll most likely spend the night in the nick!'

Chapter 2

Whatever Julia expected when frogmarched into the house, it certainly wasn't the magnificent library in which she now found herself.

The light from crystal chandeliers played on jewel-hued Persian rugs and parquet flooring. The walls were lined with glass-fronted shelves containing leather-bound books. Large landscapes hung in gilded frames. There were heavily carved oak chairs and tables, a fireplace with a ceiling-high hood upheld by stone Titans, and a deeply cushioned chesterfield upon which reclined the woman she had last seen tied over a vaulting-horse - Theona Blue.

She was swathed in an exotic silk djellaba and Gus, standing beside her, arms folded over his chest, wore a towel knotted round his hips. Julia was dragged forward and Roy kneed the backs of her legs. She fell, facedown, at Theona's feet. She had never felt more humiliated. She struggled to rise, but he kept a hand on her neck, forcing her into a submissive position.

'What's all this?' Theona said, and Julia lifted her head high enough to meet the interest in the singer's amber eyes.

'Found her looking in the window of the gym,' Roy grunted, and then jerked his thumb to where Will stood, fuming, between the two other guards. 'Ken and

Joe got him as he was taking photographs. I reckon they're reporters, madam.'

'There was no need to throw my camera in the pool,' Will raged. 'It's worth a lot. Who is going to pay for it?'

'No doubt you're insured,' Theona replied coolly, eyeing him from head to foot, 'I take no responsibility. You have no business being here. I could have you arrested. Who are you, and what's your little friend's name?'

Will threw off his captors and stepped forward. Anger blazed in his eyes as he glared at her. 'I'm Will Denton, and the young lady is Julia Jones.'

'You're paparazzi,' she sneered, her robe parting over the deep V between her breasts. 'A disgusting breed.' As she crossed one golden-tanned leg over the other the garment slithered open, revealing a breathtaking glimpse of thigh and a delicate bare foot with an arched instep.

'Not so,' Will protested, apparently unmoved by this display, facing her and her heavies. 'I work for a reputable magazine - *Hi Life*. You may have heard of it.'

'I have indeed, and what do you want with me?' Theona rose with all the agility of a pampered cat. She prowled round the kneeling Julia and sashayed up to Will, subjecting him to a heavy-lidded stare, standing so close that the tips of her breasts brushed the front of his sweater.

'I'd like to interview you and take photographs,' he answered and Julia, watching, admired his cool.

'Is that so?' Theona purred, lifted a hand and ran it casually through his hair. 'What are you prepared to pay?'

'I wasn't instructed to negotiate a fee,' he returned, and his face was expressionless, his lack of reaction to her closeness provoking her to persist in her attentions.

Her fingers wandered across his chest, finding the hidden nubs of his male nipples and tweaking them. 'But if I give you what you ask, then I'm entitled to something in return,' she stated flatly, and passed the tip of her tongue over her red lips.

'That very much depends on your price.'

'I'm sure we can come to some arrangement that's beneficial to all of us,' she said and, reaching down, held his erection, rubbing it through his trousers.

'It's a deal,' Will growled, his voice no longer steady.

'But you'll take shots of me clothed and write a sensible, career-oriented, non-salacious piece about me,' she went on. 'I may permit you to include Gus, or I may not.'

'You call the shots.'

'I always do. And now we'll play before we get down to business.' She left him abruptly and turned to Julia. 'Get up,' she ordered.

Julia staggered to her feet. She was mortally ashamed of her appearance, convinced that she looked a mess. Her stockings were wrinkled, her torn skirt barely covered her thighs and, during the tussle with Roy, the ribbons tying her panties had snapped and she had been forced to step out of them. To her eternal shame, she had seen him pick them up and take a long sniff at the tiny bundle

13

before thrusting it into his pocket.

Theona had the advantage of height, even though shoeless, and Julia was forced to look up at her. 'We meant no harm—'

'Of course you did!' Theona snapped. 'Invading my privacy! How dare you? What did you see, and how much?' She flung round to Roy, shouting, 'Destroy her camera, too. I won't be made the butt of the gutter-press.'

'*Hi Life* isn't like that!' Julia exclaimed, remembering Denise and the pride they all took in the magazine.

'I'll bet,' Theona scoffed, and narrowed her eyes, examining Julia with as much attention to detail as she had Will.

Her stare was unnerving, embarrassing and exciting. Julia couldn't rid herself of the pictures of the singer being paddled by Gus. Her own buttocks stung as she remembered the red blotches spreading over the rounded hillocks, and she wondered if Theona felt pain every time she sat down. How long before such marks faded? These thoughts obsessed her and, with Theona so close and Gus not far away, she experienced an ache within her impossible to assuage by anything except orgasm.

Then, suddenly, Theona hissed, 'Take your clothes off.'

'Me?' Julia's eyes widened and her hands flew instinctively to her breasts.

'Yes. I want to see what you're made of. You too, Mr Denton,' she added sarcastically.

'Oh, please, no formality; call me Will,' he answered, equally caustic. 'Are you sure you're ready for this? Many women find me alarmingly well-endowed.'

'I'm used to well-endowed,' she replied, and looked directly at his fly-closure. 'I'd be surprised if you had anything I haven't seen already.'

Julia waited for his lead, but Theona's ringed fingers shot up under her ragged skirt and closed round her pussy. The shock of it was electrifying and she gave a long quivering sigh as Theona started to move her index finger. She was conscious of Will and the other men focusing on her. 'Oh, stop it,' she begged, but without much conviction.

'You don't mean that,' Theona chuckled. 'Where are your panties?'

'They fell down, Roy has them,' Julia managed to gasp, pleasure overwhelming her as Theona rubbed her swollen lips and bud. She couldn't help swaying her hips in time to that sensual motion, the tide of ecstasy rising, threatening to swamp her, destroying all reason and control.

'Good, isn't it?' Theona mocked. 'I can tell you're a slave to your desires.'

'I'm still a virgin,' she protested, helpless as, at a nod from his mistress, Roy eased off her bolero jacket and slid the straps of her dress and bra down, baring her breasts.

'A virgin, eh? That's a rare commodity,' Theona cooed, and called to Gus, 'D'you hear that, lover-boy? Come over here and help me.'

In an instant Julia was pressed against him, her naked back in contact with his wide chest. His hand came round, one huge palm holding her breasts, his sinewy fingers fondling the bare nipples. They stiffened eagerly. Sandwiched between Theona and the trainer, she felt dizzy, the feel of their skin, the fragrance

14

emanating from their bodies, the pleasure they were lavishing on her almost too much to handle.

Theona pressed harder on her clit, and, with his free hand, Gus began to explore her bottom, worming into the crack and homing in on the puckered mouth of her anus. Julia shook as she felt the pressure of his fingertip at her forbidden entrance, an entirely foreign invasion. He left it, and skirted round her juicy vulva, penetrating just a little.

'She's telling the truth, Theona,' he opined, in dark chocolate tones. 'Close as a clam in both places. No one's been there.'

'But someone's been here, I can tell. Her clit's used to being rubbed. Do you do it yourself, Julia?'

'Y-yes,' she admitted in hushed tones.

'And you haven't a lover?'

'No. Men always leave when I won't let them go all the way.'

'Not even Will?' Theona looked across at him, and a winged eyebrow shot up. 'Haven't you initiated your apprentice?'

'No.' He returned her stare without flinching, though he was completely naked now, his clothes draped across a chair.

'You've wanted to,' she answered, and smiled to see his cock pointing like a spear towards the ornate ceiling. 'You do now.'

He shrugged, hands on his hips, legs widespread. 'I'm a red-blooded male. Who wouldn't?'

'One doesn't have to own a pair of balls to appreciate her youthful freshness,' Theona reminded, and bent her head, her corn-coloured ringlets brushing Julia's breasts. The singer's tongue lapped over her aroused nipples and her fingers continued to palpate Julia's clit, sometimes with a speed and force that numbed yet made it burn, then with a caress as delicate as a butterfly's wing.

Ken and Joe, large men with the battered faces of prize-fighters, had their hands down their tracksuit pants and were squeezing and pumping their cocks. Roy had gone even further, getting his out and working it, then lifting his testicles, toying with them, the ripe fruits enlarging, his prick hard as a broom handle.

Julia was surrounded by sex, breathing it in, luxuriating in it. Wherever she looked it was there. Five men and a woman, all in a high state of arousal because of her. She thrilled with a sense of purpose and power, and it came to her in a flash that virgins had always had this effect on people. There was something mystical about that innocent condition. Deep magic, earth magic, fertility rites where the elders were eager to spill the virgin blood onto the earth. The victim had a few moments of being worshipped, and then she was handed over to be deflowered.

Surely this couldn't be Theona's intention?

Somehow her dress was removed but, 'Not the shoes,' Theona commanded. 'I like the look of them, but pull up those stockings.' Julia did as she was bidden, hauling at the lacy tops till they almost reached her pubes. It was worse than being completely bare, the stockings, her high shoes and untidy blonde curls making her look tarty.

Gus had his fingers looped round her wrists, and Theona stepped back to view her, critical but smiling. 'Charming,' she said at last. 'She's like a young Marilyn Monroe. Vulnerable yet oozing sex appeal. Don't you think so, Will?'

'Now you come to mention it... yes, I suppose there is a vague resemblance.'

'And Marilyn was a naughty girl, just like you, Julia. But your luck is in. You've found me, and I can see you need to be chastised.' Theona raised a brow at Gus. He released Julia. Petrified, she put one arm across her breasts and covered her mound with the other hand. The bodyguards were still fumbling with their cocks, inspired by the sight of her, and Will maintained his impressive erection.

'Put your hands on your head,' Theona instructed. 'There's no need to be coy.' Then, with a violent change of mood she rounded on her guards. 'You morons stop beating your meat! I don't want you coming all over my carpet. Stand against the wall and leave your cocks out, but don't touch them.'

Huge bruisers though they were, reared in the tough school of the streets, they seemed to shrink under this tirade, obeying her meekly. Julia peeped at them, her arms aching from their position, hands linked on the crown of her head. Each was ugly, with shaven heads, tattoos and piercing, but their formidable appearance was rendered comical by the exposed erections with vein knotted stems and fiery helms wet with pre-come.

Gus sat down on an upright chair, and Theona said to Julia, 'Lie across his lap, bum in the air.'

'I can't, I've never...' Julia faltered.

'Then it's high time you did,' Theona sneered, and propelled her forward.

Gus, unsmiling, shifted to accommodate her, his legs parted, feet flat on the floor, phallus lifting towards his navel. He had a strap wrapped round his right hand. Gingerly, Julia lowered herself till she felt his strong thighs supporting her, her buttocks forced high. She was apprehensive and aroused. She could feel herself blushing as she thought of the lewd spectacle she presented.

The heat increased as she recalled the vision of Theona squirming under the paddle and then being rammed by Gus's mighty weapon. She squeezed her thighs together, feeling the swell of her mons against his flesh, the length of the underside of his cock rubbing her side. She was wet, love-juice oozing with each pulse of renewed passion. And, to add to her discomfort, her bladder was full and she was dying to relieve it.

'Please, before we start anything, can you direct me to the loo?' she asked meekly, gazing up at Theona. 'I need to spend a penny.'

'You'll have to hold it. All part of your schooling. You should enjoy it all the more while struggling not to wet yourself.' Theona ran a hand under Julia's breasts, pulling at the nipples and smiling at her. 'And you'd better not spill a drop, my girl. This is a library, not a public lavatory. I shall be very angry if you piss everywhere.'

She stood back, then beckoned to Will, and together they occupied the chesterfield. This was well within Julia's sight, and her excitement mounted as

Theona threw off her robe and straddled Will, impaling herself on his cock and heaving up and down on it, her breasts bouncing. Then all thought was blocked out as searing pain shot through Julia. Gus had unfurled the strap and struck her viciously across the up-thrust curve of her buttocks.

She screamed and tried to wriggle free, but Gus adroitly hit her again and again, agony shooting through her tortured backside. He didn't use his full strength, highly skilled at flagellation, going easy on her. Even so, hot tears ran down her cheeks, dripping on the rug, and her rump burned with a consuming fire that spread to her loins and aggravated her clit. She wanted to come most desperately, wanted him to stop, wanted to pee.

Theona, even in the throes of sex with Will, watched her constantly, shouting encouragement. 'That's it, girl. Ride the pain, surrender to the pleasure.'

Gus used enough force to make Julia leap at each stinging contact between leather strap and bare bottom. He moved down to the backs of her thighs and caught her across the underswell of her hinds. Her breath hissed out at every cruel blow. He stopped and passed his hands across the red marks branded on her skin, his fingers cool and soothing. Then, laying down the strap, he cupped her quim, palpating the protruding nubbin. Julia gritted her teeth, her pleasure mingling with the pain of her derrière and the ache in her bladder. Gus was insistent, rubbing her without mercy and this, coupled with the arousing sight of Theona and Will humping each other, was enough to lift her to the highest plateau of pleasure. But there she stuck, unable to progress to completion, terrified that, in so doing, she might void her bladder, drench the floor and add to her shame.

'Come on, baby,' Gus murmured, playing with her stiff nipples and continuing to massage her clit. 'Do it, girl. Do it for me.'

'I can't,' she moaned.

'Oh, you will, indeed you will,' he said, and pinched her bud between his broad thumb and middle finger.

Julia shuddered as orgasm ripped through her, and as soon as the spasms started to recede she scrambled from Gus's lap pleading, 'Where's the toilet - please?'

'Across the hallway,' he said with a snigger, indicating a door.

Julia hobbled, though needing to run, but having to keep her legs pressed tightly together in order not to dribble. She reached the cloakroom at last, just made the lavatory seat in time, sighing with relief as her urine flowed, though all too aware of the soreness of her bottom and thighs.

Julia hoped Theona had finished toying with her, but when she returned it was to find that she had moved away from Will. He was propped up on cushions, smoking, and observing Julia with amused, mocking eyes.

As soon as she stepped through the door Theona grabbed her and spun her round, examining the crimson roses blooming on her bottom. 'You did it well, Gus,' she said, and felt between Julia's thighs. 'You're very wet, my dear. I think Gus deserves a reward, don't you?' She pointed to where he was still seated on the chair, his penis thick and upright. 'Get your mouth round that.'

Julia's eyes widened and her heart thumped. 'Lick him, d'you mean? I can't. I don't want to. It's disgusting.'

He smiled and the bodyguards shook with laughter, their cocks twitching, but Theona was not so tolerant. 'Silly girl,' she said mercilessly, slapping Julia across the face. 'You'll do it, or I'll flay the skin off your arse!'

'Will, can't you help me?' Julia pleaded, rubbing her assaulted cheek, but he shook his head.

'Get on with it,' he advised, blowing smoke rings. 'Then we can get down to the serious business of the night.'

Did no one realise just how offended she was by the suggestion that she suck Gus's cock? Arlene had talked of fellatio, even described what it was like to perform it, and been rhapsodic when she spoke of the delicious pleasure of having someone go down on her, orally stimulating her clit. Julia had cringed, hating the idea of either activity, and yet pictures had sprung into her mind. They were decidedly obscene images, making her sex wet and her mouth dry.

Gus leant back in the chair, folded his arms behind his head and grinned at her. His cock mesmerised her, seeming to take on a life of its own. Slowly, Julia sank between his legs, her punished behind raised. She smelt the musty odour trapped in his crisp black pubic hair, spiced with sweat and cinnamon. She trembled, afraid to touch him, but her timid approach seemed to rouse him even more. His cock rose higher, like a serpent uncoiling to the snake charmer's flute. She stared, petrified yet fascinated at the sturdy, dark-skinned shaft, the fully emerged glans, juice seeping from the slit.

She touched it tentatively, amazed at the warm, velvety feel. Now it didn't seem abhorrent, misshapen and ugly. Instead, she wanted to tend it and make it grow. Her lips opened and her tongue poked out, needing to taste the clear dew at its tip. She licked up the bead, surprised to find it no more tangy than saliva. At the caress his cock leapt into her face. Its heat was against her cheek, the helm seeking her mouth. She started, and her fingers fumbled as she held it, and then groped for the smoothness of his balls, the cock rearing up proudly.

Gus dug his fingers in her hair, dragging her forward, holding her mouth to his prick. She steeled herself, stretched her lips wide and allowed the slippery, purple-red helm to penetrate between them. It was salt flavoured, the wet membranes of her inner cheeks and her taste buds accepting the invasion. After the first shock she overcame the fear that it might choke her. Thrills shivered through her as she instinctively serviced him with her tongue, and then dared to start sucking.

Feeding at her mother's teat, lolly-pops and ice-cream; all these had prepared her for her task, and she tried out several angles, improving her skill, finding that she was doing what came naturally. Gus groaned, slumping low on his spine, surrendering to her greedy slurping. His hands stroked her rumpled curls, and she felt empowered, in control of this mighty man. He had become as pliable as putty in her hands. At that moment he would have done anything for her. She dipped up and down, never letting him force his glans to the back of her throat, using her tongue to caress his stalk, then sucking strongly, entranced by the ridge of his retracted foreskin and the smoothness of his cockhead.

'Go for it, kid, you're good,' he muttered. 'Wow, that's it. Pinch my nipples. Yes, yes... pull 'em hard.'

She reached up and seized the blue-black nubs, but didn't stop sucking. Her breath whistled through her nostrils. This wasn't enough. She withdrew to grab in a mouthful of air, then returned to her task. She was hot, her face bedewed with the sweat pooling in his groin, her mouth filled with her own spittle and his pre-come. She sensed his crisis was near, felt the throbbing of his stem, the pulsing of his helm. His fingers curled in her hair, forcing her closer, jabbing at her throat. She threshed, realising what was about to happen and not quite ready for it. She tried to pull her mouth away, but Gus was having none of it. He clamped her to him, holding her hard against his belly. She couldn't move, her face pressed to that wildly throbbing weapon. It soared and spasmed as he neared the pinnacle of bliss.

A hot geyser of semen coated her face, her eyes, her nose, her mouth, spraying her hair and breasts as he came in powerful jerks. She tried to drag away, but he still held her, rigid in all-consuming ecstasy. She was helpless in his ruthless grip, bathed in his rapidly cloying libation. It cooled, mixing with her perspiration and tears, a pearly white trickle even managing to inch past her navel, heading for her delta.

She sank down, exhausted, resting her head against his thigh, and his fingers were gentle now, fondling her hair. She wanted to wipe his come from her face and body, but was afraid to move.

'Get cleaned up,' Theona said, linking her arm with Will's. 'Both of you dress, and then I'll get into my glad-rags and we'll do the interview.'

'We don't have cameras,' Will reminded.

'Worry not, my dear, I've equipment here that'll make your hair curl. You can borrow that. In fact, I'll make you a present of it. Come along, let's get started. I haven't got all night. Things to do, people to see.'

It was like walking into a treasure house.

As far as the eye could see the exhibition hall was filled with display stands. It was laid out like a glorified bazaar, a huge, beautiful expanse of exciting fabrics. It was the stuff of which dreams are made, samples of every conceivable material known to man - a jungle in which ardent travellers in the heady world of couture could lose themselves.

Arlene Murphy almost had an orgasm when she stepped inside; fabrics had the same effect on her as sex. She could feel cold fingers crawling down her spine and tickling her nipples into stiffness. She knew that her panty gusset was damp.

She had come in from the rain slanting across stylish Upper Street, Islington, into the Business Design Centre. After producing her pass ticket in the foyer, and picking up a presentation carrier of catalogues and other goodies, she had proceeded into this annual event, the Cloth Show.

She clipped a nametag to her bodice and worked her way through the crowd, nodding to this acquaintance and that, pleased to find that she was getting known. It had been a long hard haul, but success was within her grasp. She eyed the crowd boldly. There were soberly clad businessmen pacing slowly, their heads together in earnest talk; snappy dressers holding one-sided conversations into mobiles; designers swanning about in their latest offerings; coltish, willowy models and a couple of celebrities trailed by members of the press with cameras poised.

Arlene was confident she was every bit as talented. As always when in crowds, she amused herself by picturing people naked. From the highest to the lowest, all were brought down to a common denominator if one thought of them stripped. She'd started doing this at school, even the headmaster reduced to insignificance when she imagined him with a bare bottom, sagging balls and a three-inch dick.

She smiled as she looked around her, playing this interesting game. Everyone seemed to be talking at once and she caught several different languages. Background music drifted from overhead speakers, only slightly more upmarket than that used in food stores - a compilation of popular classics. Arlene roamed the stalls, a sensual tingle running up her arm as she handled the swatches of slippery satin, responding to the texture of plush, the misty transparency of chiffon or leopard print georgette. Her breath shortened, her heart thumped and the excitement she had experienced on entering was now visceral in its intensity. She yearned to find a man, or maybe a woman - Arlene was bi-sexual - drag them into the nearest washroom and screw them legless.

From these samples she longed to create the wildest, most fantastic outfits. This is what she had always wanted to do; use material as a painter uses palette and brushes, though she produced living works of art to be touched and worn, lived in, fucked in, instead of sterile canvas and paint.

She selected a hanger and took it to the agent's table, a suave lady wearing a tailored two-piece and a patronising air, her thickly gelled hair swept high.

'Excuse me,' Arlene said briskly, glad that she was taller than the woman, an impressive five-nine in her high-heeled cowboy boots. These complemented the American Indian theme of her outfit; suede wraparound skirt with fringes, brief top trimmed with peacock feathers, hand-painted wooden bead necklace, each item made by her own clever fingers.

'Can I help you?' the agent asked, staring at her with flinty eyes, the lids coated with blue shadow, the lashes spiky with mascara.

Arlene returned the frosty glare. 'I want to order samples of this,' and she held out a length of gold embroidered silk bearing the logo of the Parisian manufacturer represented by the agent.

'You have a business card?' the woman enquired loftily.

'Of course.'

When Arlene produced it the agent took it between the tips of her manicured fingers, glancing down disdainfully as she read, '"Arlene Murphy. Dress Designer. Pattern Maker. Garment Technologist." I can't say I've heard of you, Miss Murphy.'

'No?' Arlene retorted, her hackles rising, her colour too. 'And where have you been hiding? You're out of touch. How much is that fabric per metre?'

'One hundred and fifty pounds.'

Arlene gulped, but replied with regal unconcern, 'Can you send me sample lengths?'

With a curl of her cherry-red lips the agent said loudly, 'Oh, no, that's not our policy. But we'll send you out the set if you inform us when you have a prospective buyer.'

'Thank you, you'll be hearing from me in a few days,' Arlene lied, wrote down the details and replaced the hanger, then strolled away.

The truth was that she was strapped for cash. Oh yes, her star was in the ascendant, but she needed that lucky break which happens in the best movies when the heroine is discovered by some influential person and shoots to the top. She managed to keep body and soul together, just about, and knew she'd been fortunate to live with her friend, Julia Jones. Julia was hard up too, struggling to make it in journalism. Arlene wished she was at the show, but she'd gone dashing off on some adventurous escapade with Will Denton, being very mysterious and hush-hush. Arlene hoped she'd take care, worrying about her. Julia wasn't in the least bit streetwise and one needed to be in this day and age.

She supposed it all came down to Julia losing her parents in a tragic plane accident and being brought up by an elderly aunt. Her life had been sheltered. She'd lived with the aunt in the house she and Arlene now occupied, and had gone to a private school down the road, as a daygirl, not a boarder. College had been a culture shock, but she'd had Arlene to shield her, Arlene who came from a rumbustious Irish family. She had left Dublin to attend an English university and then gone on to the Portland School of Fashion. Both of them had settled in London, and Julia having inherited her aunt's property, it had been natural that they share it.

Arlene was like Julia's big sister. Julia was an only child, whereas Arlene was one of six. She felt responsible for her and hoped that old lecher, Will, wasn't getting up to anything.

Even though her thoughts were busy with Julia, another part of her mind was alert for bargains. She approached a short balding man who was manning the fort for another supplier.

'Can I assist?' he said, smiling too much. Arlene noted the little beads of sweat on his upper lip, the smell of cheap deodorant clinging to his person, the way in which his watery eyes roamed her breasts.

'I'd like to order samples of this,' she said haughtily, displaying a piece of forest green devoré.

'Certainly... Miss Murphy,' and he studied her nametag as if committing it to memory. 'Such wonderful stuff, so glamorous. I expect you know that devoré, literally translated, means devour. The makers use acid to eat patterns into the velvet.' He brought this out with relish, as if the very mention of devouring brought his cock to attention. His leer told her he would like to suck her nipples and lick her pussy.

'I knew, but thank you, anyway,' she said, deliberately adding to his discomfort by leaning across the stall so that the valley between her breasts was clearly displayed.

His face flushed even more. He came round and stood beside her, his portly body close as he placed a sweaty hand on hers, saying, 'I can arrange for your order to be processed at once. And there will be no charge for the samples. I'd be happy to deliver them in person, Miss Murphy. Perhaps we could go out for a drink or a bite to eat...'

'Perhaps we could,' Arlene murmured, batting her eyelashes at him. Unlike Julia, who never could get the hang of flirtation, Arlene was an expert.

'I'm Sam Watney,' he said, and she could see the thickening of his dick as it lay to the right of his flies. In her experience men who hung that side and not on the left were usually sexual inadequate. Besides which, it looked untidy, offending her designer's eye.

'Thank you for being so helpful, Sam,' she said throatily, and didn't back away as he pressed his prick against her thigh. 'I'm not in a frantic hurry for the swatches. Don't put yourself to any trouble.'

'It would be no trouble; a real pleasure, in fact, to help a beautiful woman like you,' he insisted, his cock growing, an expression of drooling admiration on his face.

'I'll look forward to receiving the samples. When I've decided on the colour and how many metres, I'll be in touch.' She didn't fancy him one bit, but had learned to get all she could out of men. If he wanted to lust after her and thought he was in with a chance, well, so be it. It would ensure he got her a good deal.

She turned away, and immediately bumped into the most beautiful man there. She recognised him, of course, but wasn't about to give him the satisfaction of knowing this. Let sycophantic followers hover in the background. Let the press be jockeying for a few words from his lips and, if possible, a picture. She chose to pretend to be ignorant of the fact that this was Marty Blake, one of Britain's leading designers. He smiled and she melted into lubricity.

He was thirtyish, tall, rangy and lean, casually but expensively dressed in loose, sand coloured trousers and a white collarless shirt. His face was tanned and classically handsome; high cheekbones, a straight nose, a firm jaw and dark hair that curled to his shoulders.

Arlene was cynical about men, thought she knew everything about them and what made them tick, was sure she could control her own reactions to them, but now she could feel heat washing over her skin as he pierced her with pewter-grey eyes.

Then he lifted one curving brow sardonically and remarked, 'We seem to share the same taste. These are the best I've seen so far, in the cheaper range, that is,' and he nodded to the hanger she still held.

'I agree,' she said, marvelling at the steadiness of her voice.

'Lovely,' he said, and continued to scrutinise her.

Was he referring to the devoré or her? 'It's French, naturally,' she answered.

'Have you seen the latest Italian textiles?' he asked, very seriously.

'No, I've not been round everything yet.' Lord, she thought, I can't bear to stand here like this, exchanging banalities. All I want to do is kiss him then fondle his dick.

It was impossible not to glance down at his thighs and the promising bulge at the front of his trousers. Was he gay or straight? She struggled to recall gossip printed in the newspapers or bandied around the shows. Before she could decide how to take this further, he took the swatch from her and held it up against her face, remarking, 'Green suits you. You've glorious hair; so dark yet with chestnut highlights, and your eyes are green, too. The fabric brings out their colour. Don't you agree, Miss Arlene Murphy? Or is it Mrs?'

'I'm not married,' she said, wondering why she was bothering to play along with this. He obviously expected every female, and probably many males, to be bewitched by his charm, his looks and his fame.

And why not? she thought, her hormones in overdrive, making her reckless. Why not have him, this arrogant, successful man? He was looking at her as if he wanted her, and all other sensible considerations fled from her mind.

His hand closed on hers and his grip was like steel. 'Shall we?' he asked, and she knew exactly what he meant. He moved upwards, cupping her elbow and leading her out through a door with a light above it saying EXIT. He knew his way around, it seemed, and walked her down a short corridor and through a door on the right. It led into a storeroom, a place illumined by a single small window.

They didn't speak and he guided her between cardboard boxes, stacking chairs, an industrial vacuum cleaner, a mop and bucket, a folded stepladder, towards a table at the back. As they walked he had his hands under her bodice, adroitly unclipping her bra, lifting both and working on her bare breasts. She gripped the top button of his waistband, undid it and pulled his zip down. He wasn't wearing anything underneath, his cock springing into her hand, and then they could go no further, blocked by the table.

Arlene reached up and he lowered his face to hers, taking possession of her lips. She put her tongue in his mouth, tasting him. There was the faint flavour of wine on his breath. She felt as if she, too, had been drinking, intoxicated by the bizarre situation, his hands on her breasts, her fist closed round the solid column of flesh poking from his fly. She was actually about to fuck Marty Blake! Her rival in the field of fashion, admired, even adored, lionised by the press and public alike.

He took his lips away from hers, and then caught her under the buttocks, lifting and seating her on the table. He pushed her legs open and reached under her skirt. She gasped and heaved against him as he fingered her cleft, pushing her panties to one side and sliding into her wet depths. She was ready, teetering on the edge, excited beyond measure by the breathtaking glitz of the show, the glory of the fabrics and now - this! Blake represented all the most glamorous, romantic and fantastical elements of the rag trade. It was as if by screwing him she was taking the whole of it into her being.

He could have been selfish, but he wasn't. He moved his finger faster and she moaned as the exquisite sensations rose, lifting her towards a powerful orgasm. It broke, filling her with shuddering, lusting, absorbing pleasure. She lolled back, resting on her straight arms, opening her eyes to see his swollen cock standing up from his open flies, his deft fingers rolling a condom over the straining stem. Protected now, he guided his thrusting prick into her slippery vulva and pushed all the way up her hungry channel in a single, powerful stroke.

'Oh yes, *yes!*' Arlene cried, lifting her legs and locking them around his waist, pulling him even deeper inside her.

'I'm going to fuck you harder than you've ever been fucked,' he warned, propelling his cock with forceful thrusts of his hips.

'Yes, do it, do it!' she urged.

Using all his considerable strength, Blake withdrew to almost the full length of his shaft, and then plunged back into her. She lost her grip on him, her legs falling open. He snarled and pounded into her, again and again, grabbing her bottom to hold her steady to meet those ravaging thrusts. It wasn't love or even affection, simply mindless, animal passion, a savage meeting of two virile creatures intent on getting every ounce of sensation from the act.

He worked his hard cock into her relentlessly, as if it was as much an instrument of torture as pleasure. Then he gasped, flung back his head, his body jerking with the overwhelming force of his orgasm. Arlene revelled in the sheer magic of feeling his cock spasm, buried deep inside her.

He bent over her, rested his head on her shoulder for a split second, then pulled out, the teat of the rubber filled with his spunk. She regained control, her breathing becoming regular, her heartbeat slowing. Blake straightened, removed the condom and left it lying on the table. He tucked in his shirt and zipped up. He was composed and quiet, recovering his control. Watching him, Arlene entered that lonely place which always awaited her after casual sex. It was chilly and barren, and she never had come to terms with it. She slipped down off the table, adjusted her knickers and skirt, then tucked her breasts into her bra and rearranged her bodice. Neither of them spoke.

Then, 'I'll leave first and you follow after a moment or two,' he said. 'Don't want people seeing us together and getting the wrong idea.'

'Of course not,' she replied, an edge to her voice. 'That would never do.'

There were a dozen things she could have said, like, 'Shall I see you again?' but this would have been playing against the rules. People like she and Marty Blake didn't do that kind of thing. She watched him leave, then gathered up her bag, her length of devoré and her carrier and let herself out into the corridor.

When she crossed the hall, it was to see him surrounded by a gaggle of admirers, cameras flashing. Staring straight ahead, she went through the vestibule and stepped out into sunshine, the street bright and new-washed by the downpour. She walked briskly, found the nearest underground station and took a tube to her workshop.

Chapter 3

'What happened next?' Arlene demanded, seated at the kitchen table, all ears as she listened to Julia.

'It was very normal, well, as normal as an interview with a celebrity tends to be,' Julia replied, running her hands through her hair, still shell-shocked by the turn of events.

'No more sex?' Arlene went to the counter and re-filled their coffee cups.

'Not a whisper. Everyone became ultra professional. Theona was a perfect person to interview; chatty, informative, and witty. And she posed so naturally for pics, fully clothed, of course.'

'And Gus?' Arlene brought back the cups and perched on a stool, long legs crossed at the knee, tiny skirt riding back over her thighs.

'He was sent about his business, as were the bodyguards. It all went like clockwork and, when we'd finished, Will's car was waiting outside for us. Roy had been dispatched to fetch it. We went back to the hotel, occupied our separate rooms, and left after breakfast this morning. You know the rest.'

She had told her story reluctantly, her face red, her body aching with remembered pain and pleasure. Arlene had been insistent and, in a peculiar way, Julia found it arousing to voice what took place. She had been too shy to discuss it in the car on the drive back to London, and Will, though smirking at her every now and again, also kept quiet. It was as if they had never seen each other nude, or indulging in sexual practices. He dropped her at her house in Notting Hill, and Arlene, home from work, immediately pounced on her, wanting to know every last detail.

'D'you mean to tell me you kept your cherry through all these shenanigans?' she said sceptically, sipping at the mug held between both hands.

'It's true,' Julia answered earnestly. 'I'm still a virgin.'

Arlene nearly choked on her coffee. 'Oh yes, very virginal, I should say so!' she scoffed. 'I'm sure you're as pure as the driven snow. Come off it, Julia. Been brought to climax, gave a guy head. Is this virginal behaviour?'

'It's true. No one has penetrated me.' Julia rushed from defence to attack, pushing back her cup and standing up. 'I thought that you, at least, would believe me.'

'Oh, don't get so uptight. Sit down. Okay, I believe you're still technically a virgin. But you haven't told me yet... did you enjoy what you did?'

Julia fidgeted, unsure of herself. 'Some of it. I don't know about being slapped and belted. I haven't made up my mind if it's really my thing. Anyway, enough about me. What have you been doing?'

Arlene grinned and said, 'Only shagging Marty Blake at the Cloth Show, that's all.'

Julia focused on her, his name ringing a bell. 'Isn't he the one who was voted Top Designer of the Year recently? I tried to get him to talk to me, wanted a piece for *Hi Life*, but he was awfully rude.'

'That's Marty Blake. An arrogant, chauvinistic pig.'

'And you went with a man like that? I thought you were into girl-power.'

'I am, but Marty has a cock to die for. Besides, he may be able to give my career a nudge in the right direction.'

'Are you going to see him again?' As usual, Arlene had managed to steal her thunder, but Julia was genuinely interested. Her friend was so talented and dedicated that she deserved to do well.

'Nothing was said, but yes, I expect we'll bump into each other in the course of our work. Stop looking at me like that. It was a fuck, that's all. It didn't mean anything to either of us.'

'That's dreadful.' Julia could feel all the conventional attitudes of her middle-class background rising in a tide. The shame of her recent abandonment made her want to find a convenient scapegoat.

Arlene laughed and tossed back her wild hair, green eyes sparkling with mischief. 'Julia, you're a hypocrite. D'you know that? Giving me grief when you're no better yourself. Come down off your high horse, lady. It's time you got to grips with reality.'

Julia could feel tears behind her eyes. She was worried about what Denise would have to say. She and Will hadn't exactly carried out orders. It was a relief to be home, the house enfolding her the moment she opened the front door. It was much as it had always been. From early childhood she remembered the brown and cream chevron tiles in the hall, the stained glass panels in the porch, the dark dado, so practical for hiding finger-marks, the plaster-work of the cornices, the central carved rose in every room holding fancy electric fittings. Her aunt had told her that once upon a time these had housed gas-lamps.

She knew she'd been extremely lucky to be left this place, which was worth a fortune on the current market, but would have much rather had her aunt alive. She couldn't remember her parents, only two when their flight to Italy met with disaster. There were no survivors. Great-aunt Mary had taken in the orphaned Julia. There had been no one else. She had been middle-aged then, Julia's father's aunt, but had done a splendid job of rearing her. Rather old-fashioned in outlook, she had been scrupulously just, loving, and ever kind, proud of this child entrusted to her. Julia missed her deeply, but blushed to think what she would have made of last night's episode.

'You'll do as you're told, Tina,' shouted the handsome, foreign-looking man wielding the whip. It cracked across her bare backside and she yelped. 'I expect absolute obedience, d'you hear?'

He brought it down again, making her spin, honey-blonde hair flying. She struggled against the bonds tethering her wrists to the hook securely screwed into a rafter. Her arms were drawn awkwardly above her head, her breasts lifted high and she scrabbled for a purchase on the floor, but her toes only just touched it. Not entirely naked, her silk blouse hung loose, nipples hard with excitement, raising it in two sharp points. She wore no skirt or panties, only a pair of smoky-

26

grey stockings with lacy hold-up tops.

'I can't betray her,' she whimpered, tears coursing down her cheeks and dripping from her chin. 'She's given me a chance, helped me out when I was down on my luck.'

'And I employed you once, Tina, remember?' Blake said, watching her from where he sat on a nearby couch, legs apart to ease his erection. It excited him to see his partner, friend and sponsor chastising the girl. He did it with such finesse.

Everything Vincent Gabor touched turned to gold, each venture flourishing. They'd been drawn to one another like steel to magnet, Gabor appreciating the value of Marty's talent and prepared to invest in him. Not only that: they shared a similar need for sexual activities that went beyond the norm. Gabor's personality was that of a dominator. Both in business dealings and his personal life, he had to be the master.

This secluded basement in the foundations of his Highgate mansion was equipped with every device imaginable for the enhancement of pleasure gained through pain. Dimly lit, sumptuously furnished with deep couches and armchairs for an attentive audience, it contained a low stage, a whipping-post, a high bench, and another lower one from which chains dangled. A glass fronted cabinet held riding crops, bullwhips and rattan rods. Further along, hooks held leather clothing, hoods and masks. Gabor smilingly referred to this place as 'the playroom'.

'Don't listen to the silly bitch,' he said unpleasantly, and replaced the whip, selecting a black malacca cane instead. He rolled back his shirtsleeves, his sinewy arms bare to the elbows, took up the rod, made a few practise cuts through the air, then brought it down with a crack across Tina's backside.

She screamed and jerked as he hit her again, new welts forming to join the criss-cross stripes left by the whip. 'Oh stop, please, master!' she begged.

For answer, Gabor laid on four more, till her bottom was flushed and blotched with angry purple bruises. 'Why are you making so much fuss? I may have to gag you,' he grunted, a savage light in his peat-dark eyes. 'It's not your first beating, and I know you get off on it.' He thrust a hand between her legs, then withdrew, his fingers glistening with her dew, adding triumphantly, 'You see? You're already wet.'

He gave her a short respite, crossing to her other side, then sent the wicked length of cane singing through the air. It landed across her back with a sharp crack. She screamed again and tensed in her bonds, her mouth wide open in shock and agony. The strokes descended like a staircase of pain across her white buttocks. She gabbled for mercy between each one, before the next blow deprived her of breath. Her slender body, her tangled golden hair, the utter helplessness and humiliation of her bondage satisfied every dark fantasy secreted in the heartland of Gabor's psyche.

Blake could wait no longer, going over and twining himself round her suspended form. She moaned with agony and desire. He bent and buried his face in her scalding flesh, kissing her buttocks, his tongue flicking over the stripes.

He sought her tight crease, prising it open, dipping inside and tonguing her furrow, lapping where the wiry hair fringed her sex-lips. She tasted of perfume and sweat and bodily emissions. Her moans became more urgent and she bore down, her pudenda pointing towards him. His tongue-tip flashed over her swollen clit, and then he closed his lips on it, dragging at the tiny button of plump flesh.

Gabor laughed, balancing on widespread legs, the cane held lightly in his strong, beautifully manicured fingers. 'You see how randy she is, my friend?' he asked harshly. 'She's your slave as much as mine.'

'Love me, Marty, love me,' she cried. 'You did so once, till you got tired of me.'

He rose, looking at her contemptuously as he said, 'Love you? Are you mad? You think I really loved a stupid tart like you?'

'Why are you so cruel?' she sighed, reproach in her tear-drenched eyes.

'You adore it when he's mean,' Gabor scoffed, and holding her with one arm, loosened the chains. She dropped to her feet, staggered and would have fallen had he not supported her. 'Now then, darling,' he murmured seductively, his hands fondling her breasts. 'You want Marty?'

'Yes.' She clung to him, hope lighting up her elfin features, a slim twenty-year-old with long pale hair and cornflower-blue eyes.

'You shall have him if you promise to do as he asks.'

She shuddered and heaved a deep sigh, shaking her head even as she capitulated. 'All right. But I don't want her to know I had anything to do with it.'

'You have the key?'

'Yes,' she muttered quietly.

'That's all we need. Give it to me and I'll have a copy made.'

He took her to the couch and bent her over one of the arms. Marty, unzipped, stood behind her, angling her so that her bottom was raised to meet his prick. He reached for her slit, spreading the copious juice over and around her anus, and then opening it with his fingers. She grunted, forced forward by the pressure, accepting the invasion. Blake wriggled his fingers inside her nether hole, and then replaced them with his stiff weapon, pushing hard till the muscles expanded to take him further. The feeling was exquisite, her sphincter closing round his shaft like a velvet glove. No virgin could have offered such delight. He drove a hand beneath her, finding her clit and massaging it as he propelled himself in and out, panting hard, feeling orgasm gathering in his groin.

He was so engrossed that he didn't register what Gabor was doing for a moment. But coming into contact with a world other than his own lust-crazed need for relief, he was aware that he was in front of Tina, trousers open, his cock aimed at her mouth. He grabbed her by the hair, dragging her towards his crotch. It became a duel, with Tina wedged between the two protagonists. Who would come first? The settee shook with the force of their frantic, two-way coupling, Blake plunging into her tightness, his cock like a ramrod, his balls tight, and Gabor, his head back, the cords straining at his neck, receiving her worshipping attentions as she sucked his organ.

Blake felt her quiver, his finger sensitive to the throb of her clit as she came. This was enough to send him over the edge and he surrendered to a powerful climax, his semen spurting into the condom. At that moment Gabor exploded too, into Tina's mouth. He withdrew, wiped his cock in her hair and looked down at the still linked pair with evident satisfaction.

'That's settled then,' he said, rearranging his trousers. 'When do you want it done, Marty?'

'As soon as possible,' Blake said, withdrawing, disposing of the rubber and buttoning his chinos.

May had begun cold and wet. There had even been blizzards in the north of England. It looked fair set to be disastrous for the sale of spring and summer clothing.

'I don't know how much longer I can carry on,' Arlene said to Julia before they set off to their respective places of employment a few days later.

'I'm sure you'll get lucky soon,' Julia assured her, looking as charmingly innocent as ever, despite the revelations in Cornwall.

'I certainly hope so,' Arlene replied, hefting up her bag and making sure it was closed, preparing herself for the jostle of the underground, where one had to be doubly careful against pick-pockets.

The new century had brought neither safety nor peace. Everyone seemed so greedy, vicious and amoral, all the old standards fading fast. Arlene could cope with this, just about; a feisty girl with a caustic tongue and lots of attitude, but it was hard to always be on the alert. No one could be trusted, even in her beloved clothing business.

She let herself into her cluttered workshop above a Pakistani store. The air was faintly spiced with delicious odours from below; curry pastes, lentils, and a hundred and one eastern ingredients. Music formed a continual background - flutes, tambour, the sitar - sounds to which her ear had become so accustomed that she barely registered them.

She had other things on her mind, seriously worried. The bills were piling up. She was owed money for made-to-measure garments, but saw little hope of payment from some of them. How could she get heavy with a recent bride whose gown she had made, when the pregnant girl had been left at the altar? Her groom's wife turned up at the church and he was being sued for bigamy. There were other cases, too, where despite her bravado, she couldn't bring herself to make demands.

Her stock hadn't sold, hanging fire in the small dress shops she supplied on sale or return. The big boutiques were unaffected by the vagaries of the weather, their customers buying for holidays abroad. The top designers, and this included Blake, had nothing to fret about, their clothes bought for the United States, following their prestigious shows.

The smouldering embers of ambition flared and she swore to be up there with him one day soon, maybe even bigger and better than he was. She was certain he'd recognised her. There had been an interest there not entirely sexual. She recalled spotting him among the judges when she entered some of her designs to be paraded down the catwalk at a recent charity function. She gained a prize - a Certificate of Merit when she would rather have had a cheque. Had she made an impression on him then? She supposed she must have done, unless it was his habit to pick up women and shag them in broom cupboards.

For some reason she couldn't fathom, his cavalier treatment continued to rile her and she paced her domain like a caged lioness, glancing impatiently at the cotton jersey and synthetics that constituted the bulk of her run-of-the-mill orders.

She grabbed up the length of green devoré and held it against her body, studying the effect in the mirror fixed to one wall. She tingled, the fine hairs rising on her limbs, her pussy aching with want. Few things made her more horny than an unsullied bolt of fabric. It rivalled the smell, feel and taste of men. True to his word, Sam Watney had sent her samples, and she had ordered several metres of the green, keeping her fingers crossed that her credit card would cope. He had phoned her repeatedly, until she programmed the answer machine to pick him up. The parcel duly arrived, and the phone calls dwindled in frequency. She hoped he'd got the message, the thought of his flabby hands and slack lips making her feel sick.

The texture of the velvet sent a frisson of excitement through her fingers, up her arms, along her shoulders and into her nipples. Echoing thrills shot down to her sex, setting a warm pulse beating. She focused on the embryonic garment she imagined creating, and promised to indulge herself, partly for the sheer, voluptuous pleasure of it, and partly to keep her mind off the daily grind. The devoré called for something space age and intensely sexy. Pictures drifted across her brain - a show of her own where important buyers, movie stars, royalty and the doyens of magazines devoted to the industry who, with a few well-chosen words, could make or break reputations, would see her collection.

It was very quiet in the workroom. Her assistant had rung in sick. Alone and undisturbed, Arlene stripped off her denim skirt and white T-shirt. Braless, she quickly removed her panties and posed for her own enjoyment. The devoré cascaded over her body and slithered down her legs, gathering in a verdant puddle at her feet. Her trainers looked all wrong, so she unlaced them and stepped into a pair of court shoes dug out from under the table. This was better, the heels adding to the length of leg seen through the semi-transparent material.

'Brunettes suit green,' she heard Blake say, and she frowned, annoyed by the way the memory of him made her clit throb.

Her hand wandered down to her dark pubes and traced over the slit between them. Her pulse raced and she shifted position, opening her legs slightly, braced on those elegant, impractical heels. Her labial lips were swollen with need. She eased her finger up and down, lifting the fabric so that she didn't stain it with her juice. Pleasure welled in her loins, fanning out in her womb. She fingered her nipples with her other hand, loving the way they lifted the velvet as they peaked. Slowly, she pushed it aside, baring breasts and pubis, caressing the soft hairy lips and petting her protruding clit-head.

She eased back the tiny fleshy cowl that guarded the ultra-sensitive tip and wetted it with the dew welling from her vulva, working round it, watching herself in the mirror, wanting the feeling to last. It was too good, however, the urge for completion too strong. She couldn't help massaging it firmly.

She gasped, moaned, twisted her head from side to side, fingers plucking at her nipples, first one then the other, as her middle digit moved in swift arousal of her clitoris. She closed her eyes, bright light blazing against the blackness of her lids, a roaring in her ears as her climax welled over. It lifted her to glory and she was totally into it, part hidden by a screen that separated her from the long cutting table, the sewing machines, the rails of garments and shelves filled with materials.

She nearly jumped out of her skin when a man stepped into sight, wolf-whistling quietly as he admired her. 'Eugene!' she gasped. 'You scared the hell out of me!'

'Sorry, baby, but *wow*, that's classy!' he exclaimed, his eyes filled with that bubbling sense of humour which made him so good to be with him - Eugene Cooper, their link was a strictly professional one, to date.

'My treat to myself,' she replied, a spasm of renewed heat warming her pussy when she realised he had been watching her masturbating. She glanced down and saw the thick bough of his cock straining against his stonewashed jeans. It was exciting to know he'd been getting a hard-on seeing her playing with herself.

'Sure, and why not?' he agreed, and came closer, staring over her shoulder at their mutual reflection.

He was tall and broad, spending his free time at the gym. Dark-eyed and dark-haired, his genes where not entirely British, despite his cockney accent. He wasn't exactly handsome, but had striking features, white teeth and an infectious grin. A market trader, he had recently approached her with an offer to sell any of her leftover clothes. He had a van and an 'in' to most of the major London markets. From the start he'd made no bones about the fact that he wanted to screw her, and now she felt herself being borne along on an unstoppable tide of lust.

She looked into his mirror-image eyes and said, 'I'd better get dressed. I'm supposed to be finishing a job,' but she made no move to leave him.

Instead, she pressed back and brushed her hips against his muscled belly. His response was an automatic lift of the pelvis, bringing the solid bar of his prick in line with her bottom crease. She wriggled and his arms clamped round her waist, pulling her closer, one hand snaking over her shoulder to cup a breast.

She sighed, watching them in the mirror, like a voyeur getting kicks from seeing a couple fornicating.

'Yummy,' he returned, and nipped her ear.

Shards of ice trickled down her spine and she could feel further moisture pooling at her opening, already wet from orgasm. Eugene's cock felt absolutely huge as it tried to force its way through his jeans. Most promising, and she'd not hungered for sex with such urgency since her encounter with Blake.

31

'You're different,' Eugene murmured into her hair. 'What's happened? You've never given me the come-on before. It must be that fabric. You look wicked in it.'

'Maybe,' she murmured, drawing in a sharp breath as his broad thumb revolved on her nipple.

'Did something happen at the Cloth Show?' he asked, looking at her in the glass as he pulled the velvet tight over the cone-shaped teat and flicked it mercilessly.

'Nothing important,' she said, and arched her spine, lifting her ribs to thrust her breasts against that stabbing pleasure.

'You must tell me all about it later. But just for now there are things I want to do to you,' he said, and spun her round till her nipples were pressed to his chest.

'Careful, don't crush it,' she warned, and pushed back a little to get rid of the precious cloth, laying it over a chair away from harm.

Now she was naked and, after admiring every inch of her, he picked a silk dressing gown from one of the rails and draped it around her, then walked her over to the sagging old sofa. There he sat down and held out his hand to her. She took it and sank into the depths with him. She was trembling with lust. It ran through her from the tips of her toes to her cortex as she touched his clean-shaven cheek. He caught her hand and kissed her fingers, sucking each one into his mouth and licking it with a leisurely enjoyment that made her clit thrum. Then he dropped a light kiss on her brow and drove his fingers into her hair, massaging the scalp till she was almost purring.

Every nerve in her body quivered. He was kind and sincere and free from attachments - no wife or girlfriend. He was as free as her, and liked it that way. She ran her hands up his thighs, and then dropped to her knees between them, pressing her face to the front of his faded jeans and gnawing at the hard outline of the swollen baton slanting beneath the denim. He trembled, and his fingers gripped the corkscrew ringlets of her hair as her breath heated the skin-tight denim and the cock beneath. Smiling inwardly, she ran her tongue around the brass buttons fastening the flies. Eugene groaned.

The buttons were cold and she closed her teeth on the top one, worrying at it, rampant to free his serpent and take it into her mouth. Glancing up she saw the intent look on his face. It increased the flow of juice wetting her quim. Her nipples were pebble-hard, her clitoris red-hot. One orgasm was never enough for her hungry little bud.

'Unbuckle your belt,' she ordered, very much in charge.

'Yes, ma'am.'

As she watched him deftly releasing the buckle, she remembered Julia recounting how Gus had leathered her. Arlene had already dipped a toe into the heady waters of S&M, but didn't think Eugene would try it - not on this occasion, anyway. Later maybe. But her bottom clenched and her skin smarted as she eyed the length of belt. She could almost hear the hiss and feel the burn as it landed on her cringing arse.

She took over, finishing the job, baring the dark dimple of his navel and the black thicket that covered his lower belly. He wasn't wearing underpants, and as the final button yielded his cock sprung out, striking her face. It was so tempting that she opened her mouth wide and took it in, all the turgid length and thickness of it, till it rammed her throat. She rocked her head, pulling on the cock with a light suction, tasting the divine flavour of his pre-come. She circled the foreskin, and pulled his jeans around his bottom so that she could hold and fondle his heavy balls in their loose bag.

He stopped her then, murmuring, 'No more, baby, or I'll shoot my load. I want to do it inside you, but not till I've given you the best frig you've ever had.'

Still exposed, his wet, fiery-headed cock jutting from his flies, he moved over and pulled her up. A shiver rocked her as he fastened his mouth on hers and wormed his tongue inside, savouring her saliva. As he kissed her he rolled and roiled her nipples and palpated the ripe swell of her mound, letting his fingers enter the cleft. She sighed into his open mouth and ground her hips against his skilful hand. Sensation poured through her. His touch was as satisfying as when she brought herself to climax but with the added rush of uncertainty. What would he do next?

Pressing her flat on the creaking settee, he opened her legs, leaning over and admiring the prominent swell of her pubis, kneading it and rubbing the thick puffed wedge of hair, before poking a finger into the wet aisle. She clung around his neck, wanting to get closer and closer. She gave short sharp cries, then became silent, the coming bliss too wonderful to be disturbed by noise.

Her whole body had become a temple of pleasure as the feeling intensified. Now she saw nothing, heard nothing, bathed in a glorious agony of passion. Her climax roared and she lifted her hips from the couch. As the tension was released, Eugene sank a finger into her spasming cunt, moving it like a penis. Then he held her close, kissing her and enclosing her hot mound in his hand.

'Now,' she whispered urgently. 'Put it in me, now.'

He knelt between her legs and rubbed his cockhead against her labia, his fingers continuing to stimulate her clit. When she was sure she was about to come again he allowed his shaft to slide into her. He started to move, undulating his pelvis, withdrawing and thrusting in perfect harmony. Arlene embraced him with her arms and legs, his every downward stroke rubbing her bud.

She could hear herself making strange whimpering noises, and Eugene grunting as his hips pistoned rapidly. His eyes were shut, his lips drawn back in a snarl. He was like something possessed and she shrieked as another orgasm electrified her.

'That's it, girl,' he urged, and came with a final lunge, then collapsed, his face buried in her neck.

She stirred, duty calling. 'I must get on,' she said, wriggling out from under him. 'I've a dress to complete before leaving. If I give the customer a ring and tell her it's ready, then I may be able to deliver it and collect the lolly. I need the basics, like bread and milk and tea bags. It's that serious.'

'I can always lend you some cash,' he offered, sitting up while she rummaged for her scattered clothes and began to put them on.

Arlene hated being obligated to anyone, particularly if it was male, but she smiled across at him and said, 'Thanks, but I'll manage. All I need are a couple of substantial orders, that's all.'

She combed her fingers through her hair, and then went to her store cupboard, an area big enough to walk into, where she kept her latest, most secret designs, along with the patterns and sketches. Lit by a skylight, it was sacrosanct. No one was allowed into this holy of holies where the most precious of her brainchildren had their being. Here she was gathering her collection, waiting for that break which would enable her to exhibit.

She stared as she entered, certain that she must be dreaming. It was empty! Anger, fear and a terrible sense of loss grabbed her by the throat. 'Eugene!' she shouted. 'Quick! Come in here!'

'What's up?' he said, taking one look at her white face and staring eyes.

'My clothes, my patterns! Everything's gone!'

'Gone? How?'

'I don't know.' She moved frantically, searching in vain, knowing it was useless.

'Was it locked?'

'Yes, of course it was locked.' She was impatient, even with him, as distraught as a mother whose children are missing.

'But it looks as if someone came in and swiped the lot,' he continued, with a shrug. 'Couldn't have got in through the skylight, so how? Unless someone had a key. I'll bet it's an inside job.'

'Why should anyone want to steal my stuff?' she asked despairingly.

'Oh, come on. You know it goes on all the time, industrial espionage and all that. Aren't clothing manufacturers always pinching each other's designs?'

Arlene drove her fist into her palm. 'You're right. Someone's robbed me of my newest creations, and I've a suspicion who. And who helped him do it.'

'Who?'

'I think it's Marty Blake, probably assisted by the big chief at the top... Vincent Gabor.'

'How can you be so sure? There are a dozen designers who could have done it.' Eugene placed a comforting hand on her shoulder but she didn't bend, rigid with fury and indignation.

'I met him at the Cloth Show. And that's not all... he'd seen my work at a charity function. If he's running out of ideas, and don't forget he's been pulling out all the stops over the past year and may be feeling pretty jaded, then what's to prevent him deciding to help himself to something of mine and rehash it as his?'

Eugene pulled a face, as if unable to contemplate such an underhanded trick. Wide boy he might be, but there was always a kind of fairness about his own dealings in the trade. Honour among thieves didn't seem to exist in the rarefied atmosphere of *haute couture*.

'You mean, he broke in here?' Eugene hadn't met Blake personally, but had read about him in the papers and seen him on television. 'Burglary's hardly his style, is it?'

'It wasn't burglary. No one's tampered with the lock. He had a key. I can't believe it of her, Eugene, but there's only one person who could have given it to him.' She wanted to break down and cry, feeling as if she'd been raped. 'That's my assistant, Tina Morris. Funnily enough, she rang to say she was ill. Somehow I don't think I'll be seeing her again.'

Chapter 4

'So you see, I've simply got to help her,' Julia said, looking across the round marble-topped table at Will, having just finished giving him details of Arlene's loss.

He pulled a serious face, humouring her in an annoying, patronising way. He lifted his pint to his lips and took a long pull, then put it down on the coaster, wiped his mouth on the back of his hand and said, unenthusiastically, 'If you say so.'

'I do say so. She's in trouble. Been robbed. Doesn't that mean anything to you?'

'Sounds like a job for the police, not us.'

'She won't do that, not yet. Wants to try it her own way first. Eugene was furious.'

'And who, darling girl, is Eugene?' Will drawled, his voice world-weary and cynical.

'He's her friend. He was there when she discovered she'd been robbed. He wants to deck Marty Blake.'

'Does he indeed? How macho. Well, good luck to him. I hope he knows what he's taking on.'

The *Flying Goose* was crowded with Saturday night drinkers. Built in 1880, on a main road where once a posting-inn had stood, it had survived a firebomb during the blitz in World War Two, and retained its Victorian opulence of polished mahogany and bevel-edged mirrors etched with ferns. One of its finest features was a stained glass panel depicting art nouveau beauties, their flowing hair entwined with the names of breweries. The air was redolent of the fermented hops and tobacco of ages, though there were plenty of non-smoking areas now.

It was Julia's local; not that she drank much, but had needed to meet Will somewhere outside the office, asking his advice concerning Arlene's problems. She had found her friend in tears last night, alarmed to see this usually level-headed girl so upset. She had calmed down after threatening to castrate Marty Blake and hang Tina up by her thumbs. Then, her face set grimly, she announced her plan, one in which Julia was involved.

Nonplussed but willing, Julia required Will's help if she was to fall in with it.

He had been happy to meet her, almost too eager for comfort and she was glad he was sitting opposite. Even so, his foot kept touching hers under the table. She moved it, but he was persistent, and she realised that had he been at her side, he would undoubtedly have had his hand on her knee by now, probably fondling her inner thigh. The thought made her hot, a flush mounting to her cheeks.

She took a sip of her gin and tonic, cleared her throat and asked, 'Can you tell me anything about Vincent Gabor?'

Will's eyes sharpened and he leaned forward. 'Is he mixed up in this?'

'We don't know for sure, but yes, Arlene suspects him. What do you know?'

'Vincent Gabor is a self-made man, son of mid-European refugees. He was born and educated in England, went to Oxford, I believe. Rumour has it he's made a fortune through wheeling and dealing, and has invested some of it in the fashion industry. He has contacts worldwide. Dips his fingers into any number of pies, and is never over-scrupulous when it comes to making a profit.'

'Arlene's suggested I get a job modelling for Marty Blake,' she said. 'He won't know I'm her friend, and maybe I can find something out.'

'And how is Denise going to take it if you have too much time off?' he asked, ever practical.

'I've a holiday due, and anyway, I thought we might sell it to her with the offer of a story, if I find that Blake's guilty.'

'That's sound. She might wear it.'

'Will you help me persuade her?' Julia asked, remembering Arlene's pep talk and pasting on her most winning smile.

It was after ten o'clock and the crowd was thicker. The pub provided a showcase for aspiring bands, the skittle alley used for gigs most weekends. Now the younger element was herding towards the improvised stage, but this didn't do much to lessen the crush in the public bar. The noise was deafening as the support band struck up, and Will moved over to the banquette where Julia sat. She couldn't slide away from him, blocked by a gangling youth with a shaven head and rings in his eyebrows.

Will, ever the opportunist, bent closer and shouted in her ear. 'Marty Blake is Gabor's protégé. I've heard they're thick as thieves, and that seems to be the case, if what Arlene suspects is true. Gabor's useful; he can get garments made in the sweatshops of Sri Lanka, and will front up the money. In exchange he enjoys all the glamour of the industry and gets to fuck beautiful models, to boot.'

Sure enough, she felt his hand close on her knee. It was like a self-fulfilling prophecy. Up it travelled, pausing momentarily to see if she would protest, then journeying on, finding the curve of her mons under the little white panties. Julia's exclamation of indignation was lost in the uproar surrounding them. Will didn't look at her, just kept on talking.

'Gabor's a big fish, Julia,' he said, and tickled the spot at the top of her cleft, where the outer labia protected her clitoris. 'It's not wise to tangle with him.'

'I must help Arlene,' she insisted, increasingly uncomfortable, unable to stop herself from resting against the back of the bench and slipping down a fraction so that her mound was lifted towards his fingers.

'Did I say you shouldn't?' he went on calmly, and she felt him easing round the edge of her knickers and starting to brush over her floss. 'Just be careful.'

'Don't,' she hissed. 'Someone may see you.'

'Unlikely,' he answered, chuckling. 'You don't really want me to stop, do you?'

Before she could answer they were interrupted by a weedy man with a ferret face and sparse, sandy hair who clapped Will on the shoulder, shouting, 'Hello there, chummy. How's your belly off for spots? And who are you, deary? What a choice bit of totty.'

He leered at Julia and she was certain his base instincts had drawn him there, just when Will was fingering her crotch. She disliked him instantly, hating the way in which he smiled as he addressed her in that disparaging tone. She escaped Will's hand under cover of the table, sat up and rearranged her skirt, all without the newcomer seeing, or so she hoped.

'Hello, George,' Will said, unimpressed. 'Sit you down, if you can find a chair. This is Julia Jones. Julia, meet George Comby. He was with me at the *Daily Courier* in our misspent youth.'

She nodded and made appropriate noises, while George continued to give her lecherous glances. With typical bad timing, the pierced and tattooed youth on her other side got up and headed for the skittle alley and the band. George instantly squeezed himself into the vacant seat and set his whisky tot on the table.

'I'm warning you, George, Julia is one of these new girls,' Will said. 'If you refer to her again as "totty" you'll probably get a clip round the ear.'

Ignoring Will's advice, George continued to subject her to his lascivious stares, pressing his bony thigh against hers. She couldn't move in the close confinement of the table and bench, crushed between him and Will. The bar was dimly lit, but she could see that both men were flaunting erections: Will's jeans were bulging and George's corduroy trousers were full beneath the fly buttons.

'What are you doing in this neck of the woods?' Will asked. 'Not your usual stamping-ground, is it?'

'Had to see a man about a dog, if you get my drift,' George answered, squeezing Julia's hand, which lay on the table. 'No, actually, it was to fix up a photo-shoot. For a skin-mag, you know. Nice work if you can get it.'

'I heard you were concentrating on photography now,' Will said, and Julia was glad to have him there, protecting her like a faithful mastiff. There was an ambience about George that made her think of dark alleys and deceitful deeds.

'That's right. I'm in with most of the top-shelf porno magazines. They like my work.'

'We've got a bit of a problem here,' Will said, picking up George's empty glass. 'Maybe you can help us. Another Scotch? Hang on while I get it.'

Julia wanted to stop him from leaving her with the unpleasant George, but he was already elbowing his way to the bar.

'And what do you do, darling?' George asked, his eyes never quite meeting hers. He always seemed to focus just beyond the person he was addressing, as if unwilling to allow them a peep into the windows of his soul, which she imagined to be black and wrinkled and hard as an old prune. And Will had once been his bosom buddy? He dropped in her estimation.

'I'm a model,' she replied, and this wasn't entirely untrue. She had modelled for Arlene in a fashion show once.

'Are you? Well, you're pretty enough and have a great figure.' He slipped an arm round the back of the seat and fastened his clammy hand on her shoulder, his fingers moving over the flesh revealed by her sleeveless crop-top. His predatory gaze dropped to where her breasts filled the white jersey cloth.

'I'm rather on the short side, even in high heels,' she said quickly, unable to shift away from him. 'Fashion models are expected to be tall and thin.'

'You're okay. I like petite, curvaceous girls,' he leered, licking his thin lips.

'Here you go, George,' Will said, returning with the whisky, and Julia had never been more thankful to see him.

'Cheers,' George said, and knocked it back in one. 'Now then, you said you wanted my help.'

'Julia's a model, but she needs pictures for her folio.'

'No problem. I'll do them.'

'I haven't much money,' Julia put in, unwilling to be indebted to him.

'That's all right. I'll get paid if any of them are used.'

'Not for porno mags?'

'Call it art, my dear,' he answered, running his tongue over his slack lower lip.

'But I want poses that will make people take me seriously as a model for clothes,' she protested, having second thoughts about the whole idea.

'And so they will. I can see you doing kinky clobber. Fetish gear's all the rage now, and you don't have to be into the scene to wear it. Leather, PVC, chains, studs, bondage straps; you can buy them in lots of highstreet stores, or something remarkably like them. You look vulnerable and innocent, yet with a hint of naughtiness, too. It'll drive the punters wild. Who are you going to apply to for a job?'

She glanced at Will questioningly, but he nodded and she said, 'Marty Blake.'

'Going straight to the main man, eh? And why not? I've found models for him before.'

'So you know him?' Will asked cautiously.

'Of course, old boy.' George shrugged and looked meaningfully at his empty glass.

Will didn't take the hint, saying, 'There you are then, Julia. When shall we start?'

'No time like the present,' George suggested eagerly.

'Now?' She wasn't prepared for this.

'Yes. Have you got your car with you, Will? I was going to get a cab back to my place.'

Will nodded.

'Right, let's go then.' George stood up. 'Ready, Julia? I'm going to make you a star,' he promised.

He took her arm as they made their way towards the exit. There he leaned closer, his unpleasant breath fanning her cheek as he added. 'I expect a return. Nothing is for nothing, girl, and I have my own method of extracting payment from lovely girls.'

Although he wanted her to sit in the back of the car with him, she succeeded in occupying the front seat next to Will.

'I'm still in the same place,' he said, as Will turned the ignition key. 'Sylvan Avenue, Wood Green. Remember? We used to have a whale of a time there, didn't we? Once I'd got rid of the wife, that is. Silly cow didn't approve of me drinking. We're divorced now. Good riddance to bad rubbish, I say.'

London was still busy but Will, who knew it like the back of his hand, took diverse shortcuts to bringing them to George's residence, a late Victorian terrace house in a tree lined street. His own car was on a hard standing in his small front garden.

Iron railings and a tiled path led to the porch and the front door, with all its original brass fittings. Inside there was a passageway, not unlike that of Julia's own house, then up two flights of stairs and into a studio that stretched the entire length and width of the attic. It smelt of cigarettes, stale booze, developing fluid and coition.

'Make yourselves at home,' George said, taking off his jacket. 'We'll start with a few shots as you are, love. Just to get in the mood. I shan't be a tick.'

He busied himself with his equipment, very professional all of a sudden, the whisky addict banished. She put down her bag and mounted the shallow step of the podium. George adjusted the back sheet, reflectors and lighting. He then retreated, squinting at her through the viewfinder.

'Now, darling... stand proud, lean on your right hip. That's it. Look at me. Straight at me. Big sexy eyes, think sexy thoughts, pout, sweetie, pout those gorgeous lips as if you're about to fasten them round a great fat cock. Lovely!'

This wasn't too bad. Julia began to get into the swing of it, remembering photos she'd seen of famous models, aping their brash confidence, the way they stared arrogantly down their elegant noses, thrust out their bosoms and arched their necks with never a crotch-shot between them, just the blatant suggestion of promiscuity.

Soon George had her take off her fleece and display her bare middle in the crop-top. 'Hitch up your skirt. That's great. What legs! Now we'll try something a little bit more daring, shall we?'

He handed her a bundle of garments and indicated a screen. She changed behind it and came out wearing a red leather skirt and a basque. Under his direction, she assumed an expression of utter boredom and indifference. She was the epitome of every man's wet dream, with her sulky mouth, and the way her heavy-lidded eyes stared defiantly into the camera as she straddled a damask upholstered chair. Her breasts were pushed high by the restrictive corset. The short skirt barely reached the tops of her wantonly spread legs, exposing the slim expanse of her upper thighs, and a glimpse of the tempting blonde floss at her apex. Black stockings covered her from toes to above the knee, fastened by fancy garters. It was a pose that was ageless: she could have been a nineteenth century whore posing for some be-whiskered photographic pioneer who'd already realised the commercial value of racy pictures.

She could feel the colour running into her face as George stared through the aperture and Will lay on the couch, smiling in an almost proprietorial manner.

George tried out other positions. 'Let's go with the flow,' he said. 'You're a natural. I knew you would be the moment I clocked you.'

Julia laid on her stomach, propped on her elbows, one leg out straight, the other bent. It was charming, guileless even, till the eye travelled to her naked buttocks, firm globes ripe for caning. In another she bent to fasten her shoe, her breasts lifting even higher as she glanced provocatively over her shoulder, her skirt riding up to show her bottom crease and the downy hair of her pudenda.

'Now lay down, dear,' George urged, and pointed to the cushioned-heaped settee at the back of the podium. 'That's it. Let's see your pussy. I want your hand down there, touching. I want your head back, your tongue circling your lips, and your eyes half-closed as if you're going to come at any minute.'

'I can't do that,' she murmured, but her hands were already on her satin smooth skin, her thighs bent outwards.

'Yes you can. Pretend you're in your bedroom and there's no one to see. Do it like when you can't help playing with yourself.' George's voice was thick with excitement, his prick distorting the front of his cord trousers. 'Come on, sweetie, do it for me,' and he waltzed round her, snapping as he went. He ended up somewhere between her feet, the camera aimed at her crotch.

She nibbled her lower lip as she obeyed, not so much him as her own urges, and combed her fingers through her pubes. She was acutely aware of the openness of her sex and of George's third eye, the camera lens. Juice glistened on her vulva, and the hot bright lamps ruthlessly exposed every frill and curl of her genitals, beating down on the sensitive cleft. And, more than this, she felt the heat on the rabid swell of her clitoris. She touched it with a fingertip, and pleasure fired through her.

'Make it wet,' said George.

His gruff words turned her on unbearably. Far from this intensely private act being something secretive and shameful, here was someone actually encouraging her to do it. He put down the camera and reached for a bottle of baby oil, and before she knew what was happening he flipped back the cap and poised it over her quim. She started at the sudden chill as several shining drops fell directly onto her clit. Any residue he massaged into her thighs and up and over her mound, the pubic hair shimmering.

For an instant his finger followed the oil and she gasped, shuddered and wanted desperately to come. Then he withdrew and took up his camera again. As if on cue Will knelt behind her. She felt his hands on her breasts, teasing the erect nipples, and an even greater thrill as he leaned across to take one in his mouth, while continuing to finger the other.

'Oh... that's good,' she mumbled, despite her shame.

'Back off now, Will,' George instructed. 'I don't want you in the frame. Julia's supposed to be doing it for herself. Come on, baby, give yourself a brisk wank... that's great... come on, I want to see you come,' he urged crudely as the shutter clicked.

She crooked her middle finger and caught the underside of her clitoris, and with every touch the waves of orgasm swept closer. She sighed and tensed, her bottom cheeks clenching. A silence fell over the studio; a watching, waiting silence broken only by the camera's whirr. She had forgotten the men, the camera, the lateness of the hour and the weird circumstances, every sense focussed on the sensations pouring through her. One giant wave, a second and then a third lifted her onto the rollercoaster and she screamed as her climax thundered, screamed and writhed and offered herself voluptuously to George and his lens.

'Oh, *boy*...' he croaked, still sliding around her, seeking ever more lurid shots. 'This'll have the boys spanking the monkey!'

At that Julia returned to reality, leaving the euphoric clouds and coming down to earth with a rude bang. 'But you said I would do fashion poses,' she protested.

'So you shall, pet. And the first pics we took of you in your ordinary gear will be fine to present to a prospective employer. Though I've a hunch Blake's sponsor will approve of these even more.'

'You talking about Vincent Gabor?' Will asked, his hands shaking slightly as he lit a cigarette, even though Julia was now sitting with her legs primly together and her nipples again covered by the basque's lace edging.

'Sure thing. He's encouraging Blake to go for the leather and kink. I'll get this developed pronto, show them the proofs and arrange a meeting.'

'Don't we get to see them first?' Will was obviously keen to protect her interests.

'If you want.'

'We do.'

'I'll give you a bell when they're ready.'

'Then, that's it?' Julia couldn't wait to get out of the corset that was nipping her waist and pinching her ribs, her breasts pushed unnaturally high. 'I can go home now?'

'So soon?' George said regretfully, his tongue wetting his lips again. 'I hoped we could... you know... get better acquainted.'

'Another time,' Will intervened, and Julia slipped back behind the screen, tearing at the lacing of the corset as she went. She heard Will and George talking.

'Don't I get to dip my wick?' the photographer asked.

'That's up to her, but I doubt it. She maintains she's a virgin.'

George gave a disbelieving bark of laughter. 'Pull the other leg, Will, it's got bells on.'

'I'm telling the truth.'

'You mean to say you haven't fucked her?'

'No. And I sincerely believe no one else has, either.'

'But she'll do other things, give head or a hand job?'

'Yes, though never with me. But I've watched her at it.'

'Have you?' George wheezed eagerly. 'I've got the most monumental stiffy. It refused to lie down all the time I was shooting her, and still won't. So now what

41

am I going to do with it?'

'Sorry, but that's your problem,' said Will coolly. 'I'm in the same state and we'll both be doing the five-finger exercise tonight.'

Julia stepped from behind the screen wearing her own clothes, glad the session was over. 'Thank you, George,' she said, and sort of meant it. Posing had been embarrassing, surprisingly exciting, and would provide her with pictures, but she didn't think she would care to repeat it.

'Okay, Julia, if that's how you want it,' he said regretfully, then shrugged and added, 'Maybe things will be different next time we meet.'

'Don't come down,' Will said. 'We'll find our own way out.'

George saw them to the door, then retreated to the darkroom adjacent to the studio and removed the film from his camera.

'That's wicked!' Marty exclaimed as he watched the leggy, coffee-coloured model stalk down the centre of the long, high-ceilinged room. 'Absolutely ace, Cressida. You've caught the mood perfectly. Marta Hari... spy, dancer, harlot. It'll be a showstopper. If Mrs Hooper-Jones doesn't buy it, I'll get a job down the mines.'

By now he had conveniently forgotten that this stunning, sequinned and beaded gown, a la the 1914-18 war, was not his at all, but Arlene Murphy's. He was so powerful, or rather Gabor was, that he took chances that would scare an ordinary person. All he had to do was move a spangle here, a few diamantés there, and he could justify putting his label in it.

'That fat old broad,' Cressida said, her voice like rich dark chocolate, her slanting agate eyes heavy with scorn, 'is like a sack of potatoes tied up in the middle,' and she fondled her own eighteen-inch waist.

'Ah, the intolerance of youth,' he said blandly, lounging in the chrome and black leather armchair, one trousered leg crossed over the other. 'So she is, but never mind, dear, I always seduce her into a double think, urging her to dismiss the nubile models from her mind. I suggest that though they show the clothes, it takes someone like herself to give the garments pizzazz.'

He caught sight of himself in the large mirror screwed to the red brick wall of this fiercely expensive riverside apartment. It had been part of a derelict factory before conversion by one of Gabor's building companies. It was high fashion. So was Marty.

He would have been the first to admit that he had done things of which he wasn't proud in order to reach the highest echelon of the fashion world. He'd recognised at art school that talent, even sizzling talent like his, wasn't enough. What was needed was a large slice of luck, a conscience that wouldn't keep one awake at night, and the ability to seize life by the throat before it got you.

With the cool for which he was famous, he made a critical note of the fit of his Madras cotton shirt, which, along with his baggy trousers, were top-sellers from his couture range. Branching off into menswear had been one of Gabor's inspirations. Now every go-ahead executive worth his salt had at least one Marty Blake suit in his wardrobe - classy, sexy, and pricey.

'How can she be so stupid?' Cressida said, pursuing the subject of Mrs Hooper-Jones as she paced across the polished wooden floor and came to rest in front of him.

'Her husband's a millionaire. That gives her the right to be any goddamn thing she pleases, including stupid,' he answered nastily, running a hand up Cressida's thigh.

She was so close he could smell her costly perfume and the scent of her highlighted dreadlocks. His cock stirred, trapped in his trousers. Her breasts were nearly as flat as a boy's, but her umber nipples jutted out like organ stops.

The gown she wore was stunning and he marvelled how Arlene had managed to do it on a shoestring. The girl had imagination, flair and guts, and the memory of their encounter in the storeroom fired his lust even as he directed it towards Cressida. But though he had penetrated Arlene and brought her to pleasure, it hadn't stopped him robbing her, though, creative artist that he was, he understood just how deeply this would have wounded her.

Barbaric, outrageous, the dress would be a blockbuster, selling to the highest bidder when he showed it. The bodice was made of thick gold mesh, slashed to the navel. The sleeves were scalloped and asymmetric, trailing jet beads. The black silk-chiffon skirt clung to Cressida's lean hips, clearly defining the deep crease between her buttocks and giving him thoughts of whips and canes, paddles and tawse. She would be a willing party, he knew, though with her height, strength and attitude, she preferred the dominatrix role. It was slit so high on each side that every movement showed her stocking tops. Her height was increased to six foot four inches by her stilt-heeled ankle boots. She wore no panties, the shadow of her mound visible, carefully depilated, except for a line of black hair that accentuated the division of her sex-lips.

Marty parted his legs to give her easier access to his cock. It was rock hard. Besides being one of the world's highest paid models, she gave superb head. As he lay back, anticipating the moment when her plum-coloured lips would fasten round his helm, he dwelt on Mrs Hooper-Jones. Even in the heat of passion his thoughts were never far from his other lust, that of making money.

She was his best customer, spending thousands of dollars a year in his West End showroom, ordering half a dozen ensembles a season. Though a middle-aged, dumpy New Yorker, by the time he'd finished smooth talking her she was convinced that the mannequins were mere mirages - substitutes for real women. He told her that it was only when an inspired garment was actually cut on the customer that it could finally achieve perfection. And she, besotted by him, believed it.

'D'you know, Cressida, I feel almost sorry for those rich, pampered bitches,' he said, as he fingered her smooth pussy flesh. 'What they really want is to have their cunts stroked, like this. They're lonely and frustrated and their husbands are workaholics. I'll bet a dime to a dollar that Mrs HJ goes back to her apartment overlooking Central Park, all alone after some glitzy charity function, and plays with her pussy as she looks in the mirror, thinking, "I'm wearing a Marty Blake". Then she wanks until she can't stand.'

43

'They've all got the hots for you,' she said, and gave a deep-throated chuckle as she rubbed her clit against his fingers. 'What d'you want me to do? Suck you off or fuck you?'

'In a minute you're going to do both, but I'm enjoying this. Part those lovely legs and let me get at your quim,' he growled, his eyes narrowed to tigerish slits.

She stood with her crotch on a level with his face, hiked back the skirt and her beautiful, tapered hands came down each side of her labia, the deep blue lacquer on her almond-shaped nails contrasting with the strip of inky fur fringing her slate-dark lips. She stretched the wings and her clitoris protruded, red as blood and well developed.

Marty leaned forward and extended his tongue, flicking over the erect bud, his balls clenching as he heard Cressida's indrawn gasp of pleasure. She opened herself wider and the juice welled from her vulva. He could taste it, salty and strong, and ran his tongue over her delta while one of his fingers moved higher, finding the puckered moue of her anus and pushing against it, gaining entrance to her rectum.

The little mouth yielded, and he sank his forefinger inside to the second knuckle, feeling the taut muscles gripping it, and remembering the blissful sensation of thrusting his upright tool into that dark, secret tunnel.

'My tits,' she pleaded, still holding her petals apart.

With his tongue lapping her clit, he reached up and found the two ardent points poking through the mesh. As he moved from one to the other he wondered if he could alter the cut of the bodice so that they were always on display. He teased them, made them swell even more, and she pressed against his tongue, mewling like a Siamese cat on heat as she convulsed in orgasm.

Marty's cock pressed urgently against his trousers and his balls felt tight in their hairy purse, aching with the need to discharge their contents. He slouched low on his spine, and Cressida took her long nails to his zipper and ran it down. He relaxed as her hand lifted his heavy cock from inside. Then, with feline agility, she lifted her skirt up out of the way, sat astride his lap and sank down slowly, holding herself at the tip of his cock and rubbing her swollen slit against it. He grabbed her legs and hitched them up till her ankles rested on his shoulders. The force of gravity pressed her down so that his dick plunged into her, burying deep. Holding her firmly under the buttocks, his fingers indenting the smooth brown haunches, he lifted her up and down over his pulsating length.

Cressida took her weight on her arms, clinging each side of the winged chair. Her face was contorted like an African mask, full lips pulled back over her even white teeth, her eyes fierce and unfocused. Her body heat swept up like a miasma, and he breathed deeply of its odour.

He closed his eyes as the first spasm shuddered through him. Sparks danced, sensations scorched and he erupted, and amidst the volcanic outburst he was aware of Vincent coming into the room, encouraging him.

Marty dropped from nirvana and tumbled Cressida off him. He tucked his cock away and did up his flies. Vincent continued to grin, clad in a knee-length white towelling robe, loosely girded, his stoutly muscled calves supporting him,

44

his phallus, impressive even in repose, showing through the opening. Larger than most, naked of foreskin, the exposed helm was a dark purple. It slanted to the right, the black pubic thatch glistening with the pre-come juice weeping from its single eye.

He was flanked by girls.

Two walked with their heads down, hands clasped behind their backs. Their hair was waist-length, one toffee-gold, one a brunette. They were barefoot and naked, except for a tiny suede cache-sex and a spiked collar fastened tightly round their necks. Slender and shy, their colour was high, their attitude one of shame, their rose-pink nipples crimping at the drop of temperature. Behind them strode a pair of strapping Amazons in black leather catsuits. They were as tall as Cressida, big breasted, wide-hipped, their hair piled high, strutting arrogantly and swishing whips that trailed several knotted cords. Careful not to strike Gabor, they flicked the girls' rumps, making them yelp, though never daring to look up or protect themselves from these stinging blows.

'The jacuzzi is the best thing since sliced bread,' he announced, jerking a thumb at his slave girls who immediately crouched at his feet and towelled his legs. 'You should have joined us. Plenty of room for all. Aren't you glad I insisted it was included when we designed your conservatory?'

'Of course, you always know best,' Marty said, though his sarcasm was lost on Gabor. This was one of the few things he could do better than his foreign sponsor. No one dispensed irony like the British.

Gabor was hardly listening, standing with his legs spread, his wet soles making imprints in the rug. He was studying Cressida with shrewd eyes, then said, 'Is that one of the dresses you've recently acquired?'

'I don't know what you mean,' Blake prevaricated.

'Then it is an Arlene Murphy,' Gabor said, admiringly. 'It's superb. She has style, that little nobody.' Then he glared down at the honey-haired slave. 'Mind your manners, slut. Did I give you permission to touch my cock?'

'I'm sorry, master,' she quavered, sinking low and placing her mouth on his foot.

'Punishment time,' he announced.

The leather-clad women hauled the girl up and dragged her to a stool, a plain thing of metal and thin upholstery. She was forced to bend over it, her knees on one side, her outstretched arms on the other, her hair streaming down to touch the floor.

'Oh please, don't hurt me,' she sobbed, but Gabor strolled across and placed a hand on her raised hindquarters, then had the women open her cheeks wide so he could penetrate her fissure. He examined it with brutal fingers, making her cry out. She was helpless to move, her ankles gripped and pulled apart, her hands roped and tied to the stool.

'Marty, would you like to do the honours?' Vincent said, with a sly grin.

'What a splendid notion,' he replied, his lust momentarily appeased, yet his cock already stirring at the sight of the trussed and naked slave.

'Give him the whip, Kay,' Vincent Gabor commanded and, after the tallest of his Amazons had done so, he had her stand beside him so he could finger her shaven mons and pierced nipples through conveniently placed openings in her catsuit.

Marty Blake's palm closed round the smooth haft and balanced it. Short and strong, it supported the long wicked plait that ended in a dozen knotted thongs. It would hurt, he knew, no stranger to the kiss of the lash. Submissive or dominant; he selected whichever role appealed at any particular time. It depended entirely on his mood and what was happening in other areas of his life. Now, he longed to see Arlene stretched over the stool. What right had she to be so clever? No one should be more talented than him.

He took up a position behind the girl's bare posterior, flexing his arm. He knew Vincent was watching him critically, a past master at chastisement. He wanted to acquit himself well. As in everything else, a certain rivalry existed here between the two men. Lifting the whip high, Blake struck with measured ferocity. His aim was as accurate as when he used his cutting-out shears. He had the eye of a perfectionist, and soon raw red bars striped the slave's quivering flanks. Her hips writhed and rose, to be held down remorselessly by Kay and the other Amazon.

Power raced through Marty: he felt himself to be omnipotent.

He'd stolen Arlene's work and no one was any the wiser. Tina wouldn't tell. She daren't. Besides, she was in love with him. And he suspected that Arlene, too, had been bewitched that one time he screwed her. And this little creature threshing and screaming under the whip was the recipient of his rage and passion. The blows fell across the backs of her thighs, the underhang of her buttocks, and she begged for mercy, her struggles subsiding to reflex actions at each cut.

'Enough,' ordered Gabor, and Blake allowed the whip to fall to his side. 'Kay, take the wretched girl and put her under the shower. And you,' he pointed at the other slave, who was trembling lest she follow the same fate as her friend, 'fetch Miss Cressida a cup of coffee. Quickly, or you'll be bending over the stool yourself. Come over here, Marty, we've an important matter to discuss.'

He moved to where a settee stood near a low glass and teak table. Blake sat and watched as Gabor took up a large manila envelope and drew something out. 'Take a look at these,' he said, handing the contents over. 'It's a new girl who wants to go into modelling. George sent me the proofs. Don't you think she's charming?'

Marty had seen hundreds of CVs and folios from aspiring mannequins and, at first, he only glanced through these, then his attention sharpened as he looked at the blonde, blue-eyed girl who seemed to return his stare with amused precocity. First, she was in a denim skirt and crop-top, pretty, almost wholesome looking, yet with a certain naughty gleam in her eye. The next pictures confirmed her double personality. Wearing a red leather basque and miniskirt she became a tart, albeit a well brought up one.

She was gorgeous, and he eyed every pose closely. It was always exhilarating to discover a brand new talent, and now Marty held it in his hands. But he wanted more than just pictures - he wanted *her*.

'What d'you think?' asked Gabor, smiling knowingly.

A nod of approval from Blake spoke volumes. 'What's her name?' he asked.

'George rang to see what I thought of the proofs. Her name is Julia Jones. Nice and simple, eh? We'll let her keep it, and I think we should see her as soon as possible. Don't want some other designer signing her up.'

'When?' Blake felt a hot rush of excitement, a boy again waiting for Christmas morning to come.

'Tomorrow,' Gabor replied decisively, the pictures in one hand, his other disappearing inside the robe to fondle his erection. 'We'll invite her for an audition.'

Chapter 5

Julia wasn't familiar with the Highgate area of London. All she knew was that it contained a famous cemetery where many celebrities of the past were interred, including Karl Marx.

It was a place where only those with money could afford to live. George had given her Vincent Gabor's address and told her to arrange to go there for an interview with him.

'He's over the moon about your pics, sweetie,' he had crooned down the phone. 'Can't wait to see you in the flesh.'

'And Marty Blake will be there?' she asked, unsure whether to be pleased or sorry that she'd made an impact.

'He'll be around, for sure, but it's Gabor you've got to impress.'

She pulled up at the gates of Hazel House. They were open and she drove her old banger along the drive and stopped outside the main entrance. She mounted the steps and pressed the bell, meanwhile looking up and around at the impressive building. It was a solid house set foursquare in a large piece of ground. It had stood there for a hundred years, and the monkey-puzzle and cedar trees were well established, as were the azalea bushes and privet hedges. The garden was immaculate and the mansion maintained to a high standard. The car she shared with Arlene looked battered and seedy in comparison with a Mercedes and Jaguar parked nearby.

I shouldn't have come, she thought, hearing the bell go ding-dong deep within the building. She was acutely nervous, even though Arlene had advised her on her outfit and she was wearing a skirt and top in caramel linen, with a cashmere cardigan. A conservative ensemble, but the cut was superb, one of Arlene's own creations. Neat shoes and beige stockings completed the picture, and Arlene had also worked on Julia's hair, making the most of the bouncy curls, and helping her with her make-up, too, emphasising her English Rose complexion and darkening the lashes that framed her violet-blue eyes.

This increased Julia's confidence yet made her oddly uncomfortable. She wasn't used to wearing dressy clothes. Although these were quite casual, she

47

much preferred trainers or terrain sandals, jeans and T-shirts or shorts in warm weather. The stockings clung, upheld by white ribbon suspenders attached to a narrow, lace-trimmed garter-belt. Ordinarily she would have had bare legs, for the day was warm, a hint of approaching summer borne on the balmy breeze that lifted her curls and ran impudent fingers up inside her skirt and around the coffee lace trim of her French knickers.

She heard footsteps coming along the hall and the two halves of the double door were flung open with a flourish. Julia had a quick impression of height and severity, finding herself face to face with an intimidating woman, who said without a smile, 'Miss Jones?'

'Th-that's me,' Julia answered, stumbling over her words.

'I'm Grace Pennick, Mr Gabor's personal secretary and assistant,' the woman went on, and stood to one side so that Julia might enter. 'Please come in.'

'I had thought that perhaps he'd want to see me in his office,' Julia gabbled on, following Grace across a hall as big as a ballroom.

'He works from home a great deal,' she answered crisply, her demeanour not one that encouraged small talk. Julia found her formidable. She was dressed in a charcoal-grey suit, the jacket severe and the skirt calf-length. Her sheer black stockings fitted flawlessly and she wore lace-up shoes with high heels. Her hair was cut short and swept back from her plain, broad-featured face. Her flat cheekbones were rouged, her eyes outlined by kohl and mascara, and her mouth was a wide scarlet slash. The use of cosmetics did nothing for her, too heavily applied to be soft and feminine. When she twisted her lips into a sneer, her expression was one of cruelty and rapaciousness.

She opened a door at the rear of the hall and they entered a large panelled room. It was filled with tapestries and antiques. Whoever Vincent Gabor was and where he fitted into the equation, there was no denying his exquisite taste. Julia gazed in awe at the collection of bronzes that stood on tables and plinths. It took her a second to take in their content. Sculpted and cast by master craftsmen, they were executed in the style of Ancient Greece. There were muscular men having intercourse with naked, buxom goddesses; hairy satyrs with goat legs and massive phalli penetrating the quims of slender, nude nymphs; men copulating with men, women pleasuring women, and mixed groups indulging in the penetration of every orifice.

Julia, staring at them dumbstruck, wondered if they were originals thousands of years old and worth a fortune. Her eyes kept returning to one in particular where a voluptuous girl bound with chains was on her hands and knees. Her bare bottom was lifted towards a grotesque, dwarfish figure with an enormous cock, who was brandishing a whip. Stripes had been carved on her back and buttocks, tears made to trickle down her cheeks. The piece was so lifelike that Julia almost expected to hear her scream.

'What a collection,' she said in awe. 'I've never seen anything like it.'

'Nor will you,' Grace answered with almost personal pride, and a lustful look in her eyes as she stared at Julia. 'Mr Gabor is a connoisseur of art. He specialises in erotica. You appreciate them? That's good. He'll be pleased to know you're responsive.'

'I've come about a modelling job, nothing else,' Julia reminded her, but was disconcerted when Grace, hatchet-faced and unsmiling, reached out, slid a hand under her cardigan and started to fondle her nipples.

'So?' the woman said, unbuttoned Julia's linen top, and with stunning presumptuousness freed her breasts from her lace and satin bra, displaying their ripe roundness and luscious tips. 'What better way to begin?'

Julia was stunned, feeling unsteady on her high heels, aware of the heat of the room, the heat of Grace's fingers, the heat welling up in her loins. A hand slid down, lifting the hem of Julia's skirt and stroking her thighs between her stocking tops and knickers. Not really knowing what to do, she stood perfectly still under the woman's caresses, her arms hanging limply at her sides, and she felt fingers worming inside the leg of her knickers.

She gasped, moved back a step and, with a mocking twist to her lips, Grace released her. 'W-when will I meet Mr Gabor?' Julia blurted, her heart racing, her mind in a confused spin. 'Are you going to tell him I'm here?'

'I shall interview you first. He trusts my judgement, and we're very impressed with your photos. Have you brought along your CV?'

'Yes,' Julia said, pulling a folder from her bag. It contained her hastily concocted history of modelling work to date. Will had dreamed it up on his word processor.

'This looks interesting,' Grace said, sitting on the chintz-covered window seat and browsing through it. 'Though it seems you aren't very experienced.'

'That's true, but I'm willing to learn,' Julia insisted, wondering if Grace guessed the CV was a fabrication.

It had been Denise's idea. After a few moments of doubt she had agreed with Will's suggestion that it would be a great story if Julia could pull it off, and had given the project her go-ahead. This was the chance to prove herself for which Julia had been praying, and she knew she could always rely on Will if she got into situations too hot to handle. Mobile phones were a blessing in disguise to people like them, who worked on a knife-edge and often needed an instant response and support.

To her further embarrassment, Grace reached for an envelope lying beside her and started to leaf through George's photographs. Julia could feel herself blushing. This was far worse than when she had been posing. Then it had seemed as if some other girl was performing those rude acts, not her.

'These are splendid,' Grace said, a hectic flush adding to her rouge, her pupils unnaturally large as if she'd been using belladonna. 'I'd like to see you modelling similar garments in reality, as it were. I've some here, brought along specially. Take off your clothes.'

Oh dear, another one wanting Julia to undress. What was it with people? But, certain that she must comply in order to be accepted and then spy for Arlene, she slipped her arms out of her cardigan, then took off her top and bra. She unzipped the skirt and let it drop. Now she only wore her knickers, suspender belt, stockings and shoes.

'Let me help you,' said Grace, her voice husky, and she knelt at Julia's feet, her strong hands undoing the tiny pearl buttons at the waistband of her satin drawers.

These slid down with a seductive whisper and Julia lifted her feet, one by one, so that Grace could take them off, along with the shoes. She held the silky undergarment to her face with sensual delight, then put it to one side and unclipped Julia's suspenders, front and back, and rolled down the nylons, careful not to snag them. Naked, Julia was aware of Grace's breath on her skin. She went to unhook the garter-belt, but Grace slapped her fingers away.

'What?' Julia squealed, the backs of her hands stinging.

'I shall undress you,' Grace replied sternly, and imprisoned Julia's outer labia between thumb and index finger, and walked her middle digit between the soft inner lips, finding her clitoris and starting to stimulate it.

Tingling excitement made Julia gasp. Grace smiled knowingly, then stood up and went to where articles of clothing hung on the back of a chair. She took up a wasp-waisted corset of black satin, trimmed with scarlet, and brought it over.

'I wore something like this for George,' Julia said as Grace wrapped it round her, settled her breasts in the half cups and started to pull on the lacing at the back.

It was extremely restrictive and growing tighter as Grace hauled, pausing only to snap, 'Hold the couch - I need to get a purchase. Come on, breathe in...'

'Oh... ah...' Julia grunted, bending to cling to the scroll back of the chaise longue, legs apart, the fair floss hardly covering her chubby lower lips protruding between.

She was conscious of Grace behind her, tugging as if her life depended on closing the gap of the corset to the limit. The more Julia protested, the air leaving her with a rush at every forceful jerk at the laces, the more determined Grace became.

Finally, satisfied that she couldn't reduce Julia's waist any more, she tied the ends and tucked them away. She prowled round to the front, pinching Julia's nipples till they swelled like raspberries over the basque's upper edge.

'Gorgeous,' she muttered, and bent her head to lick each one, her tongue as rough as a cat's, causing a frisson of lust to race through Julia's nervous system.

She caught a glimpse of herself in a mirror over the mantelpiece, and was struck by how extreme she looked. The black corset contrasted with her paler skin, nipping her waist to doll size, thrusting her breasts high. And, below the edge of the garment that ended at her navel, the swell of her belly and the outrageous sight of her golden fuzz sliced through by her labial slit.

'I couldn't wear this on the catwalk,' she gasped, with some difficulty.

Grace commenced running her hands over Julia's rounded buttocks, so shamelessly displayed. She wove her fingers into the valley, playing over the crimped anus, and then going lower to the damp vulva.

'You could, with a few modifications and a few additions.' As she spoke, she gave full rein to her imagination, adding a length of silk to form a skirt, or a long stole, a swathe of sable to cover naked nipples, an exotic turban on Julia's tousled hair.

She was right, transforming the revealing basque into a bodice suitable for wearing to the most star-studded première, naughty but acceptable. 'You could have been a designer yourself,' Julia said, and Grace nodded.

'Perhaps,' she agreed, whipping away the improvised skirt. 'But we can't all be prima donnas. Someone has to keep the nuts and bolts of life together. I know my place and am happy to obey Mr Gabor. There are many perks, not the least of which is this,' and she cradled Julia's sex, spreading her fingers in and around the wet delta, holding the petals apart and concentrating on the juicy button of her clitoris.

Still clinging to the walnut frame of the brocade-upholstered couch, Julia surrendered to the pleasure sweeping her towards orgasm. Grace was holding her from behind, and she hissed in Julia's ear, 'I'm going to make you come, but you're not to do it till I say you may. It's all par for the course. Our models have to be pliable and submissive.'

'W-why?' Julia was struggling to sound rational, her traitorous desire increasing, that artful finger tormenting her needful bud.

'It's a house rule,' the woman said in husky tones. 'Whoever works for Marty Blake and Mr Gabor has to know his or her place.'

'Even you?' Julia sighed, her eyes closed, and then the fingers between her thighs were too much and her pleasure peaked, her orgasm shattering into a million fiery sparks.

Then she was cruelly jarred back to reality as the woman administered a harsh slap on her bottom. 'Bad girl!' she admonished. 'Did I say you could come?'

Reeling with shock, Julia was propelled to the chaise longue and thrust down. Grace rucked up her grey skirt, revealing a forest of wiry black hair that sprouted from her mons. She knelt over Julia, spreading her thighs, the lips of her labia protruding from the thicket, crowned by a large crimson clitoris. 'Now you'll bring me off,' she grated, lowering herself till she was squatting over Julia's stunned face.

She was appalled yet fascinated by the woman's brazenly exposed and demanding sex. She had never been in such a position before, never been so close to another woman's genitals. She was disgusted yet shamefully excited, tentatively kissing that pink sliver of flesh, using her fingers to peel apart the hair-fringed folds, then sucking strongly. Grace's flesh tasted unexpectedly sweet, her juice coating Julia's cheeks and chin.

Julia found it difficult to breathe, enveloped in female flesh and female essence, while Grace was grinding her hips to match the rhythm of the enchantingly naïve lips and tongue palpating her clitoris. She was losing control, her body shaking, hands inside her blouse. 'Ah... ah!' she cried, her voice rising to a howl. 'Oh... yes! Yes! I'm coming... that's it! Oh, I'm there!'

She writhed then went rigid, and Julia felt the clitoris pulsing against her tongue and knew Grace had attained her zenith. Then giving herself no time to recover, the woman climbed off Julia and stood, her skirt falling into place. 'Get up,' she snapped. 'Don't think you're forgiven. You didn't wait to come till I gave you permission. Such disobedience can't be ignored.'

'This is silly,' Julia complained. 'Don't you want me to model more clothes?'

'No need; this is part of the test. Now, over the table - at once.'

Annoyed, apprehensive, yet with a dark skein of excitement coiling inside her, Julia did as she was told. The table was narrow, the surface highly polished, and Grace pushed a hand into the small of her back, making her lean across it. The wood pressed against her breasts, swelling over the basque, forced high by her posture.

'Grip the edge of the table,' the woman instructed.

'No,' Julia refused sulkily.

Grace grabbed her wrists, and there was a metallic snap as fur-lined handcuffs closed around them, fastened to a length of chain bolted underneath. Julia tugged, to no avail. She cringed, haunted by vivid pictures of Theona Blue as she had seen her through the window of the gymnasium. Was this cruel woman about to whip her? Fear gripped her, coupled with a reprehensible and inexplicable throb of anticipation.

Then, without warning, Grace viciously smacked her bottom. Julia yelped and clenched her buttocks, pain robbing her of breath. But this didn't stop Grace from hitting her again, her hand harsh, leaving a scalding trail. She paused and Julia, sobbing in spite of her resolution to show no emotion, hoped and prayed she had finished. Silence yawned and she strained her ears to listen for movement. She could see nothing but the carpet, and hear nothing but birdsong filtering in through the window.

Something swished behind her and she screamed at the impact as Grace struck her with a riding crop. It bit into Julia's rump, excruciating agony rising to a crescendo. Before she had time to recover the lash fell again. She clawed at the table, absorbing the pain, and when three more stripes joined the first she no longer shrieked, making mewing noises instead, choked by tears, aware of the pain yet conscious of something else - a throbbing deep inside her that resembled sexual desire.

What was happening to her? Was she becoming totally depraved?

'Ah, she's perfect. Fresh, artless... I like her.' Gabor sighed, giving a tug at the gold ring threaded through the piercing in Cressida's clit-hood. He looked down and added, 'I really must give you a diamond to go there. A diamond stud, to enhance your wonderful pussy. Would you like that?'

'Thank you, master,' she replied meekly, the feisty girl reduced to a slave in his presence.

They were in a recess built between the library and the reception room where Grace had taken Julia, where Gabor was able to spy on visitors. The mirror that hung over the fireplace was a two-way one, and he'd been watching everything his aide and the new girl had been doing. He had heard them talking, heard the whip singing, the niche wired for sound.

He stripped off his T-shirt on entering, and his finely tuned body was tanned and muscular, kept in trim by a rigorous workout routine orchestrated by his trainer. He was olive-skinned and tanned easily, his chest and limbs coated with dark hair, pectorals crowned by wine-red nipples. A scribble of hair ran down from chest to navel and there fanned out to join the black bush from which his penis rose from his rolled-down jogging pants. While observing Julia at every stage of her interview with Grace, he had ordered Cressida to kneel and press her breasts together, forming a channel for him to use for his lust. He thrust his cock between her nut-brown orbs, but hadn't come until he'd raised her, spun her round and made her stick out her rump so he could plunge into her receptive vagina, which fitted round him like a velvet glove.

Julia deserved a diamond too, he thought, watching her climb stiffly but still with innocent grace from the table and begin dressing. His cock sprung up again as he admired the red marks scoring her bottom, and he knew that very soon he'd enter the room, put on his business head and talk to her, all the while remembering her in the throes of orgasm or pain. He would hire her, of course, making her feel privileged to be a part of his team, then slowly and using all his powers of persuasion, he would seduce her. The idea of her being a virgin intoxicated him immensely.

Then he changed his mind, saying quietly to Cressida, 'On second thoughts, it would be better to keep her dangling. Wind her up and then let her go. She'll be so wired if I leave it a day or so, that she'll agree to any terms. She'll model Marty's clothes, but I also want her to join my team of artistes who entertain influential foreign customers.'

He picked up the intercom and spoke to Grace. 'Tell her to come to my penthouse suite at two o'clock tomorrow afternoon,' he said brusquely, aware of Cressida coiling herself, snakelike, round his legs, her nimble fingers forming a ring which she passed over his shaft. It stiffened and, as he gave Grace his orders, so she rubbed his escaping jism over the helm.

'You can't see her today? Very well, sir, I'll tell her,' Grace responded and replaced the phone.

Gabor heard her informing Julia that he was busy and couldn't get away till tomorrow. He noted the flicker of disappointment that passed over the girl's lovely face, and his penis swelled under Cressida's ministrations, but his thoughts were with his interview with the virgin Julia the next day.

'Did you see Blake?' Arlene demanded as soon as Julia stepped inside the door.

'No,' Julia said, dropping her bag on the hall floor and kicking her shoes across the tiles. 'Jesus! What a trek. The traffic was evil, road-rage all over the place. I hate driving through the city and I've to do it again tomorrow. I didn't see his high and mightiness, Vincent Gabor, either. I'm ordered to attend him tomorrow afternoon, in his office in town. Apparently, he was too busy to see me.'

'So you don't know if you've been taken on?' Arlene paced about restlessly, from hall to sitting room and then out through the conservatory to the garden.

'Well, not finally, I suppose, though his assistant, Grace Pennick, looked at my CV and had me wear a brief costume. She did other things, too,' Julia added, her face heated with more than a hectic and frustrating drive through the busy streets.

'Oh, and what were they?' Arlene asked, but she was still wrestling with her annoyance because Blake had not turned up to the audition.

It wasn't simply the loss of her designs that was bugging her. She was finding it hard to cope with her own strong feelings concerning Blake. She was furious with him, naturally, but memories of their one session in the broom cupboard continued to plague her. Eugene had been with her almost constantly and she was grateful, but no matter that they were screwing each other brainless, she still couldn't blank Blake from her mind.

'I'll tell you all that happened, in a minute,' Julia promised, and Arlene could see that she was tired, so fixed a tray of tea and carried it out to the patio.

The sun was warm, beating down on their loungers, and she stripped off her clothes and applied a generous helping of screening oil, enjoying the rays in this secluded corner, far from prying eyes.

'Aren't you going to get your kit off?' she asked, pouring tea and taking her own cup back to her lounger, spreading it with a beach towel and then lying down, her face shaded by a parasol clipped to the backrest.

'I suppose so,' Julia said, surprising Arlene with her reluctance.

She wriggled out of her skirt, top and bra, but was hesitant about removing her French knickers. 'You'll spoil your base tan,' Arlene warned, staring at her lower half severely. 'Like me, you usually insist on a seamless, all over brown. Now is the time to start, ready for the heat wave. What's the matter with you? You're not usually shy. Have you got the curse, or something?'

'No, it's not that,' Julia answered, obviously highly embarrassed. Then she suddenly dropped her drawers and presented her posterior to Arlene, almost defiantly. 'It's this. Look.'

Julia's firm but luscious bum was bright red, marked by long stripes. Arlene winced, yet a hot spasm of longing forged through her sex. 'You've been whipped!' she cried. 'Who the hell did this?'

'Grace Pennick,' Julia said, and gingerly lowered her bottom onto the padded seat.

'Blimey,' Arlene gasped, astonished and riven with a sudden burst of envy. 'You said you'd tell about what happened this afternoon. I want every detail.'

Julia reached for the sun oil and applied it to her limbs, breasts and stomach, and then she plunged into the story. 'It was all right at first. She took me into a magnificent salon in Gabor's house. No one else was there. She said she usually interviewed applicants on the first occasion. She looked at my CV and copies she had of the photos, then she asked me to undress, and when I'd done so, laced me into this corset thing. It was so tight I nearly passed out.'

She fell silent and Arlene, idle under the heat, looked sideways at her. Julia, obviously lost in a dream of the afternoon's activities, raised her knee, and her thighs, no longer pressed together, drifted apart. Arlene tried to see between them, but Julia's hand wandered down and sought her clit, stayed there for a moment, then rose, uncovering the labial groove. She played over her cleft, descended, slipped along her delta, and returned with a finger glimmering with dew. She repeated this action, but only her middle digit was lowered, the others gracefully lifted, like the open wings of a dragonfly.

Arlene's heart was pounding and wetness seeped from her vulva to soak into the towel under her bottom. Julia was her friend, but now she had become an object of sexual desire, too. 'What else did Grace do?' she managed to croak, having a fair idea of Julia's reply. Something or someone had excited her beyond decorum or modesty. Arlene had never seen her masturbating before. She'd always been modest, but recently events had taken place that had brought her out of her shell.

'Oh, she undressed me, and fondled me so expertly that I couldn't hold back. I came before she told me to and, as punishment, she sat on my face and had me suck her, then she spanked me and used her riding crop on my poor arse,' Julia said haltingly.

Her finger pressed down on her bud, flicking it, hesitating, and then circling it with gentle movements. Arlene sighed, her own pussy throbbing with longing.

'Have you done this to a woman before?' she asked.

'No,' Julia whispered. 'I felt so ashamed, but it was good.'

Arlene relaxed, closed her eyes and separated her pink slit with two fingers. 'It is good, different than with a man, more satisfying in many ways. And when she whipped you - was that arousing?'

'I'm not sure. I think so. The pain seemed to connect with my sex. I pretended she was a dominating man - a tall, dark and handsome master. It's always been a fantasy of mine.'

Bloody hell, wonders would never cease, Arlene exalted.

As if inspired by visions of her demon lover, Julia's fingers fluttered over her clitoris and she started to moan. Her thighs opened and then closed on her hand. She pumped her hips up and down against her imprisoned fingers, then cried out and fell back, panting.

Arlene sighed too, senses inflamed. She started to caress herself, thinking of the burning stripes on Julia's buttocks and sharing her need for a man who would command her and subject her to the kiss of the lash.

A replete Julia propped herself up on one elbow and stared at her. 'Can I watch?' she asked sweetly.

'Of course,' Arlene said huskily, and it seemed as if the two of them were alone in the entire universe. She slipped her hand down to her entrance, wishing for something with which to penetrate it. She would come through rubbing her clit, but longed for a large vibrator to stuff into her channel just on the point of climax. This always added to her joy. With her legs apart, one finger in her cunny and another rubbing her nub, she was transported, keeping up the smooth movements until she was caught up in the tidal wave of release.

Julia felt extremely anxious as she entered the palatial portals of Gabor's superb office block in the heart of the city. It was called Abby Reach. A uniformed porter asked her for identification and, when she'd given it, nodded and took her to the elevator. This in itself was impressive, lined with gleaming mahogany, its gates constructed of intricate ironwork, a curiously old-fashioned touch in so modern a building. Within seconds she was whisked up several floors. When the lift stopped and the gates parted, she stepped out into a foyer, and Grace was there to meet her.

'You're on time,' she remarked. 'That will please Mr Gabor. He's a stickler for punctuality.'

As yesterday, she was wearing a functional tailored suit, buttoned high at the neck, with a skirt that reached to below the knee, but the fact that she wore stockings of so fine a texture that they resembled a smoky mist hinted at the sexuality Julia now knew lay beneath this almost puritanical exterior. Yet she was treating her as if this was their first meeting and that intimacy had never taken place between them.

'Is this his office?' she asked, butterflies in her stomach.

'No, he owns the building and has various branches of his business activities housed here, but this is his penthouse suite. He chooses to stay here sometimes, particularly if he's entertaining.'

Julia was as overawed as she had been in Hazel House. She had never met someone with so much money and power. The room into which Grace conducted her was spacious, made larger by its minimal décor; white rugs spread over highly polished teak, a white leather couch big enough to seat six, low glass-topped tables, spotlights overhead and windows giving a magnificent view over London's heartland. Two beautifully proportioned and extremely ancient bonsai trees in shallow, earthenware pots, formed a cool green counterpoint to so much white.

Music came from tall thin speakers that resembled sky-scrapers and were correctly placed for surround sound - classical music, a slow, haunting aria delivered superbly by a soprano voice.

'What is it?' Julia asked, a dunce when it came to composers, her taste eclectic. She knew what she liked, be it pop or highbrow, but was usually at a loss concerning titles or performers.

'*Casta diva*, from Bellini's opera, *Norma*,' Grace said, face uplifted to the sound, hands clasped against her breasts. 'Wonderful, isn't it? So sad, so lyrical. It makes me cry, and makes me randy.'

This was astonishing coming from a woman who Julia already thought of as the Ice Queen. Was she, perhaps, in love with Vincent Gabor, her boss and master?'

'It is a so wonderful work, and the rendition is perfect,' said a deep, accented voice from behind her. She swung round and nearly gasped aloud. There stood Prince Charming in person, her dream come true. She got a quick impression of height and strength, of pronounced cheekbones, a patrician nose and a wide mouth. The upper lip curled disdainfully, but the lower was full and sensual. His face was framed in blue-black hair that coiled around his collar, and she found herself staring into the most unfathomable eyes. Though dark-lashed and beautifully shaped, rather like a wolf's, there was something about the expression in them that caused a shiver to chase down her spine to her sex.

'Julia, this is Mr Gabor,' said Grace, and her voice was slightly unsteady.

'How delightful,' he said, and bowed over her hand. He didn't kiss it, but his lips hovered over the back, warm breath giving her goosebumps. 'I've been so looking forward to our meeting. I watched the video of you, taken yesterday afternoon, and I think you're just what I'm seeking.'

Julia's heart missed a beat. She'd been filmed? Had this included Grace seducing her and then beating her, and her own response to lesbian love? One glance into Mr Gabor's eyes convinced her that he had seen everything. She had nowhere to go, nowhere to hide. What must he think of her?

She felt small and insignificant, underdressed in her floral print frock that was no more substantial than an under-slip. It reached to just above her knees, had spaghetti straps and a scooped neckline, back and front. With her bare legs and sandals her attire was more suitable for the beach than town. Hot and bothered as she drove in, she had been glad that she'd opted for something informal, but now regretted it.

Vincent Gabor, however, smiled at her saying, as he held on to her hand, 'This is the look for summer; carefree, casual and bold. It makes a statement.'

'Does it?' she quavered, unable to pull away, mesmerised by him. His suit was faultlessly tailored, his open-necked shirt pristine, forming a contrast with his coppery skin. He even smelt expensive, though there was an underlying hint of his own personal body odour and the scent of his hair.

He smiled again with a flash of perfect teeth. 'Of course, all clothing reflects the manners and mores of the time. This is the age of women-power. They are like gorgeous butterflies emerging from the chrysalis, vital and full of force. The males have had to do a re-think, and maybe the women sometimes regret no longer being subjugated. There are those among us who seek to redress the balance.'

He had lost her; she couldn't understand what he meant by his last sentence. But she wanted to please him, so said, 'I'm sure you know much more about what is fashionable. I simply follow the magazines and have had some training in deportment.'

'Tonight I'm holding a small exhibition of Marty Blake's newest, most innovative designs, and the audience will be select,' he went on. 'I want you to be one of the models.'

'Me? But I thought it would be some time before I actually appeared in public,' she gasped, her heart dropping like a stone to the pit of her stomach.

He chuckled and put an arm around her in a gesture that should have been avuncular, but was far from that. 'This isn't the public, just a few of my friends and customers. You'll be fine.'

Oh, Julia cried inside, trembling with fright, where are you Aunt Mary? I need you or Arlene, or even Will. What have I let myself in for?

'Is this an audition, or are you about to offer me employment?' she asked, pulling herself together and trying to control that weakness of the knees brought about by her trepidation and his close proximity. His arm was like a steel band, though lightly placed, and she knew she'd be powerless to get away.

'I've already seen you in action, remember?' he teased, and pressed against her, making her conscious of the fleshy baton lying in his trousers. 'And Marty Blake watched the video, too. He was *most* impressed.'

She should have broken free, but couldn't. She was furious, shamed, and despite her predicament, aroused. Gabor was smiling so enticingly that she forgot to be angry, every sensible thought fluttering out the window. 'What... what time shall I come back?' she whispered shakily.

He arched an eyebrow at her. 'Come back? Did I say you could leave?'

'But I need to change, and um, do my hair and make-up,' she stammered, reduced to a jelly as he casually lowered his hand and lightly touched her bottom through the thin dress.

'There's no need for you to go anywhere,' he drooled silkily, dragging the fabric across the flimsy triangle of her panties. 'Everything you need is here, my dear.'

'Oh, I see,' she said quietly, her breasts rising firmly against the thin fabric that tightly encased them as she breathed deeply to calm herself, 'then you must tell me what to do...'

'Grace will take care of you,' he said, and moved away, picking up the phone and dialling a number. He waved a decisive hand to his aide, adding, 'See to it. She's to have everything she wants and to be ready by eight. Now, leave me.'

'Yes, sir,' Grace said stiffly. She prodded Julia in the back and hurried her across the vast floor to a door near the windows. It led to a smaller room, with French windows leading onto a balcony. Three girls idled there in the sun, completely naked, on deckchairs and cane basket-swings. Their skin was oiled to promote a tan, their hair up and kept in place with clips. Julia was shocked to see that two of them were pierced through the nipples, navels and labial wings. She didn't know quite where to look, though they seemed unfazed. She noticed that a copy of *Hi Life* was being passed around.

'Mr Gabor's seraglio,' Grace remarked, with a contemptuous sniff.

'Stuff off, you sour old cow,' retorted a redheaded beauty with legs that were long and slender. 'You're only jealous - though whether of him or us, it's hard to tell. Who's this, your new plaything?'

'Keep your spiteful mouth shut, Gina,' Grace snapped coldly. 'This is Julia, and she'll be modelling tonight.'

The girls laughed and Gina strutted over to Julia, magnificently naked and whiplash lean, her breasts full, the hard teats rising from brownish-pink aureoles, her pubic mound completely hairless, drawing attention to the dark cleft of her sex.

'We're all models here,' she sneered. 'But sometimes we're told to do more. Are you prepared for that?'

'I don't know what you mean,' Julia replied, as afraid of these brazen girls as she had been of the bullies in her school playground, to whom she'd always come off worst.

'You don't?' Gina sneered again, hands on hips. 'Well, neither did we. Isn't that so, girls?'

'That's right,' they chorused. 'We went like lambs to the slaughter.'

'I told you to be quiet,' Grace insisted, and lifted the short cane she carried, slashing Gina around the thighs and backside. Then she seized Julia's arm and marched her towards another door.

Julia hung back, frightened of what lay ahead, but Grace would have none of it, dragging and thrusting her into the next room.

Chapter 6

It's going to be all right, Julia kept telling herself as she submitted to Grace's rigorous grooming.

First she was stripped and pushed into the shower, washed all over with scented gel, rinsed off, then told to step out. She was wrapped in a large warm towel, and Grace was utterly scrupulous about drying her.

The luxury of her surroundings, the pampering lavished upon her, the fragrances, the soft samba music in the background, all conspired to ease Julia's mind and arouse her senses. Wherever she looked she could see Mr Gabor's face, and his deep voice seemed to mingle with the pulsing beat of the Afro-Spanish rhythms. When Grace sank to her knees before her and parted the damp fluff bordering her labia, she imagined it to be him. Grace's tongue became his, coaxing her swelling bud, and it was his long brown fingers that reached for her nipples, not the woman's.

They were in a dressing room. There were racks where clothes hung; daywear, evening gowns, and a large collection of garments made of leather and PVC. She could see trousers and catsuits, split crotch panties, basques and corsets, and weird contraptions that resembled a pony's harness. Accessories were on stands close by; hats, broad-brimmed or pill-box shape, some with alluring veils, and shining helmets with ostrich feather plumes; cloaks and masks and bull-whips, paddles and tawse and birches. The shoes ranged beneath were extraordinary and theatrical; high heeled courts and mules and, most fascinating to Julia, thigh-high boots with lacing at the outer sides, stack heels, sharp pointed toes and spurs. Metal glinted on the clothes and footwear, studs and rings and zips.

'Is this part of Marty Blake's collection?' Julia asked innocently.

'Not exactly,' Grace answered, straightening up and unwrapping the towel, so that Julia was naked, pink from the shower and glowing with outer warmth and inner arousal. 'But you'll be wearing something like them. Mr Gabor has important customers coming tonight.'

'Buyers for big stores?'

'Don't ask so many questions,' Grace said abruptly, and gave her hip a light slap. 'Yours is not to reason why, but to do as you're told.'

Then the woman had Julia sit on a stool in front of the dressing table mirror and commenced to massage her with body lotion. Soon she felt limp, as if she was floating in a rose-scented cloud. Grace had a magic touch, her capable hands becoming marvellously gentle, yet with a firmness that brooked no

59

resistance.

It was while she was skilfully applying make-up to Julia's face that the other girls burst in, chattering and laughing, brandishing a list of what they were to wear and in which order. Gina seemed to be the ringleader and she stood close beside Julia, staring threateningly at her in the mirror.

'Leave her alone,' Grace warned, calmly but with menace. 'She's not for you, or for me.'

'Who then?' Gina demanded like a spoilt child.

'I have my orders,' Grace informed her, brushing Julia's lustrous hair. 'Mr Gabor wants to put her through her paces.'

'What's so special about her?' Gina asked spitefully.

Grace said no more, but simply continued brushing Julia's hair.

'Come on, darlings,' called a magnificent person who shimmied in on enormously tall stilettos that added six inches to his already considerable height. 'Stop frigging your fannies and get into your gear. We can have a quick rehearsal before the curtain goes up.'

'Oh, Roberta, must we?' they complained in unison, but the stranger would have none of it. He strutted around them, running a critical eye over them from top to toe.

'You certainly must. I've been too lenient with you, I can see that. Discipline is needed, and that's what you're going to get. Come on, chop, chop! You too, Gina. You didn't think I'd let you get away with laziness, did you?'

The stunning figure scrutinised Julia. 'Is this her - the new one?' he asked Grace. 'Mr Gabor's been telling me all about her.'

Julia stared, open-mouthed, as the person beamed at her. He - and she assumed he was a he - had the bearing of an empress. His skin was smooth and unblemished, and he wore a short skirt that finished mid-thigh. His legs were superb, his make-up faultless, his eyes emphasised by kohl and mascara. His hair was out of this world, mainly dark but with reddish streaks and a number of little plaits ornamented with colourful glass beads. One of his slim hands reached out and tipped Julia's chin up with a long talon that matched his gold eye shadow.

'This is her,' Grace confirmed, pride in her voice as they viewed her handiwork in the mirror.

'And your name is...?' he asked the bewildered girl, missing nothing as he assessed her face and figure.

'J-Julia...' she faltered, nonplussed by his strangely intense interest in her. 'Julia Jones.'

'Cute breasts and a pert little tush,' he commented. Gina and her friends, blonde Katie and dark Vesta, were watching like hawks, hoping to see her discredited, but Roberta smiled with a flash of white teeth, patted her shoulder kindly and added, 'You'll do fine, love. I've a wonderful scenario worked out. Get her into the white outfit, Grace, and she can strut her stuff during rehearsal.'

The room became backstage, with everyone concentrating on donning their costumes, doing their make-up and hair, and quarrelling like children until

Roberta lost it and told them all to shut up. The warm façade vanished and he was suddenly cold and cruel, and Julia shivered as she imagined incurring his wrath. He might look like a glamorous leading lady, but he had a vicious temper and the strength of a man.

The first ensembles selected were quite conventional, next spring's fashions in spice and sand, lit by flashes of citron. Grace didn't attire Julia in the white costume, not quite yet. First of all she had to put on a dressing gown to go out to the reception room where an apron-shaped platform and a long catwalk had been set up.

'Get your mind off pussy and your hands off cocks!' Roberta shouted to a pair of slouching engineers who were eyeing the models with intent. 'Music! Lights!'

At once everything was transformed as the houselights dimmed and the spots were aimed at the stage. Gina appeared, swinging her hips, ribs lifted, breasts jutting, wearing an orange see-through sarong, a tiny G-string, and strappy sandals with thin heels. Raunchy disco music pounded out and she moved in time to the beat. Julia, watching from the wings, thought her superb, but Roberta wasn't pleased.

'No, no, not like that,' he shouted. 'You're walking as if you've got a prickly pear shoved up your quim. Put some zing into it. You know how to walk... like this.'

He made an entrance, paused for full dramatic effect, and then moved down the catwalk with all the fearsome grace of a hunting leopard. Julia forgot he had originally been a man, for he was so svelte, so sinuous, elegant, aristocratic and sexy, that he might have been born a female. The only giveaway was his height, the size of his hands and feet, and the flatness of his bum. Apart from that, he was a female by nature rather than surgery and hormone pills.

'Watch closely, girls, especially you, Julia,' he demanded in a high, bossy voice. 'One, two, three, pause, legs apart, give 'em a thrill, then twirl, turn, hands on hips, up stage we go. Walk, walk, face the audience one last time, and off. Have you got it? Right, come on then. Julia, with me, walk, walk...'

This was nothing like the time when Arlene had drilled her in a church hall. She felt clumsy and totally inept, and deeply regretted being drawn into her friend's hare-brained venture. It was Julia who'd had her dresses stolen. It wasn't her who had the hots for the alleged perpetrator of the crime. So why was she there, being taught how to walk like a model by a giant transsexual, and possibly in danger if the little ruse was discovered? This wasn't her scene at all, but then, she wanted to be a recognised reporter, and this venture could be a great step for her...

Roberta clamped a firm grip around her arm and directed her to follow his moves. She began to get the hang of it, responding to the exciting beat that shot straight down to her epicentre. She stalked, she paced, she stared haughtily at mere mortals. She might not be dressed for the part, but by the time she'd walked the catwalk for half an hour with Roberta, she had the edge on the others.

'And rest,' he said at last, and took her back to where Grace waited. 'The bride

61

gown,' he instructed, and they exchanged a significant glance. 'She'll be in the finale. In fact,' he added, a little sinisterly, 'she'll be the finale.'

Grace nodded enigmatically and a faint smile flickered in her eyes. 'Do you want her shaved?' she asked.

'I think not, at this point. Mr Gabor didn't mention it. But later, no doubt he'll let me do the honours.'

'Shaved?' Julia gasped, staring from one bizarre face to the other - Grace so gaunt and unfeminine, and Roberta a brazen parody of a woman. 'But I don't want to be shaved.'

'Whilst here your wants have nothing to do with anything,' Roberta said dismissively, any trace of beneficence gone from his features; he now looked as stern as Grace.

Julia had a job to do, she reminded herself. Will wouldn't crack on a story, and neither would she. That's what investigative journalism was all about. 'You're right,' she said, drawing her shoulders back determinedly. 'I'm sorry.'

At once Roberta changed, visibly relaxing. 'I do,' he said, smiling. 'Obey me from now on, and we'll get along just fine.'

He strode to the catwalk, clapped his hands smartly together, and took the models through the routine again.

The air was charged with a heady excitement, and this increased as the girls prepared themselves. Much spring water was consumed, alcohol being banned before a show, but they puffed edgily on innumerable cigarettes and consumed more chocolate and sandwiches than anyone harbouring the idea that models were anorexic would have believed.

And eventually it was time for Grace to dress Julia in the white gown they'd all spoken of.

Bridal dress or confirmation attire, Julia wasn't sure which it was, and doubted that it mattered. The important thing was that it symbolised purity, an innocence that someone, probably Vincent Gabor, couldn't wait to besmirch. She stared at herself in the pier-glass, no longer Julia Jones, self-styled super-sleuth, but transformed into a male fantasy of feminine virtuousness. The gown was a simple length of silk chiffon with long full sleeves, reminiscent of that worn by a medieval princess in a fairytale. It was buttoned to the throat, but of so sheer a weave that the outline of her nipples could be seen, and the faint shadow between her thighs showed as an indistinct triangle through the diaphanous pleats.

This teasing display was more arousing than if she'd been naked, and despite her concerns, she thrilled at the sensuous sight and feel of it.

Grace pinned on a beautiful corsage, then topped the whole with a floating white veil that covered Julia entirely. She resembled Demeter, the goddess of fertile crops, or a young maiden about to dedicate herself to a god.

'You look lovely - doesn't she, Roberta?' Grace said as the glamorous transsexual appeared in the dressing room.

'Perfect,' he gushed.

Now Julia could hear the murmur of voices from outside, and the compelling beat of soul music. Her heart began to thump, and once again she was reminded of her predicament and swamped with nerves.

She was shaking as she stood with Grace in the wings, waiting until the other models had displayed their first costumes. She listened to the ripples of applause and murmured comments.

During the intermission the girls changed into outlandish gear, which might have been supplied by a back street sex shop, not a respected fashion guru.

'You ready for this?' Gina mocked, as she stood close to Julia.

Her glossy red hair was piled high, and she wore a shining black patent leather bustier opened down the front and fastened with criss-cross lacing, her breasts lifted high, their upper slopes bare. Black and gold suspenders stretched to clip her stocking-tops, framing her pubis, which was part-covered by a pair of scarlet, open-crotched panties. Elbow-length black gloves and ankle boots with zips and stilt heels completed her outfit.

Vesta and Katie also wore provocative attire. Vesta's blue satin corset finished under her breasts, the upper curve decorated with chains that chaffed her teats and made them crimp. Her pussy was bare, and so was her generous bottom, apart from leather straps that ran across her navel to part her cleft on either side, pushing it into prominence, then disappearing into her crease, over her anus and up to the back of her waist.

Katie's costume appeared ordinary enough, at first glance. She was wearing sports gear: a tiny white skirt, suitable for tennis, except that every time she moved it was to display her naked beneath. Her top was tiny, a mere strip of jersey cotton stretched over her breasts, and to complete the picture, her coltish honey-brown legs ended in white ankle socks and trainers.

There was a general buzz of approval when they walked onto the stage. They postured and preened, and while they entertained, two stagehands quietly manoeuvred a wooden triangular frame - one angle at the bottom, the other two at head height - to the back of the stage. And then Roberta, wearing a spangled, figure-hugging gown, a pink feather boa and a ringletted, platinum blonde wig, stepped to the fore.

'Now for the high spot of the evening, gentleman,' he announced, flanked by the beautiful girls. 'The *pièce de résistance*. We're about to present Julia, our very own virgin bride. Yes, gentlemen, I tell you no lies. She truly is a virgin - our sacrificial virgin.'

Julia didn't like the sound of that at all. Her stomach knotted with trepidation, and she was on the verge of bolting when Gina and Vesta grabbed her arms and pulled her into the unremitting glare of the spotlights. None of this had been rehearsed. 'Wh-what are you doing?' Julia whispered frantically. She could see nothing in detail beyond the lights, the auditorium black, cigarette and cigar smoke drifting in layers above the shadows that sat there - watching.

'Just be quiet and don't resist,' Gina hissed, and the two girls moved her to the front of the stage, where she stood, in full few of everyone. This was a show put on for fashion buyers? Somehow Julia doubted it. She was on to something more than the theft of her friend's designs here.

Gina lifted the veil, laying it back over Julia's hair, to general murmurs of approval from the inky shadows.

Roberta tossed his shimmering mane and snapped his fingers at Gina, who held Julia's forearms while Vesta snapped two metal bands to her wrists. Roberta snapped his fingers again and the macabre wooden crosspiece was trundled forward and positioned precisely in front of Julia, who stared at it, eyes wide with dismay.

Chains hung from the cuffs, and as Julia stood aghast at the scene that was unfolding - with her as the main attraction - Gina and Vesta lifted her arms and attached the chains to the crosspiece of the triangular frame, pressing Julia's cheek to its smoothly polished surface in doing so. Her ankles were gripped, forced apart and fastened with two more metal bands and chains that, in turn, were fed through iron rings at the base of the wooden structure. She was at their mercy, arms strained out to the sides at head level, her ankles parted wide and also secured. It was uncomfortable, her arm muscles already beginning to ache, and the cross felt somewhat unstable, cunningly contrived so that it was rooted in a turntable.

Somebody was close, pressing against her back, and without opening her eyes Julia knew it was Vincent Gabor. He was there behind her; she knew it, could sense it, and instinctively accepted that it was he who was to lead her through the ordeal. She could feel him, erect against her buttocks, even through his trousers and the material of her dress, and she instinctively eased back a fraction against it. For some reason, despite the horror of her situation, she wanted him; yearned for his mastery.

'Shall I take your virginity like this?' he whispered, his dark velvet voice filling her head. 'Here, in front of all these people? Or later, in private?'

'I...'

'Whatever I decide,' he went on, so quietly she could barely hear him, 'you must be chastised first. You know that, my dear, don't you?'

'I... why?' she managed, choking back the sobs that threatened to overwhelm her. 'What have I done wrong? Why would you punish me?'

'Because you need it,' he murmured enigmatically, and then withdrew, leaving her, eyes closed and holding her breath with apprehension... and inexplicable excitement.

Strong hands lifted the skirt of her dress and fixed it just above her waist, and then he moved away, leaving a chill where his warm body had been. The onlookers waited with a menacing, brooding, quiet. The music was no more. The cross was slowly turned, until it faced the back of the stage. Roberta was there, one hand on hip, one leg thrust out through the slit in his dress. Grace was with him, an austere figure in black. Their unblinking eyes were fixed on Julia, pinning her as effectively as the chains that held her to the odious frame.

Through her anxiety and confusion Julia was vaguely conscious of a stirring in the air behind her - not so much a sound, as a breath of movement... and it was followed by a searing explosion of agony. Too shocked to cry out, she convulsed against her bonds. Vincent Gabor had laid the lash low, deliberately catching her in the crease between toned buttock and thigh, and before she could recover a second blow bit mercilessly, placed an inch higher than the first. This time a howl was wrenched from her lips. Her buttocks were bathed in fire, the heat spreading down through her loins and up to her breasts, her clit and nipples echoing the pain, but on the brink of twisted pleasure, too.

Julia's world shrunk to that moment, as though she and Gabor were in the eye of a hurricane and everyone else had vanished. Alone, just the two of them, the teacher and his pupil, the master and his slave. And for some bizarre reason she would have had it no other way, even when the whip bit into her flesh again, and again, and again. She embraced the crosspiece, welcoming its solid support, nearly fainting as she slumped there feeling the drag on her wrists and the discomfort of her ankles, and the breathtaking pain of the brands Gabor had whipped into her as surely as if he'd used a hot iron. They would fade physically, but their marks would remain imprinted on her soul for all eternity...

Julia was vaguely aware of hands freeing her from the frame and someone - she knew it was Vincent Gabor - carrying her away from the scene of her cruel ordeal.

Now she was somewhere quiet, too drained and bewildered to open her eyes, but feeling a soft mattress under her, as he laid her on her front. An astringent coolness laved her stripes, taking away the heat, and he was spreading lotion over her buttocks, massaging it in, his hands gentle - hands that, a short time ago, had brandished the whip, punishing her most cruelly. He was an enigma, and she was intrigued, falling ever deeper under his spell.

She dared to open her eyes, squinting sideways, her tearstained cheek pressed into a satin pillow. The light was subdued, but she glimpsed a carved bedhead and, to one side, drapes pulled across the windows. Of course, it would be dark outside by now. She had been in the penthouse suite for hours. Would Arlene be worried and send out a search party, headed by Will? For some inexplicable reason, she rather hoped not. She and Vincent Gabor had unfinished business.

'You took your introduction to pain very well, my dear,' she heard him say, and felt his hands lightly working the balm into her skin. 'Don't worry. This is a secret prescription made up for me by a Chinese doctor. The welts and bruises will fade in a day or two.'

He rolled her over. The finest linen caressed her tender rear, and she smelt the aroma of herbs and spices, oils and incense. It was pungent, almost narcotic, and she relaxed, wanting never to leave this place. Vincent Gabor sat on the side of the bed, smoothing her hair back from her flushed forehead and looking deeply into her eyes. The throbbing of her bottom receded, the ointment working as he promised. He lifted a glass of wine from the nearby bedside cabinet, supported her while she sat up a little, and she drank gratefully. It was red and full-bodied, and delicious.

When she'd finished he replaced the glass, then gently and skilfully removed her clothes. Feeling too lethargic to utter a sound or move a muscle, Julia watched him, the wine making her a little woozy. In her investigative mind she wondered dreamily if he'd added anything to it, but no longer cared, content to be gazing up at a very powerful and very attractive man.

Then he stood and, without taking his steely eyes from her supine form, started to undress himself.

The evening jacket came off, and the crisp white shirt was unbuttoned and tugged from his waistband. He had the body of an athlete, kept in superb condition by regular training. Broad shoulders tapered to a narrow waist, and his skin was copper-brown. He was hirsute, but not unpleasantly so, chest furred, arms as well, but not on his back or shoulders. Julia was glad of that; hairy men were not her favourite.

His shoes and socks were slipped off, his trousers unfastened and lowered over his trim hips and down his muscled legs, before being discarded where they fell in a crumpled heap. Now he wore nothing but the briefest of pouches, the front weighted by the size and hardness of his tumescent penis.

Julia propped herself up on one elbow, the better to see him, and a dart of desire pierced her to the womb. Thumbs hooked into the brief garment, eased down, and his manhood sprang from its snug den, thrusting potently towards her. Brown-skinned and veined, it curved upwards with no foreskin to protect the swollen twin lobes of his glans. He let her look for a while, and then knelt on the bed, looming over her.

His face lowered towards hers and then her took possession of her mouth, his tongue performing a dance of desire with hers. She moaned against his lips, and heaved her body up so that her naked breasts met his softly pelted chest. His kiss was perfect. She'd never known anything like it, aching with longing, her nipples peaks of passion, and her clitoris hard and needy.

He raised his head and swept a hand down over her breasts, her tensed tummy, and down between her thighs. He found her clitoris and teased it, then dipped into her entrance, testing it with two fingers. She wriggled against the invasion, wanting more.

'Oh, yes... please,' she gasped, the discomfort in her buttocks augmenting the pleasure as he took her to the heights with all the skill of an experienced lover, carrying her upwards on liquid wings until her orgasm peaked and shattered.

He eased his knees between her limp thighs and she felt his cock nudging at her. She wanted it, hooked her legs around his waist and pulled him in closer. Her hands slipped up and down the sinews of his arms, her nails dug into his back, and he rocked against her, then thrust hard, his cock slicing into her enveloping depths. She felt her membrane resisting and the pain was intense. She closed her eyes and bit her lip, sobbing, but not prepared to let the moment slip away.

He thrust harder, pushing his cock with his lithe hips. There was a moment's pause and then he prevailed, sinking into her.

She whimpered, her stripes and her plundered vagina combining in pain. She was overwhelmed, his huge penis stretching her narrow channel, the bulbous tip butting harshly against her cervix.

'You're too big...' she moaned.

'Don't be silly,' he grunted, moving more rapidly, dragging his cock out then plunging back in again.

And, gradually, the pain melted into a dull ache that turned into utter pleasure as his pubic bone ground against her clitoris and she felt his heavy balls brushing the insides of her thighs. He was moving in a steady tempo and without conscious thought, and she kept up with it, tightening her legs around him, wanting more, embracing the size and girth of his shaft. She could feel the sweet beginnings of another orgasm. She had never known such ecstasy, the feel of his cock inside her an awesome sensation, until she wanted to remain linked with him forever, her life dedicated to his service.

And Vincent Gabor was showing great passion and a need that matched hers. She revelled in the feel of him, the smell of him, the joy of that rigid muscle pistoning inside her, and she didn't care when suddenly all gentleness was gone. He took his pleasure ruthlessly, and his roughness excited her unbearably. She squeezed even tighter with her legs, wanting to get closer and closer, even if it meant he speared her to the heart.

She sobbed into his mouth as her crisis came, sending fiery arrows throughout her writhing body. He gave a harsh bark and stiffened, head back, body arched, and she felt the heat of his seed erupting deep inside her.

Julia gave a deep contented sigh, happy to be crushed beneath him, his face buried against her throat, his rasping breath gradually returning to normal.

Then he raised himself, resting on his elbows and staring down into her face, his spent penis slipping from between her legs. 'Now you know what it's all about,' he said casually.

'Can... can I stay with you tonight?' she asked carefully, sensing him becoming distant, making her feel cold and empty.

'No, I've business to attend to,' he said dismissively. 'But I will see you tomorrow; we have much to discuss, and a contract to be drafted and signed.'

Chapter 7

'And?' Will pressed.

'And what?' Julia responded, and he didn't much care for her defensive tone.

'And, aren't you going to tell me what's going on?'

He hated being hard on her; he was nothing like as tough has he liked to portray. This lovely girl with the big round eyes that could change from blue to violet according to her mood had really got to him. He'd even had a furious row with that sleazebag George, who'd been angling to sell the nude pictures of her to a porn magazine.

Julia and Will were in the *Hi Life* office. She was reporting to him during Denise's absence, who was away on business for a few days. Julia sat in front of his desk, looking mouth-wateringly gorgeous as usual. Will leaned back in his operator's chair and his neglected monitor automatically switched to screen-saver. Two spacemen drifted across a black, star-spangled void, to the accompaniment of bleeps and blips and what the designer had obviously imagined were sounds heard in the far reaches of the universe. I don't think so, Will concluded, and turned the volume down.

Julia fidgeted, her denim skirt riding up over her silky thighs, and the tiny white triangle of her panty gusset winked at him as she crossed her legs. His cock stirred with that familiar ache he associated with his frustration concerning this nubile nymphet. He concentrated on her body language, and it told him that she wasn't too happy.

'It's all going fine,' she said at last. 'I'm really in there. I'm seeing Vincent Gabor again later today. He wants me to model for Blake, who'll be there, too, I hope. In fact, if I take to the life, I might give up journalism and embark on a new career.'

'That's bollocks, and you know it.' He scowled across his desk at her, annoyed at the sudden cold chill that invaded his heart. Lose her to the fashion trade? Never!

'I don't know any such thing,' she retorted loftily, standing and going over to stare out of the window at the uneven rooftops, then down into the crowded lane. It bordered Soho and Wardour Street, home of films, printed sensationalism, and sex, and not far away from London's theatre-land.

Will could not resist the temptation to leave his chair and stand behind her. 'Fine view, isn't it?' he said quietly. 'Can't you feel the energy, the crazy tempo, the get-up-and-go? I wouldn't want to work anywhere else on earth.' He hardly knew what he was saying, simply giving himself an excuse to be close to her without exactly touching. Her hair smelt delicious, reminding him of the hay fields of his boyhood, fragrant with poppies and meadowsweet. Then there had been his grandmother's cottage near the sea, where the front door bore a garland of honeysuckle throughout his summer visits, his townie nostrils seduced by the scent that somehow mingled with the tang of ocean spray.

Unable to control his emotions or his burgeoning penis, he leaned down and kissed the tender nape of her neck. He felt her stiffen and cursed himself. He'd got the timing wrong - again. She moved away, putting space between them, glancing at him from the tail of her eye. 'Don't push it, Will,' she warned gently. 'I like you; you're a good friend...'

'But,' he finished the sentence for her. 'There's always a "but" in there somewhere.'

'But, I'm not ready to make a commitment just now. There's too much happening in my life.'

'Okay, but just tell me one thing,' he said. 'Have they fucked you?'

She turned her eyes to him, and despite the glint of anger there, he could see a defensive uncertainty as well. 'I don't think that's any of your business,' she said without conviction, and then turned to leave. 'Tell Denise that I think this story will blow the roof off, when it's completed.'

'Bugger!' Will cursed, sat down again, eased his erection into a more comfortable position, and opened a file. He was writing an astringent article concerning cosmetic surgery, and breast implants in particular, but for once the words simply refused to flow from his fingertips to the keyboard. Breasts; surely

68

one of his favourite topics, but all he could see were Julia's; so firm yet succulent, not too large and not too small - just perfect. He groaned and gave up the battle to write, elbows on the desk, chin in his hands as he stared at the taunting cursor on the screen and saw nothing but Julia being spanked by Gus. It was a scenario he had relived over and over, using it as a masturbation aid, and coming when he got to the bit where she sucked Gus's cock and he ejaculated over her face and hair.

Will needed relief now, so he went across and turned the key in the lock, then unzipped his trousers and lifted out his engorged cock. Some people condemned wanking as something only frustrated teenagers needed to indulge in, but Will disagreed. Whether in relationships or out of them, he had always indulged. It was so easy, so uncomplicated and immensely satisfying. He loved women and everything about them, of course, but his cock was always there for him, loyal and true.

He slumped low on his chair, legs spread, flies agape. His weapon rose from his groin like a splendid fleshy spear; he was very proud of its length and girth. He stroked it affectionately with his right hand, and reached lower with his left to rummage inside his underwear and fondled his balls. They felt like sap-filled fruit.

He hadn't had sex for several days and they were more than ready. He massaged them, and pretended that Julia was on her knees between his legs, cupping his testicles in her dainty fingers and licking his cock. He squeezed his shaft and pumped briskly, drawing down the ridge of skin that collared his helm, then sliding up and over it, anointed by the bead of juice that hung from the eye. Will sighed, and watched his hand and fingers performing the ritual. He knew precisely how much pressure to use and for how long, and when to let up to stop himself peaking.

But it wasn't wise to delay too long when doing it in the office; someone might knock on his locked door and wonder what he's up to. Besides, after the recent closeness of Julia he wanted instant completion. He increased the rhythm of his fist, tight around the stem, the helm appearing and disappearing, his fingers slippery with pre-come juice. He couldn't stop now. He could feel the force gathering, chasing down his spine and into his loins. It surged and he pumped his cock furiously, dreaming of it cocooned in the deep warm valley between those luscious breasts of sweet Julia. He stiffened, groaned quietly, and felt the spunk pumping from him, coating his fingers and wetting his shirttail. He came in several glorious spasms, then replete, rested for a minute before wiping himself with a tissue and tucking his diminished penis away, zipping up quickly.

Composure regained, Will unlocked the office door, and lust appeased for the moment, settled down to his unfinished leader.

'I've done it,' Julia cried excitedly, rushing into the sitting room. Arlene was lounging on the settee, watching daytime television. 'Why aren't you in the workshop?' Julia added, then getting no response, raced on. 'I've just popped in to change; I've got a date with Vincent Gabor.'

Arlene turned her head sharply, looking at her friend inquisitively. 'You have?' Julia nodded eagerly. 'You like him, don't you?'

Julia blushed and lowered her gaze to the carpet. 'Yes,' she admitted meekly. 'I think I do.'

'Well I hope you haven't forgotten the object of the exercise; my stolen designs,' Arlene reminded her curtly. 'I don't like that starry-eyed look of yours.'

'I'm not starry-eyed,' Julia protested, pouting sulkily. 'You don't understand—'

'So what about the plan?' Arlene cut in. 'What about my designs.'

'I told you,' Julia remonstrated, and Arlene half-expected her to stamp her foot like a tetchy schoolgirl, 'I'm meeting Mr Gabor today to discuss a modelling contract, and I think I'm being introduced to Marty Blake. Apparently they're planning a big show, and I want to be part of it because it'll give me an opportunity to find out if Blake's pirating your stuff.'

Arlene eased off, realising that Julia was actually doing very well in her undercover role, but still concerned about the potentially dangerous attraction she could see developing towards Gabor. 'So, what's Vincent Gabor like?' she asked, encouraging her friend to talk.

Julia elegantly lowered her bottom onto the edge of the settee, winced a little, and looked suddenly unsettled, as though she wanted to tell Arlene something, but wouldn't. 'Well, he and his friends don't live as we do,' she began. 'I'm entering an entirely different world to anything I've known before.'

'Such as?' Arlene probed, placed a reassuring hand on Julia's knee, and listened with growing concern as her sweet friend opened up and told her everything about the dubious events that had taken place at Gabor's penthouse.

Julia prepared herself for the forthcoming evening with a great deal of consideration. Nothing too brash, she decided; Vincent Gabor was to treat her with respect, and so was Marty Blake.

She chose a simple outfit that suited her personality. She hadn't the confidence to put on something that was overstated, even though Arlene put her considerable wardrobe at her disposal, mostly her own designs and making.

She settled for a midnight-blue dress, the snug bodice of which showed off her breasts to perfection, moulding her cleavage into a deep, dark shadow. The skirt was cut on the cross, and she admired herself in the mirror, pirouetting so that it swirled around her legs. Yes, it was lovely and feminine... just right.

She drove the short distance to Highgate, her car representing independence. If things got too alarming she could always leave, beholden to none for a lift. With a scrunch of wheels on gravel, she parked outside Hazel House and sat for a moment, gathering her thoughts. Her mind had been filled with Vincent Gabor all day. It was as if he'd cast a spell over her, invaded her very being. She hadn't been able to eat, her stomach full of butterflies. In the bath, and whilst dressing, she had viewed her body as if it belonged to someone else, a vessel which she was oh so willing to sacrifice to him. She was infatuated, totally and dangerously.

But she had a mission to complete, and she would surely discover that Marty Blake, not Vincent, had perpetrated the crime.

The front door was opened by a voluptuous maid wearing a short black taffeta dress that clung to her generous breasts, pinched her waist and flared into a short frilly skirt, a white apron and lacy cap, fishnet stockings and high-heeled shoes that beautifully enhanced her shapely legs. 'Can I help you?' she asked brightly.

'I've an appointment with Mr Gabor,' Julia announced, surprised, for she had expected Grace to be there.

'Yes, miss,' the girl answered. 'He is waiting for you.'

'I'll see to this, Penny.' An androgynous figure appeared at the maid's side. It was dressed in black leather from head to foot, a close-fitting hood covering its head. 'Follow me, Miss Jones. I'm Kevin Dean, by the way, Marty Blake's PR and advertising consultant.'

It was hard to come to grips with the idea of him attending board meetings, yet the whole sequence of events was taking on a bizarre quality. It was even stranger than when she had first entered Hazel House and, as she walked behind Penny and the sinister person in black who called himself Kevin, she wondered what she had taken on. The shadows of evening were silently filling the hall and she had a strong urge to turn tail and flee, to seek the sanctuary of her beat-up old banger. But she was fired by curiosity and desire, and couldn't resist seeing what was round the next corner. Somewhere inside her head a continual film was filling up with images, recording every detail. Later she could re-run it and write it all down.

Would they take her to the reception room or had another place been chosen? Apparently it had, for they didn't pause, conducting her to the back of the house. Kevin stopped and pressed a button near a pair of cedar wood doors. They slid open, revealing the entrance to a lift, and Kevin gestured to Julia, who stepped inside. He followed, and so did the maid. It began to descend smoothly, then stopped with a slight jar. The doors hissed quietly open again, Kevin stepped out, followed by Julia and the maid.

Ahead of them was a dimly lit passage. It was chilly and damp. Had it once been a cellar? Was this still its role? Maybe Vincent Gabor stored rare wines there, knowledgeable when it came to vintages. She knew she was whistling in the dark; rare wines weren't the reason the lift had been installed, the walls re-pointed, the stone floor swept.

'Where are you taking me?' she asked, addressing Kevin's thin back, for he insisted on walking ahead of her.

'To meet the master,' he replied evenly, the foreboding tone of his voice causing her to shudder with trepidation. *Master.* The very word chilled her more than the dingy damp passageway he was leading her along.

A door set in an arch loomed before them. It was made of solid oak and heavily studded with nails. It had an ornately worked iron keyhole. Kevin rapped on the panels with his knuckles, and a voice called for them to enter. Kevin pushed open the creaking door and stood aside so that Julia might go first.

She was aware of darkness shot through with scarlet, of the persistent hum of a heating system in the bowels of the house, of the tall, powerful man silhouetted against the flames of large ecclesiastical candles standing in carved sconces.

'Welcome, Julia Jones,' Vincent Gabor said, the timbre of his voice scraping down her spine like sharp fingernails on slate. 'Come to me.'

She couldn't speak, every vestige of sense deserting her. Gabor didn't move, willing her to go to him, but she couldn't, having lost the ability to walk. Her knees had turned to jelly.

Then Grace emerged from the shadows, as severe as ever in an immaculate grey suit.

'Don't keep the master waiting,' she snapped, and dug her fingers into Julia's arm, marching her across the stone-flagged floor to him.

'But... but I thought this was to be a business meeting where I'd sign a modelling contract,' Julia began, daring to raise her eyes to his face and drowning in the hypnotic glint of his ink-black pupils.

'So it is,' he stated. 'Are you wearing any panties,' he asked suddenly, the forthright question taking her by surprise.'

'I - um - yes, I am, but I don't see—'

'Then you are breaking the rules of my house. You are to wear no panties when in my presence,' and reacting instantly to the click of his fingers, the maid lifted her short skirt and bared her beautiful bare bottom.

'Oh, but I wasn't told,' Julia said, her wide eyes transfixed by the six fading parallel welts etched on the girl's lovely pale buttocks.

'Nonetheless, you will be punished,' he insisted.

'But, Mr Gabor, that's not fair,' Julia protested, looking back to him.

'Do you dare to question my decisions?' he said, then called over his shoulder without freeing her from his stare. 'Marty, come and meet Julia Jones, your latest model... You've just earned yourself six lashes, my dear.'

Things weren't going as she'd hoped and planned, and Julia felt sick as Marty Blake appeared.

He took her hand and led her to the middle of the vault. 'Walk up and down,' he commanded, scrutinising her closely. 'I watched you last night, being whipped,' he disclosed, and although she'd suspected as much, it still made Julia feel even worse to think this arrogant man had witnessed her public chastisement and humiliation. 'It made me extremely horny, and it's your very quality of injured innocence that will appeal to the punters. I recognised it the moment I saw those first pictures of you - and don't worry; we'll acquire the negatives from that creep, Comby. He won't be flogging them on the porn market.

'I see you as the rising star of the woman's magazines,' he went on. 'Beautiful, talented, the face of the millennium. And you'll be wearing my designs, too.'

'I...' Julia felt she should say something, but didn't know what, and so she just stood there in the flickering candlelight, the word caught in her throat, her moist lips slightly parted, as she gazed at each of them in turn.

'But before all that,' Gabor broke the tense silence, 'she must be punished, as I just explained. Take off the offending garment, my dear, bend over, and grip your ankles.'

It was on the tip of Julia's tongue to refuse; if the whole scenario wasn't so alarming it would have been ridiculous, but then she glimpsed Grace's taut expression and knew there was nothing she could do but obey. She blessed the shadowy twilight in which they existed, the candles more discreet than the glare of electricity. But even so, as she slipped her hands beneath her dress, hooked her thumbs into her panties and bent over from the waist, easing them down her legs to her ankles, she was terribly conscious of the soft blue hem rising up the backs of her thighs, certain that all in the dank chamber could glimpse a sight of the undercurves of her buttocks.

Somehow she just knew she was expected to lift the material higher and fold it over her hips, and as she did, despite her misgivings, her nipples were erect and sensitive, and then she waited, holding her breath and trembling, for the first cut. Somehow it was worse than when she was bound to that horrible wooden frame, because there was nothing tangible to stop her from refusing to take her undeserved punishment... nothing except the inexplicable devotion she now felt for Vincent Gabor, her bewildering need to be controlled by him, and her incomprehensible desire to yield to him, body and soul. She prayed he would be the one to chastise her, not Blake, Grace, or the other weird creep.

The cellar had gone eerily quiet, and when the lash finally exploded on her vulnerable flesh with vicious severity, its crack roused the echoes. Julia thought she was ready for it, but was unprepared for the white-hot agony that forced a wail from her throat. The pain wrapped round her, across her tummy and down into her groin. Before it had time to settle the whip hissed and bit again, making her jerk, almost rocking her off her feet. She wanted to scream but held it back, gripping her ankles till her knuckles drained white as the pain built in her poor bottom.

Run, her mind frantically urged. You don't have to endure this.

But that dark sensual side of her that she was only just discovering insisted she stay. Vaguely she heard the others through her inner turmoil, and then wailed a feeble protestation as the cruel whip struck again. Julia clung to the thought that he had said six strokes, no more. She cried silently, fighting to hold back the tears that were squeezing from her tightly shut eyes, not wanting the onlookers to see them.

Then Gabor stopped and she felt his hands stroking her ravished buttocks, caressing the reddened orbs that had taken so much punishment. Fire radiated through her welts, and she longed for the balm he had used before.

'Get up,' he ordered, and groaning, she straightened, feeling weak and dizzy and distraught. He put a strong arm around her trembling shoulder. 'Are you feeling it?' he asked. 'Is your bottom stinging?'

'Yes... intensely,' she gasped, hardly able to speak.

Gabor nodded and looked pleased. 'I'm pleased to hear it,' he said. 'I think you'll be a valuable member of our team. Don't you, Marty?'

'I think so,' Marty Blake concurred. 'But I'd like to test her further, in my own way...' His eyes glinted hungrily and he leered at her from the shadows cast by the candles.

'This is my room whenever I stay overnight,' Marty Blake conversationally told Julia, as he checked she was properly secured to the four-poster bed. Her forearms and knees sinking into the soft mattress, she strained to try and see him over her shoulder. She was naked now, the blue dress a tiny crumpled heap discarded in one dark corner of the room.

'What are you going to do?' she asked timidly. She didn't trust or like Marty Blake at all, and wished Vincent Gabor was with them, but he'd dismayed her by permitting his friend to bring her up to the room, just the two of them.

'Don't worry, my dear,' he crooned from behind her, 'you'll love it... as I will.'

He appeared beside her, naked, climbed onto the bed and shuffled forward on his knees, his semi-erect penis swaying between his thighs. Without pausing he gained a grip in her hair, lifted her head, prised open her mouth with his free fingers, and fed his cock into her mouth.

'Good girl,' he grunted. 'Now suck... that's good...' and he started to move her head back and forth as she obeyed his commands, his swelling erection stretching her lips wider and wider. 'Ooh,' he croaked, slipping his fully erect cock from the haven of her warm wet mouth, 'too much of that and I'll miss out on my special treat.'

Blake moved away, and Julia whimpered as the mattress sank again, this time between her bound and parted ankles. He edged forward. His erection bobbed against the back of her thigh and then her buttock, leaving a sticky emission there, and she buried her face in the silk coverlet, defeated and waiting for the man to take his pleasure from her body. Deep down she'd always known her undercover work made this very happening highly likely, and she'd succumbed to Vincent Gabor quite contentedly, but Marty Blake was a different animal altogether.

He leaned over her, covering her back, his penis lodging itself between her buttocks. 'Have you ever been fucked in the arse, my dear?' he whispered harshly in her ear. 'I know you were a virgin until Vince got his hands on you, but what about your arse?'

Julia was stunned, her stomach knotting with horror. 'N-no,' she blurted. 'No, I haven't!'

'Oh good,' he gloated, anointing his penis in the juices that were seeping from her traitorous sex. 'Then your virgin arse will be my little treat to myself,' he sniggered, and licked her cheek, leaving it horribly wet with his saliva.

'But - aaahhh...' Julia's protest faded as Blake stabbed expertly with his hips and lodged the lubricated and swollen tip of his cock just inside the tight muscle of her anus. The shock forced the air from her lungs and her back arched, making her breasts and erect nipples available for his groping hand. She tried to rock forward, but he followed until she was sandwiched between the enveloping mattress and him. Then he raised himself on straightened arms, his weight on his hands and knees, the tip of his cock the only contact between them, and gazed down at her lustrous hair, the beautiful curves of her shoulders, back and hips, and the soft buttocks moulded around his spear of an erection, which disappeared into the deep valley between them.

'I... I don't think I can...' she mumbled, almost incoherently, into the mattress. 'Don't make me... not that way...'

'But you are, dear Julia,' he gloried. 'Now, be quiet and enjoy...'

As Marty Blake's hips sank Julia clutched the coverlet desperately. The pain was intense, but as his hairy groin nestled down against her buttocks and her bottom was fully impaled, it rapidly eased and transformed into undeniable pleasure. He paused for a moment, allowing her to get accustomed to the new sensation, and savouring the tightness of her virgin rear passage, not wanting to spill his seed too soon and deny himself such sublime delight.

'That's very nice, my dear,' he grunted. 'You're a natural, and no mistake.' And then he started to move, just his hips, nothing more, the muscles of his arms knotted as they took his weight.

Julia moaned feeble protests, her head rolling from side to side on the bed, and then, very slowly, she began to lift her bottom, tentatively meeting his thrusts.

'Good girl,' he gasped. 'I told you you'd love it. *Hell*, you're so lovely and tight!'

His crude words suddenly triggered something inside her, spurring her on. 'Don't stop,' she sobbed desperately, her orgasm upon her. 'Please don't stop!' and as she shuddered in blissful release Blake grunted, stabbed aggressively with his hips, and came deep in her clutching bottom.

Chapter 8

The pace was hotting up. Marty's collection was to be shown at Mayfair's prestigious *Majestic Hotel* in a week's time. Tickets were on sale, the proceeds to go to charity.

Julia spent most of her days and much of her evenings rehearsing in Gabor's penthouse. Roberta was at a high pitch of tension that transferred itself to the models. He and Kevin were always getting at each other, two bitchy queens who were jealous as hell. If Blake gave one too much attention, the other threw a tantrum.

'It's fun, but exhausting,' Julia said to Arlene over coffee in a corner café where they had paused for a rest between browsing in boutiques and charity shops. It was Saturday and they were catching up on themselves, doing the mundane chores like food shopping, washing and cleaning house.

'Have you seen anything that looks like my work?' Arlene asked anxiously, her hair coiled up and kept in place by fancy plastic clips.

Julia knew her friend's anger wouldn't be appeased until justice had been done. She'd lived with her long enough to be aware of the paranoia that existed amongst designers. Terms like copying, templates and ripping off, underpinned

Arlene's conversations. 'Not yet, but I'm not called to be in every session,' she said. 'I know Blake's planning something special, which is strictly under wraps.

'I know what you're thinking,' Arlene said, scowling through a haze of cigarette smoke, so strung out that any attempt at giving up on nicotine had gone to the wall. 'For every designer having a successful season, there's a rival convinced that his or her idea, style or whatever, has been hi-jacked. But I don't care. This isn't the case with me, and Marty Blake won't get away with it, the bastard.'

Julia looked longingly at the counter where, under little glass domes, a selection of iced cakes, gateaux piped with cream and crumbly pastries beckoned. She had to refuse their seduction. At this stage in the preparations Roberta would go berserk if any of the girls put on as much as an ounce.

'I'm doing my best to trap him, but it's not easy,' she told her friend. 'He has his special people about him and no one can get through if they're not meant to.'

'I hope you are doing your best, darling. I'm not talking counterfeit T-shirts here; those items that were stolen from me were my babies, my hope for the future. He had no right - no right at all to take them.' Arlene glared balefully at her coffee. 'And if I ever catch him out, then he won't know what's hit him.'

'You'll report him to the police?'

'Oh, no,' Arlene mused slowly. 'I have my own way of dealing with Mr Marty Blake. Leave that part of it to me. But first I need proof. Can't you get close to him?'

'It's difficult, Arlene. I *am* doing my best, but he's so aloof.'

'I know, I know,' Arlene said quickly, knowing it was unfair to badger her friend, who was doing her best, she knew. 'Come on, we've still got the crush at the supermarket to negotiate,' and she finished off her coffee and stubbed out her cigarette in the foil ashtray that had been grudgingly provided by a waiter.

Julia was saddened by the bleak look in her friend's eyes and, having now met and experienced Marty Blake, could understand how much he had upset her. He was too handsome for his own good, and despite his unscrupulous tendencies, Arlene had admitted to fancying him something rotten.

And so Julia set about attempting to capture his attention again when she next paced the catwalk. He arrived late, the rehearsal halfway through before he put in an appearance. Kevin was with him, carrying a briefcase and wearing an air of importance, as well as a loose jacket and baggy shorts that had come from Blake's workshop. His shaven head glistened with a light patina of sweat.

Roberta huffed and tossed his beaded mane, glaring disdainfully at Kevin, but restraining his cutting comments concerning tardy timekeeping. Blake was top dog, and could only be reprimanded by Gabor.

Gina had swung through her routine, wearing one of next spring's ensembles, a saucy little number, brief and made of easy-care cotton. It exemplified youthful insouciance, and undoubtedly chain store buyers would purchase it. Blake catered for these as well as for the shiny set; those rich women who appeared at every event that involved fashion.

Vesta was ready to go as Gina reached the head of the catwalk. She was modelling a suave and elegant cream linen day-dress, with a wide-brimmed hat. When she returned to the stage Julia took her place, sashaying towards Blake who stood at the end of the walk, looking up at her. She knew that her youth and vibrancy contributed to the success of the beach outfit she was modelling. It consisted of a short, fringed sarong in a jungle print, and a low-cut vest finishing just above her navel. She had sunbathed all day Sunday and deepened her tan, adding zest to the spicy tones of the fabric, which were repeated in the bold, chunky necklace and pendant earrings.

When she reached the end she paused, legs parted, feet balanced on mules with high soles. She guessed that from this angle Blake could look straight up her skirt, even catch a glimpse of the red lycra G-string that cupped her mound. She was angry with Vincent; he played hot and cold, only speaking to her when he felt like it. He hadn't made love to her since taking her virginity. He was hardly ever there, didn't attend rehearsals and was always jetting off on mysterious trips, to do with business, so Grace said.

Blake, on the other hand, was very much in evidence. This was his show and he was obsessed with success. Now would be a good time to get closer to him, and what could be closer than having sex with him? She still didn't like the man, but it would help her undercover work, and she hoped Vincent would get to hear about it and be hurt.

Blake was observing her closely, a slight smile curving his finely chiselled lips, and so she decided to put her plan into action. The sarong was loosely fastened, one end tucked into the waistband, so it was a second's work to unhitch the loop, accidentally on purpose, and the skirt unwrapped itself and slithered down round her ankles.

'Oh, I'm so sorry, Mr Blake,' she squealed. 'I hope this doesn't happen on the night!' She adopted a demure pose, her knees pressed together, a hand with fingers spread wide as if seeking to protect her modesty, covering the little red triangle that barely hid her mound. She turned away from him, knowing that her bottom still bore the marks of punishment, and wanting to remind him.

'We'll have to see that it doesn't, won't we, Julia?' Blake said, his grey eyes gleaming like steel 'Safety pins are a great asset to any model who isn't too sure of the security of her clothing. You would do well to remember that.'

'Yes, Mr Blake,' Julia said, pouting innocently and, while bending to retrieve her sarong, gave him a tantalising flash of the delicate strip of red fabric nestled tightly between her thighs that stood between her and his devouring gaze. 'Thank you, Mr Blake.'

'Get into your own clothes and we'll go for lunch,' he said, decisively.

'But Marty, we've only just got here,' Kevin protested, shooting bitchy daggers at Julia.

'What about the other girls?' Roberta put in, standing theatrically in all his magnificent glory of form and height, a petulant scowl on his heavily made-up face. 'Don't you want to see which ones are wearing what? Your opinion is of the essence, as you know.'

'You just hold the fort,' Blake said, in a tone that no one cared to dispute. 'I'll be two hours, tops.'

A taxi took them to an ultra-smart redbrick building fronted by a quay, beyond which the River Thames flowed. It was one of several that had been converted into offices and much sought after apartments. Half a million pounds would not be enough to buy one of these. But despite the money that had been spent and the planning that had gone into improvements, to Julia the frowning structures would never be anything other than factories in dockland.

'You live here?' she asked, seeking a topic of conversation. All the way there Blake had done nothing but stare at her, silent as the grave.

'Yes, and I have my atelier on the floor below.'

'How convenient,' she observed, thinking of Arlene's shabby little workroom above a shop, whereas he could afford a well-equipped studio on hand. He wouldn't even have to go out of the building in order to get there.

They reached his door and he pressed a series of computerised buttons to admit them. Once inside, Julia forgot the original use of the place. It had been cleverly renovated, and she wondered if he could be persuaded into letting her view that hive of industry where his machinists and pattern cutters would be working non-stop in order to bring his collection together on time.

She would ask him in a while, she decided, when they'd had lunch and done whatever he'd brought her there to do. Her chest tightened and her nipples crimped. She might be falling under the spell of Vincent Gabor, but Marty Blake was undeniably attractive too, and she couldn't forget the feel of his cock in her mouth and the shameful delights she experienced when he plundered her virgin bottom.

'Do you want a drink?' he asked, crossing the terracotta-tiled floor to a Peruvian style cabinet. Made of roughly carved wood, with blackened and deliberately rusted hinges, this piece and the chairs and table that went with it, looked as if they should be gracing a dining room/kitchen in a hacienda.

'Orange juice, please,' she said.

He fetched it from the large American-style fridge and carried it to the table. Then he took out a salad, a dish of tuna and pasta, garlic bread and yellow butter and a cheese board. 'My housekeeper prepared this earlier,' he said. 'A useful Tai boy, a wonderful cook and a wizard when it comes to ironing my clothes and generally looking after me. He's pretty, too, and sometimes models my menswear.'

'I see,' she said, nervous of him, disliking him, yet secretly aching to feel his avaricious touch again.

'Do you, Julia?' he said, and sat close to her at the octagonal table. Hewn from a solid block of wood, it stood on a central pedestal and was spread with an embroidered cloth. 'And what do you see, I wonder, with those wide blue eyes?'

This was an ideal opportunity and she knew she mustn't blow it, so she put on her best look of doting innocence and smiled sweetly. 'I see a very clever and successful man who is letting me model some of his clothes, and I'm more than

78

just grateful,' she said.

'You intrigue me,' he answered, serving the tuna salad and a tangy mayonnaise. 'You came along at just the right moment; I needed a fresh face.'

'Do you ever think of anything except your clothes?' she asked, idly touching the rim of her chilled glass with the tip of a dainty finger.

'Hardly ever. I'm like any creative person, one-pointed and egocentric. I live and breathe my designs. When everyone has gone home at night, I pop down to my workroom and spend hours adjusting the toiles draping the dummies. I'm rarely satisfied, and putting on a collection is a monumental strain. I brought you here to help me relax. Don't let's talk about work. Tell me about yourself, Julia Jones. Are you attracted towards Mr Gabor?'

She nearly choked - was she *that* transparent? - dabbed her lips with a paper napkin, looked at him quizzically, and said, 'What makes you think that?'

He chuckled, moved behind her to top up her glass, then suddenly eased down her shoulder straps and the bodice of her dress shimmered down a little, almost exposing her nipples. 'He excites you, doesn't he?' he said smoothly. 'He's so masterful, so cruel. I'll bet you never dreamed you could be so submissive.'

'I don't think I want to talk about it,' she said, trying to readjust her dress.

'No, sit there like that,' he insisted. 'I wish the public were ready to accept some of my more advanced ideas for women's designs. There's nothing more beautiful than the dishevelled look, almost - but not quite - allowing the observer to glimpse the perfection of a beautiful pair of naked breasts. It looks so sluttish - so wanton. It is absolutely enticing.'

His intensity made Julia begin to wonder if he was slightly eccentric, if not mad, but there was nothing she could do if she wanted her plan to succeed. 'No more, thank you,' she said, when he offered the salad bowl.

When they had eaten he removed the dishes to the kitchen area and came back with a large bowl of strawberries. 'These early fruits are always the sweetest,' he purred, put down the bowl, closed his hands round Julia's waist, and guided her up to sit on the edge of the table.

Without resistance he parted her smooth thighs, reached between them and beneath the skirt of her dress, and plucked the gusset of her panties between finger and thumb, his eyes staring deep into hers the whole time. He pulled. The delicate material resisted, so he picked up a dinner knife and, as Julia froze and watched it with alarm in her wide blue eyes, nicked easily through the fragile, slightly damp panties. They fell apart, exposing the full, luscious petals of her labia, and she gasped as he explored her sex lips, holding them open, his fingers sliding on the clear moisture wetting her vulva, and spreading it over the swollen sliver of flesh that crowned her delta.

'How beautiful you are,' he complimented. 'So soft and succulent and fragrant.' His fingers worked with more intent between her thighs, and through her turmoil of conflicting emotions, she sensed he was referring to that secret area that was responding so traitorously to his touch. 'You make me want to eat you... fruit and cream... mmm, a delicious combination.' His voice was low, almost hypnotic, his breath ruffling the soft hair on her lightly perspiring brow.

Her mouth opened in surprise as he picked a plump red strawberry from the dish and inserted it into her vagina. It was icy cold, straight from the fridge, and she gave a quick gasp. He pushed the succulent chilled fruit deeper inside her, and rested his thumb on her clitoris, which thrummed in response to the exciting sensations: cold and hot, soft and firm. She longed to come.

He grinned knowingly, and applied a further strawberry to one of her nipples, which bunched delightfully at the sudden cold. He sucked the fruit between his lips and munched slowly, then leant down to lick the red-stained flesh of her aureole.

Below, in the dark confines of her channel, she could feel the fruit warming in her heat, but this was suddenly chilled again when he inserted more until she was filled with a delectable summer harvest. He suckled at her breasts again, and a tingling feeling emanated from her clit. It spread to her groin, her womb, the base of her spine, the intense excitement making her moan and arch her neck, staring at the ceiling through misty blue eyes.

Blake sat on a chair between her legs, leaned closer, his cheek resting on her thigh as he watched her labia turning the colour of the berries, her clitoris a shining pearl at its crest. He tickled it, circled it, manipulated it until Julia felt herself rushing towards completion, and then she gave a low-pitched sob and shuddered on the table, fingers clawing his hair as she climaxed. Her fruit-filled sex convulsed, pulping the softened contents. A trickle of crimson juice ran from her like blood, and Blake caught it on his tongue.

He lapped at her, drinking the delectable nectar of fruit and pussy juice. His tongue entered her vagina and curled around a strawberry. He sucked it out, swallowed it, and then probed avidly for the rest of the sweet harvest. Feeling drained Julia lay back on the table and let him do as he willed with her. She was still quivering from the mighty orgasm, relaxed and utterly replete, her sex lips glowing with the warmth of his tongue and soothed by the slippery sweetness of his spittle.

He stood, loomed over and kissed her, and she could taste strawberries and her own fragrant juices on his lips. With an arm around her, he led her into the lounge, a place with modern art on the walls, a hi-fi console, a forty-inch television screen, white carpets and white leather armchairs and a deeply cushioned white leather couch. The French windows opened onto a conservatory and rooftop garden. It all simply reeked of money.

Blake discarded his shirt. He was staggeringly beautiful and well muscled, the planes of his chest leading down to the hard, washboard ridges of his belly. He slipped out of his designer toe-post sandals, and then took off his trousers. Julia had already experienced his handsome penis, but couldn't quite recall it being so big, and as he walked to where she sat spellbound on the couch, it bobbed in time with his stride, and his balls swung beneath it in their scrotal sac.

He stopped in front of her, his cock pointing threateningly straight at her face. 'Touch me,' he said.

She hesitated a moment, but then lifted a hand and closed her fingers around the impressive erection, marvelling at its smoothness. He narrowed his eyes and watched her efforts closely, and drew in a sharp breath of pleasure. Emboldened by this, she rubbed with more confidence, working the foreskin up and over his glistening helm.

And then his hand clamped around hers and he whispered, 'I can't take much more. I want to fuck you now.'

He lay with her amidst the leather and his thumb skilfully found her clit. She came quickly, consumed by pleasure so intense that she had to clamp her mouth to his shoulder to smother the scream that threatened to wrench itself from her lungs. As if this was his cue he positioned himself between her thighs and filled her with one decisive stroke. Her legs lifted around his hips and locked there, drawing him in. She wanted to pull him closer, glorying in the smell of him; the scent of his hair, aftershave and body lotion that barely masked fresh sweat and the stronger odour of aroused male.

But he wasn't Vincent Gabor, and no matter how she tried, it was he who held her in thrall. Even as Marty Blake ground deeply into her and used her harshly, intent on his own satisfaction, so she remembered each and every detail of the time when Vincent Gabor took her virginity.

When it was over Blake left her abruptly, and she wondered what would happen next. She heard the shower, and soon he returned, drying himself in a large towel.

'Time to go,' he said matter-of-factly. 'I told Roberta I'd only be a couple of hours. He'll have my guts for garters if I let him down.'

That was it then. His attitude was almost rude, and certainly dismissive. That was how he had treated Arlene at the Cloth Show. Such arrogance matched Vincent Gabor's and Julia's heart went cold. She pulled down her skirt and adjusted her top. 'May I use the bathroom?' she asked, trying to appear unruffled and not to show her hurt at being dismissed so casually.

When she had cleaned up and refreshed herself, she realised that her panties were now useless. She'd have to go back to the rehearsal knickerless, and try to keep the hem of her dress discretely low. She shrugged, ran her fingers through her hair and returned to the lounge.

Blake was fully clothed once more. 'All set?' he said.

'Yes, but I did rather want to see your atelier,' she replied, putting on her most appealing, little-girl-lost look.

'Sorry, darling,' he answered as she picked up her bag and he strolled with her to the door. 'Can't possibly disturb my workforce. Another time, perhaps.'

Julia was convinced he didn't want her poking her nose in. What, she wondered, was he up to? She would have bet money that he'd got his secret agents copying Arlene's dresses. However, it hadn't been an entirely unsuccessful mission. She was confident that she'd discovered a few chinks in his armour. Next time, she would get into that studio if it killed her!

'I'm very pleased with you, Julia,' Vincent Gabor said, in the dressing room at the end of the day. They were alone, and he leaned over and placed a kiss at the nape of her neck. She smelled delicious and her skin was baby-soft. She melted into his arms. There was no doubting the instinctive warmth of the girl or her welcome.

'How so?' she asked, breaking free and idling her fingers through her curls. 'I wasn't expecting you to be here. Grace said you were away.'

He drew up a stool beside hers and, sliding a hand onto her knee under her robe, started to move upwards, caressing her thigh all the way. He needed her hot and malleable. 'I was able to return earlier than expected. I've been talking to Marty, and he told me about your lunch date.'

He was amused and aroused by the way her cheeks reddened and the shy manner in which she kept her eyes fixed on her hands folded in her lap. She was feeling guilty, and he liked that. Contrite, she'd be all the more eager to accept punishment for her unfaithfulness. His fingers climbed higher and he parted her thighs, sliding over her wet cleft and finding her bud. He felt her shiver, and strummed on her tiny organ. Her labia opened like petals in the sun and her clit enlarged.

'Don't worry, Julia,' he continued, using his most persuasive tone. 'What you did pleased me. I like you to be nice to my friends. You want to please me, don't you?'

'Yes, of course I do, Mr Gabor.' She lifted her eyes to his and they sparkled with a clear sincerity that almost touched his conscience - almost, but not quite.

He kept up the pressure on her clit, bringing her closer and closer to orgasm. She swayed on her seat, her face flushed, but timing it to perfection he removed his hand from the warm dark valley between her thighs before she had reached her orgasmic plateau. She moaned frustratedly, leaned towards him, tried to keep his hand there where she needed it most, but he calmly withdrew. His fingers were coated with nectar. Its oceanic odour rose between them in a sweet wave and his fully erect penis throbbed. He was sorely tempted to take her, but had other matters to sort out first.

'Bearing in mind your desire to please me, you will do whatever I command after the showing of Marty's collection,' he said firmly. 'There will be a formal party when it is over, and an informal one later on. I expect absolute obedience, Julia, no matter what you're asked to do.'

There was a moment's pause, and then she answered, 'Yes, Mr Gabor, I understand,' and then, despite loathing her weakness, she couldn't prevent herself from reaching blindly for the bulge in his lap, covering it with her small palm and rubbing through the immaculate cut of his trousers, her robe falling open over her nakedness.

'Punishment first,' he said quietly.

'Punishment?' she asked, in a voice weak with consternation and frustration. 'But, what have I done now?'

'You hesitated when I demanded that you obey me to the letter, without question,' he told her sternly.

'I'm really sorry, Mr Gabor,' she said. 'I really am. Don't whip me, please.'

'I am prepared to be clement,' he said. 'Not on you're account, however, but because we don't want you marked in any way before the show.' Placing his feet firmly on the floor, knees a little apart, he pulled her to him until she was lying across his lap. The robe tangled under her and he eased it away, running his hands over her shoulders and back and buttocks, the feel of her unblemished flesh, the helplessness of her position, making the lust rise urgently within him.

He paused, to excite himself further and let the tension build, and then, without warning, his right palm smacked down across her bottom, making her whimper and her hips bounce from the shock. He let the smart sink in, and spanked her again, his hand burning with the sharp contact of palm on rump. He did it thoroughly and for several minutes. At first she protested and writhed in a futile attempt to make herself a difficult target, but soon her response changed and he knew she was awaiting each slap with anticipation, her bottom glowing red, the heat no doubt spreading to her clitoris, making it pulse greedily.

He loved spanking a female and watching how it changed them - tamed them. Chastising a female, and the inevitable sex that followed, was almost - but not quite - as satisfying as concluding a business deal - particularly if that business deal was at the expense or ruination of someone else.

Julia pushed her bottom up, silently begging for more. He slipped his free hand under her belly and his probing fingers found her wet delta. He buried it in her vulva and then withdrew, anointing her clit with juice. He moved it up and down as he continued to chastise her, his palm slapping down on her scarlet bottom cheeks.

Each blow landed close to the former one, leaving a glow that her wriggles and yelps told him were adding to her wanton pleasure. His finger worked the hard button of her bud. Her lovely hair swept the floor and she whimpered piteously. He changed pace, whacking three more slaps across her cleft. He never relented in his brisk attention to her clit and she gave a muffled scream, her convulsions announcing that she had reached her crisis. She slumped across his lap and he ceased his assault on her hinds, allowing her to lie there for a moment, his hand gently cradling her mound.

'How on earth am I going to get in?' Arlene raged, hands thrust into her wild dark hair, green eyes as dangerous as a lioness's. 'It's tickets only, isn't it? Top whack tickets, only available to the rich, famous and influential. Just the kind of people I'd be brown-nosing if it was my show instead of his. Which it should be if there was any justice in this world.'

'I'm going, representing *Hi Life*,' Will told her again, alarmed by her bitterness. 'I've a pass as a member of the press. Why don't I say you're with me... assistant photographer or something?'

'That's a good idea,' agreed Eugene, obviously eager to smooth her ruffled feathers.

They were seated at a table in the *Flying Goose*, awaiting the arrival of Julia. Each was keyed up in his or her particular way. Marty Blake's much-advertised event was taking place the following day. It was early evening and the bar was filling, patrons beginning to trickle in, dropping by for a pint on the way home from work, or already making a night of it. Members of the pub team had requisitioned the dartboard, and others were gathering for the weekly quiz in the lounge bar.

'Could we get away with it?' Arlene asked Will, crossing her slim legs in tight stretch jeans and lighting up another cigarette.

'You could wear a wig,' he said light-heartedly, and was rewarded with a freezing glare. He was never quite happy in her company; she was too fiery a woman for him, though she did remind him a little of Denise.

'A wig,' Arlene sneered scornfully. 'Blonde, I suppose, to convince the men that I'm an empty-headed bimbo.'

'Julia's a blonde,' Will pointed out, finding himself instinctively protective of the sweet girl.

Arlene shrugged and spread wide her hands, 'I rest my case,' she said. 'Julia's a darling and I love her to bits, but she's not exactly the brain of Britain, is she? And she'd be the first to admit it.'

'That's not fair,' Will said, surprising himself at how determined he was to fight her corner in her absence. 'She's very loyal and very brave. It takes guts to do what she's doing right now.'

'Modelling?' Arlene replied sarcastically.

'No, trying to net a couple of suspected villains, and on your behalf, might I remind you?'

'Okay, you win,' Arlene conceded. 'So, I'm to wear a wig, change my style and become your assistant - is that it?' she asked, moving the subject away from Julia and back to the agenda.

'That's about it,' Will said. 'Anyone care for another drink while you ponder the idea?'

'Mine's a pint, please, mate,' said Eugene. 'And is there any chance I could come along, too - just to keep an eye on things, should they get rough? If Arlene spots one of her gowns, which he's saying is his, then I don't reckon much for his chances. She'll gouge out his eyes and be done for assault.'

'I wish,' she said darkly, then added, 'I'll have a lager,' and looked anxiously towards the door; she would be on tenterhooks until Julia appeared.

'Number twenty - *Springtime in Paris*,' said the commentator, standing to one side of the stage, microphone in her hand. 'Number twenty-one - *Rio Carnival*.' And so on and so on, as she continued to introduce a dizzying procession, each model displaying a Marty Blake creation.

The cameras clicked, recording the girls' progress along the catwalk. At the top each girl turned, revealing the whole of her outfit - the patter of shutters and the beat of soul music an accompaniment to her haughty stride. The tide of beautiful females wearing outrageously new ensembles seemed to go on forever.

For two hours the audience, sitting on small gilt and red plush chairs, watched the procession gliding by in burgundy silk crêpe, cream grosgrain, quilted damask, a heady flurry of hot spice and curry colours for the beach and tropical nights. There were ballgowns and dresses for every hour of the day, or night, and a sprinkling of male models outlandishly attired in kilts and sarongs, and skin-tight trousers that left nothing to the imagination. Hats, shoes, jewellery, even a new perfume called *Body Talk* had all been designed by the maestro, Marty Blake.

'Isn't he just *wonderful*,' gushed a short, overweight and overdressed American matron. She had a seat in the front, but Arlene had managed to wedge herself to the fore, with the help of the camera she hefted and the press badge she wore pinned to her chest. It all seemed to open all manner of otherwise closed doors.

'You know him?' asked Will, her stalwart backup, his journalist's head glued firmly in place. Eugene brought up the rear. Both of them wore suits, and that in itself made Arlene all the more conscious that this was a momentous occasion and one which would be remembered; the start of Marty Blake's downfall, she thought, irritated by the fat woman's drooling admiration of such a charlatan.

'Oh, yes, I've been a customer of his for years. I'm Mrs Hooper-Jones, from the USA.'

She levelled Will a searching stare, taking in his press badge and adding, 'Are you a newsman?'

'I work for a popular magazine called *Hi Life*, Mrs Hooper-Jones,' Will said, using his considerable charm. 'I'm here to report this event. Anything you can tell me about Mr Blake and his work will be of enormous value.'

'Have we got a couple of weeks?' she gushed again, her bouffant hair, her extravagant but passé gold brocade two-piece more suitable for a wedding than a late afternoon fashion show. Without awaiting Will's reply she rushed on. 'Why yes, honey, he's been designing my clothes for several years,' she willingly disclosed. 'And this collection... *my*, but he's excelled himself! So new, so daring. I can't wait to take some of the things home and show them off to my girlfriends. They'll just die! But hush now, here they come again.'

She adjusted her pink-framed spectacles and looked at her programme. As the music beat out a rhythm the applause swelled and three more models stalked and turned and trod the catwalk.

Arlene stared, half expecting this but stupefied when it actually happened. She thought she'd spotted several of her designs earlier, but these were blatantly, undeniably hers. Evening or party wear, when she had given full rein to her imagination. She'd used synthetics, PVC, and Lycra to create slinky, daring outfits, vaguely Egyptian in concept, certainly space age fantasy gear. Will leaned forward with his camera and clicked away at a bodice like a cellophane-wrapped bouquet of carnivorous flowers.

'Get all these,' Arlene hissed under her breath. 'They're mine. Marty Blake is a thieving, conniving bastard!'

The girls retired and the lights dimmed. There was a hush, an expectant pause as the commentator announced, 'And now, just before our final item which is the traditional wedding scene, we have great pleasure in presenting Marty's latest and greatest, which he has called *Queen of The Night*.'

Someone had changed the music tape. Now the mighty chords from the *Space Odyssey* blared forth, the lights went up and the audience gasped and started to clap and cheer. Arlene stared and stared, her emotions in turmoil; hatred of

Marty Blake, pride in this piece of her own work, and a blazing fury forming a combustible volcano within her.

Cressida posed, allowing the furore to die down before moving. Tall Cressida rendered seven foot tall by the addition of a towering jewelled headdress and stack-heeled silver boots laced to the thigh. Her make-up was barbaric, and she looked like a sexy, alien warrior queen. The gown scintillated, a diaphanous skirt slit front and back, the flaps dangling from the heavily encrusted belt drawing attention to, rather than hiding, her shaven mound and shapely taut buttocks. Tooled metal armbands stretched from wrists to elbow. Arabesque bra cups that left the top half bare upheld her firm breasts, and a jewelled collar drew the eye to her stiff nipples.

Cameras flashed all over the long, high-ceilinged banqueting room, and the distinguished guests, drawn from among the aristocracy, the world of entertainment and *haute couture*, leaned forward on their seats.

'*Don't!*' Eugene warned in urgent, hushed tones, grabbing Arlene's arm and preventing her from leaping up onto the catwalk.

'But it's mine!' she gasped, tears of rage smudging on her cheeks. '*Mine!*'

'I know, I believe you, but there are other ways of tackling this,' Eugene insisted, glancing anxiously around to see if anyone had noticed the intensity of Arlene's reaction. 'Pay Blake a visit after the show. Will and me'll come with you.'

'Oh, my word!' Mrs Hooper-Jones exclaimed, unaware of anything except her pent-up emotion and frustrated desire centred on Marty. 'Will you look at *that*? I must have it for the Ladies of Louisiana Charity Ball at Thanksgiving!'

Chapter 9

The atmosphere backstage was one of nerve-jangling tension. Roberta and Grace were possessed of an extraordinary, unnatural calm, far removed from their frantic behaviour at the rehearsals. It was as if, now too late to do anything to avert disaster, they had reached a stage of stoical acceptance.

Julia had only appeared in the beach outfit. It had been decided to keep her for the grand finale, the wedding sequence that always ended any show worth its salt. She had been selected as the bride. Roberta had made her practice until she was giddy, having nightmares of going down the aisle, or in this case, the catwalk, hearing Mendelssohn's *Wedding March* ringing in her ears, her arm linked with that of Lee, Marty Blake's houseboy. He had been chosen to act as her bridegroom. He was an exotic figure in a colourful cotton kanga, a frilled white shirt and a dinner jacket. This, coupled with thonged sandals, fuchsia-pink toenail varnish and camp gestures, made him a very odd choice indeed. Apparently he was popular with the punters; the older women wanted to mother him.

Julia's single foray into the public eye had been enough, and she was shaking like an aspen leaf as Grace settled ten thousand pounds' worth of wedding dress round her. She was in awe of it, yet knew it to be bottom of the range; it would have to be a very well heeled daddy indeed to lead his million-dollar princess to the altar wearing one from the top end.

Julia was in the lap of luxury. The hotel the girls were staying in was extremely grand and very expensive. All gilt and mirrors and cut glass and crimson plush.

'More like your traditional whorehouse,' Gina had commented acerbically. 'And I expect there's a fair bit of whoring goes on inside it, too. Can't fool me with all this pomp and circumstance. It's a load of old cobblers.'

They had been permitted one run-through in the banqueting room consigned to them. The hotel manager let it be known in no uncertain terms that only because the event was to be patronised by certain members of the royal family had he allowed such a rabble of riffraff and mountebanks to enter its sacred precinct.

'Fuck right off,' Roberta had commented under his breath, sticking up a stiff forefinger at the pompous little man's retreating back. 'Swivel on that, baby! Charity my arse; the hotel's costing a fortune to hire. The good cause, and I'm not sure which one it is, will get the leftovers after every one's had a slice of the pie.'

Cressida returned, flushed with success. *Queen of the Night* had brought the house down. Foreign buyers already besieged Blake, though the show was not yet over.

'Keep it on, darling, keep it on!' Roberta squealed with barely controlled hysteria. 'You know you'll be poncing about out there again, as soon as the wedding thing is over, to let them have another look.' His voice rose shrilly. 'No, don't sit down!'

'Stuff off!' Cressida spat, her feline eyes elongated by black liner, her full red lips parted in a snarl. 'I need to have a piss.'

'Then I'll come with you,' he insisted. 'To hold up your skirt and make sure you don't piddle on it.'

Julia surveyed herself in the full-length mirror. She was almost unrecognisable in this gorgeous, fairytale gown fashioned of silk faille, and decorated with seed pearls and lace. Vincent Gabor had called in a favour from Armand, a famous stylist with a salon in the West End. He had come to attend to the models' hair. He attached the wreath of orange-blossom and stephanotis to Julia, and was now fussing round her, adding the finishing touches.

'Beautiful, beautiful,' he murmured, a distinguished man with silvery wings of hair sweeping back from his temples. His manicured hands fluttered around her, adjusting the veil that drifted to the floor like a gossamer cloud.

She wondered uneasily what she would have to do at the late night gathering Vincent Gabor had planned, and if she would wind up with him when it was over. Longing welled up in her, sex-juice dampening the gusset of her white panties.

'Are you ready, darlings?' Roberta carolled and, as the fanfare began, Julia walked up the stairs leading to the stage.

She was aware of little, concentrating on managing the trailing bouquet whilst lifting her skirt so that she didn't trip over it. Two models were dressed as bridesmaids and, as she reached the top and came out into the blaze of spotlights, Lee was there, his arm extended so she could take it and pace down the narrow walk with him. Blinded by the flashing of cameras, it took a second for her eyes to focus, but then she saw Will, and with him was Eugene and a dowdy looking, fair-haired person wearing an unbecoming hat and horn-rimmed glasses, who she knew to be Arlene in disguise.

At last the ordeal was over and Julia gratefully retired from the limelight, almost catching her heel in the billowing gown's hem in her haste to reach the dressing room and get into her own clothes. She passed Gina on the way, and Vesta, Katie and several other girls, lining up for the parade. She could hear the deafening applause as each one took a bow, then the cheers as Cressida stalked on in her *Queen of the Night* attire.

Marty Blake was with her, and the storm of clapping increased. He took the microphone from the commentator and addressed the audience.

'Thank you so very much,' he said clearly and loudly. 'I'm quite overwhelmed. You've received my collection so kindly and I thank you again from the bottom of my heart. Of course, such an event could not have taken place without the untiring work and support of my team. And none of it would have been possible had I not had such beautiful and accomplished models.

'And last but by no means least, I'd like to thank my advertising wizard and general factotum, Kevin Dean, and my sponsor, Vincent Gabor. I hope very much to be speaking with you personally at the cocktail party in the ballroom to which you are all invited.'

More cheers. More speeches, this time from Gabor and a representative from a fashion magazine, and by the time it was all over the wedding gown had been replaced on its hanger and Julia was wearing her new dress, a black sequinned number.

The slinky skirt reached her ankles, and bootlace straps held up the low bodice. She fluffed out her hair and decided to keep on the make-up, which had been applied more generously than usual. Beneath the dress she wore nothing but a pair of hold-up stockings, and this lack of underwear showed. Her nipples raised the spangled chiffon, and the fabric clung to her posterior making any viewer aware of an absence of knicker-line. She slipped her feet into strappy black sandals with high, pointed heels. She felt wanton and confident and brazen, now wanting to do the show all over again. Had Vincent been watching her with special interest? She rather thought he had, and her excitement mounted in anticipation of the evening to come. It was filled with promise, and she had high hopes of ending up in his bed.

Lost in a daydream in which he was at first masterful, binding and whipping her, and then tender, using his considerable skill as a lover, she was rudely awakened by a rumpus in the corridor outside. The door crashed inwards and Cressida came flying through, pursued by Arlene.

'Take if off!' Arlene was screaming. 'Give me back my dress, you bitch!'

'Hey!' Roberta shouted, standing foursquare between the two women. 'What's going on? No unauthorised persons are allowed in here.'

'I'll bet they're bloody not!' Arlene screeched. 'That cheating piece of lowlife wouldn't want anyone knowing he's stolen my designs. Marty Blake's a fraud and a liar!'

'Who the fuck are you?' Marty Blake snapped, striding into the melée.

Arlene dragged off the hat, wig and glasses, her own gypsy ringlets tumbling down. 'Now d'you recognise me, bastard?' Her voice was ice pick sharp, and Julia shuddered, sure that if Arlene had one in her hand Blake would be a dead man.

The colour drained from his face, but he managed to keep his calm admirably. 'I think I've seen you around somewhere,' he said condescendingly, lifting his nose with arrogance.

'Bloody right you have, you snake!' Arlene continued to fume. 'At the Cloth Show, remember? And before that you'd seen my designs on display - not these perhaps, but others. What's the matter, *Marty?* Are you running out of inspiration? Have to steal my work, do you, and pretend it's yours?'

He had recovered swiftly, backed up by the formidable Roberta, Grace and the mannequins, all of whom would support him even if they suspected that Arlene was telling the truth. It was more than their jobs were worth to question his professional integrity.

Julia froze, and Will, right behind Arlene, gave her a silent signal of warning. If she wanted to remain on the investigation she must hold her peace and pretend she didn't know them. She was glad to see Eugene edging forward, and that he was alert enough to have fallen into a fighter's stance, fists bunched.

'What's going on?' Vincent Gabor demanded as he pushed his way in amongst the seething throng. 'Marty, who is this woman?'

'A nobody,' Blake replied dismissively. 'An unsuccessful designer who's jealous of my fame.'

'We can't afford any trouble,' Gabor said. 'Get her out of here. Marty, you've to put in an appearance at the party. Now, Marty, they're waiting for you.'

He signalled to one of the many hired security men. He was built like a tank, and he nodded and advanced on Arlene. 'Her badge says she's press,' he grunted.

'It must be a forgery,' Blake insisted.

'Come on, miss, time you were going,' the security man said, and gripped her arm in his massive paw. But Arlene kicked his shins smartly and launched into a karate move, winding a leg around his and chopping at the hand that held her. He crashed to the floor. Julia wanted to jump on him and finish the job, but Will's eyes told her not to interfere - not yet, at any rate. Time enough for action later, when they had the evidence they wanted.

'Call the hotel's security,' Gabor ordered grimly.

Arlene straightened up, filled with righteous indignation. 'Don't worry, Mr Gabor,' she said. 'I'm going. But this isn't the end of it, not by a long chalk. You'll be hearing from my solicitors.'

'Tch! And what good will that do you?' Marty Blake sneered, then leaned closer and lowered his voice. 'You haven't any proof. There's not a damn thing you can do about it. But stir up trouble for me and I'll make sure you never work again. A designer? Forget it.'

'You can't scare me off, and you'll live to regret this,' Arlene promised with conviction, and then turned on her heel and marched from the dressing room. Eugene glared around belligerently, and then followed her.

'And you?' Vincent Gabor said to Will. 'Are you a part of this?'

'Not at all,' he answered promptly, camera bag over one shoulder. 'I'm here on behalf of *Hi Life*. My editor briefed me to take pictures of the show. It's quite an event in the social calendar. One of our writers is out there reporting on it.'

Gabor gave him a steady stare. 'Okay,' he said carefully, 'you'd better come along and do the party. There's plenty of celebrities who can't get enough of seeing themselves in print.'

Shaking off the restrictions imposed on them by the gathering in the ballroom, Vincent Gabor's select seraglio gave vent to hilarity and exuberance when they reached the building which housed so many of his business ventures and his apartment. Even Julia was still caught up in the excitement, though fretting about Arlene. The scene in the dressing room had reinforced her belief in her friend and refuelled her desire to help her. Marty Blake had behaved like a monster, and she was now fully convinced of his guilt. As for Vincent? She could no longer blind herself to the fact that he may have had a hand in it, too. She had managed a word with Will during the celebration, where women with shrill voices and too much money monopolised and idolised Blake.

'What now?' she murmured, pretending an interest in posing for the camera.

'We dig deeper; the ball's in your court tonight,' was all he said. 'I don't see any way I can worm my way into his private bash.'

Duty done, having entertained the media, the aristocracy, the English thespians and Hollywood starlets, the girls bundled into cabs and cars and headed for Abbey Reach. The tower block gleamed, a constellation in the darkness, every window lit. Julia was sharing a cab with Gina. It drew up near the entrance to the huge parking complex, which yawned like a cave mouth and, as on other occasions when she had parked her own car there, Julia was impressed by its activity. No matter how late the hour, there were always men loading or unloading the long-distance lorries that regularly arrived or departed. She hadn't been able to get to the bottom of Vincent's commercial enterprises, but gathered that they were legion and mostly run from the nerve centre at Abbey Reach. But no one in his employ seemed willing to talk about it.

'What's this party in aid of?' she asked, once they were in the elevator travelling heavenwards. 'More charities?'

Gina and Vesta exchanged a sly glance with Katie, and then Gina rested back against the lift's mahogany walls and slid her hands down to her crotch, wrinkling up her skirt and exposing her denuded pussy. The others smiled and relaxed, Vesta pinching her own nipples and Katie aping Gina's action and touching her clit.

'It won't be like that dull thing we've just survived, all those people going gaga over the clothes. No, Julia, this is held for Vincent's other crowd. You know, the ones that were there the first night you joined us... big boys in big business who play for high stakes. They'll be bringing along their tarts or rent boys, but they'll want us, too. We don't ask questions. Get it?' Gina moaned softly and rubbed herself briskly, adding to no one in particular, 'I wonder if I can come before the lift stops.'

'The only bright spot at the other do was Theona Blue and her band,' Vesta chipped in. 'Who had the bright idea of hiring her? I bought one of her CDs. They were on sale in the foyer.'

'No Theona Blue tonight, I fear,' Katie said, as they stepped out of the elevator. 'We may get some eastern flutes and bongos and belly-dancers, but I guess we'll be too busy to notice.'

'Oh... oh... bugger it! I didn't quite make it,' Gina grumbled, and then brightened. 'Never mind. There'll be plenty of good sex for all concerned when the party gets going.'

At first nothing much happened. People took their drinks outside and strolled on the terrace, where a kidney-shaped swimming pool and an abundance of exotic potted plants made one forget that the opulent location was way above the city. Several of the more daring guests were skinny-dipping.

Though quietly drinking and talking, the majority were wearing what Julia took to be fancy dress, until she scrutinised the guests more closely. Some of the men were in monks' habits, the hoods pulled over their heads, the fronts opened to show naked chests and bellies and cocks, some drooping, some stiff. A few women were dressed as nuns, complete with black robes and wimples, this demure attire rendered immodest by the slits in the bodices where nipples poked through, and the skirts that were hitched high, displaying luscious bottoms and cunts. Others wore leather or satin tightly laced corsets, and split-crotch panties, pussies exposed, clits and nipples rouged and sometimes pierced, with thin chains linking them. Their make-up was theatrical, their hair tousled or slicked back, and their footwear was extreme, always high of heel.

Julia recognised the strapping dominatrix, Kay, and her partner. They strode among the crowd, wielding whips and meting out punishment to the submissive waiters and waitresses. Vincent's two meek servant girls had been stripped and chained to pillars, heads drooping, long hair concealing their breasts, but nothing could hide the floss at their forks, and anyone could touch them, dive a hand between their thighs and stroke them to orgasm. Reluctant they might be, but they couldn't prevent themselves from coming.

Gina had been right about the music. The sounds of flute and tambour came from judiciously placed stereo speakers. Two dusky-skinned, buxom women were dancing, their hips gyrating, their large bottoms shaking, their breasts wobbling, the tassels attached to their jutting nipples swinging from side to side. A regal looking man in a striped kaffiyeh had ordered his bodyguards to position his chair so that he would miss nothing of their performance. As he watched through lowered lids, a young male slave in chains and leather straps bent over and presented his naked posterior, and the hawk-faced man poked his fingers into the proffered anal hole.

Julia found herself isolated from Gina and the rest, wandering that large room. A buffet had been set up. Professional caterers provided caviar, smoked salmon, a range of delectable gourmet dishes, along with pyramids of fruit and a generous selection of puddings, mostly served with cream and apricot brandy sauce. There were ices, chocolate and various, and a seemingly endless supply of champagne.

As she went further the wailing music was drowned out by the sounds issuing from the massive television screen at the far end; groans, cries of pleasure, the noise of bucking and grinding. Guests lounged on divans watching a pornographic movie where couples strained in ecstasy, their antics blown up and exaggerated as they performed the sex act in a variety of ways. The male actors were handsome and muscular, their penises large and their balls impressive. Some of the women had perfect figures, while others had obviously had breast enlargements. They rubbed their obese tits, making the nipples stand out. Winding their legs round their screen lovers, they squealed and grimaced, impaled on those spear-hard cocks.

The audience watched in silence, sipping champagne and groping their genitals, or those of the person closest to them. Soon the movements of the actors were being reproduced in Vincent Gabor's reception room as more were drawn towards the television screen. Like the actors, they started to explore every desire. Julia saw one woman whip up her nun's habit and lay on the floor with four men. One stuck his cock in her sex, another pushed his erection into her mouth and the remaining two knelt either side of her so she could take their rearing erections in her hands and masturbate them.

Julia shrank back against the wall, though her newly discovered self wanted to join in. She saw women licking one another's breasts, clits and forbidden holes and men buggering other men. Restraint had gone to the winds, the visual stimulation, the strong drink, the licentious atmosphere combining to encourage the participants to yield to their basest desires and most erotic fantasies.

'Don't you want to do what they're doing?' said a husky voice in her ear, and arms wrapped around her. She was pulled back against a rearing cock, while hands lifted her skirt and delved between her thighs.

'Mr Gabor,' she gasped, sighing and relaxing in his arms. 'I want you...'

He chuckled throatily and bent at the knee, his naked cock pressing into her bottom crease. 'I know you do,' he crooned into her ear. 'The succulent wetness I've discovered between your thighs tells me so. Hush now and be patient. If you're very good and do exactly as I say, then later you can have me all to yourself.'

'What do I have to do?' She was willing to agree to anything, buoyed up by his promise.

He let her skirt slither down, tucked his penis away and zipped himself up. 'There's a gentleman here who has expressed an interest in you. He saw you the first night you performed and also watched you this afternoon. Please him, and you please me.'

He turned Julia to face him, and was looking extremely distinguished in tight white breeches, riding boots and a red jacket, a frilled jabot at his throat. He carried a riding whip with a silver stock. He was a ringmaster, or leader of the hunt. She could deny him nothing, unable to stop staring at the bulge that strained against his flies. He took her by the hand and they weaved through the throng to where a man of Latin appearance sat; a fat oily individual, and her heart plummeted.

She clung to Vincent's hand, but he merely gave her a little shove forward. 'Senor Lopez, this is Julia,' he said, ignoring the look of utter disgust freezing her expression. 'You requested that I introduce her to you.'

The South American didn't rise, as a gentleman would. Two pebble eyes stared up at her, the epitome of evil. He stripped her with that glance, making the outspoken lust of normal men seem pure in contrast. Julia came out in goosepimples. She was sickened at the thought of his hands touching her, by his wet lips and tongue slobbering on her, by his aura of power and ruthlessness.

'Come closer, senorita,' he said in a thickly accented, guttural voice.

'Do as he says,' Vincent urged, and moved back.

Julia stood in front of Lopez, confusion swamping her, as he reached behind her and cupped and mauled her buttocks. What was expected of her? Despite the revulsion she felt towards the ox of a man, should she, in her efforts to please Vincent Gabor, suggest she and the Latin go somewhere more private?

But she was given no choice in matters, as Lopez's face split into a lecherous leer, he nodded at Vincent and smacked her bottom with unnecessary harshness.

'Take her to the bed!' barked Vincent.

Curtains were drawn back to reveal an alcove with a large divan in the centre. It was covered in a quilt of matched jaguar pelts, and heaped with cushions in ecclesiastical hues. Despite their absorption in sexual pursuits, the nearest guests stopped what they were doing and stared. Julia stared too, fear and excitement warring within her.

Kay guided her across the floor, sat her down and snapped the bootlace straps. The bodice slid to Julia's waist and she tried to cover her breasts, but the bizarre woman wrenched them away. 'Lie down,' she ordered.

Julia couldn't prevent her from seizing her wrists and chaining them to the bedhead. Her legs were spread and fastened by the ankles with ropes attached to the barley-sugar twist posts at the foot. Kay hiked up the black sequinned skirt, exposing Julia's fluffy fair bush, then smiling triumphantly, she feasted her eyes on that damp, fragrant area, and parted the plump wings with a knowing finger.

Julia squirmed in pleasure and shame, but was helpless to prevent Kay from tickling the sensitive head of her clit till it swelled and rose from its cowl. Kay then left her, and Julia moaned with trepidation and need. A heap of pillows were thrust beneath her buttocks, raising her pelvis so that her hungry pussy was fully visible. Kay searched under another pillow and drew out a vibrator. It buzzed as she switched it on. Julia waited breathlessly, familiar with the bliss such an instrument could bring. Kay wetted the tip in Julia's dew and let it play on her bud, and the feeling was even more exquisite than Julia remembered.

A shadow fell over them, and she stared up into Gabor's dark eyes. He took Kay's place, the vibrator weaving a magic spell over Julia's clitoris, plunging into her channel, twisting, then withdrawing and entering her anus. She could feel the sensations mounting, but couldn't quite reach the peak.

'Stay with me, Mr Gabor,' she pleaded. 'Take me away from here, somewhere we can be alone. I only want you.'

At once he withdrew, leaving her bereft, empty. 'Do you dare question me?' he asked. 'I have given my orders and you will carry them out.'

'Don't be angry,' she begged. 'Forgive me...'

He moved away, she saw a sudden movement, and pain ripped through her thighs as he lashed her with the riding crop. Too stunned to cry, she heard the whip whistle and she jerked, the lash landing across her belly. His arm rose again, and this time she screamed as the fiery tip of the crop struck her pubis.

Through the mists of pain she heard him say, 'Now she's ready for you, Senor Lopez.'

'Screw her... fuck her... whip her again...' the watching guests chanted rhythmically, and the wave of lust emanating from them was frighteningly tangible.

'See to him,' Vincent Gabor ordered, handing Kay a prophylactic.

Lopez stood with his flies open and Kay rolled on the condom. His erect penis was of extremely large proportions.

He positioned himself between Julia's spread legs, and she looked up into his swarthy face and shuddered at his brutal expression. A string of saliva hung from his slack lips, and his rank breath fanned her cheek. His eyes were reptilian, soulless and black as pitch. Taking his enormous cock in one hand, he ran the helm over Julia's exposed sex lips, and then returned to prod her anus. Perspiration beaded her brow, and for one dreadful moment she thought he intended to stretch and breach this narrow passage, but he returned to her clit, massaging it with the large, smooth, purple head.

If she kept her eyes tight shut she could almost imagine it to be Vincent attempting penetration. She strained up for Lopez, urging him closer, but regretted it instantly as he succeeded in pushing his huge helm into her.

'Ooohhh...' she whimpered, her eyes opening, seeing his face like a pockmarked moon looming above her.

He grinned and wedged his cock in further, the foreskin slipping right back over that monstrous head. Here it stuck. She was wet, but he was huge, out of all proportion to the size of her vagina. She'd not be able to accommodate him without discomfort. Her welts hurt, her pubic mound was sore, but Lopez obviously cared nothing for this. In fact, the more discomfort his massive tool caused the more aroused he seemed to become. He thrust again and gained ground, his glans sinking further. He shifted her on the bed impatiently, as if she was nothing more than a rubber sex-doll. He angled her hips, already raised by the pillows, her wrists and ankles chafed by the bindings.

Clearly inspired by her murmured requests for leniency, he rutted harder. Julia felt as if she was being rent asunder, appalled by his selfish haste. He was

94

almost embedded within her, but not entirely, his weapon too long and too thick. Three-quarters in and he was butting her cervix. She felt stuffed, the pressure too great to be pleasurable. She tried to draw back from him, but was too tightly impaled and too well bound. Her struggles undoubtedly spurred him on. He muttered something in Spanish, the veins standing out on his bull neck, his face red and sweating.

His fat hips pistoned and he suddenly sank fully into her, stabbing her to the vitals, his wiry black bush meeting her soft down with a jar that reverberated through her body. She thought she might faint with intolerable shame at having the ugly brute ravishing her for his own gratification, and at having so many witnesses to her ravishment. Indeed, she prayed that she would faint; anything to escape his suffocating weight, body odour, and savage, animal brutality.

Lopez snorted. He pumped his organ in and out, transported by lust. Julia, flattened beneath him, could do nothing but endure. With fierce shunts he rammed at her, his movements becoming more and more erratic until he reached the point of no return. He came, grunting like a pig, neck arched, his eyes rolled hideously up in their sockets with nothing but the whites showing.

Through her disgust Julia rejoiced; it was over. She became aware of comments of approval and people crowding in, drinking in every moment of her ravishment by Lopez. He heaved his bulk from her, got to his feet and, with a proud smile, took a bow. His semi-flaccid, latex-coated dick started to lift under so much praise, the tip, full and heavy with his seed, sagging down and swinging as he raised his arms in appreciation of the crowd's adulation. In an instant he was surrounded by a bevy of beauties, all eager to make him fully erect again. They drew him away, out of Julia's sight.

'And what was your little friend doing on the catwalk?' asked Theona Blue. 'I thought she was a reporter, not a model.'

She and Will were immersed in the square sunken bathtub in her suite at the *Majestic Hotel*. Dumpy perfumed candles were ranged round the sides, their glimmer reflected in mirror tiles. He sat at one end of it and she at the other. As she talked her toes found his balls and wriggled against them. He could feel the blood surging warmly into his groin and his cock poked its head through the bath foam, a creature seeking its nest.

She had sought him out after the cocktail party, invited him to the rooms that had been placed at her disposal, and the rest had taken its natural course. They hadn't fucked yet, but it was only a matter of time.

'Julia's always wanted to be a model,' he answered cautiously, though discretion was getting difficult to maintain. The more her naughty toes toyed with his balls, the more his resolution to keep silent faded under the desire for relief.

'And there's nothing more to it?' Theona probed, smiling inscrutably, her tawny hair piled on top of her head, perfect breasts and shoulders rising from the soapy bubbles, nipples peaking invitingly. 'She's not hot on the trail of some sensational story, then?'

'Well... maybe,' he conceded, opening his legs and sliding them each side of hers, so that she was encased and unable to do other than continue her frottage of his testicles.

She reached for the crystal champagne flute standing on the tiled surround and lifted it to her lips. 'Come along, tell auntie all about it,' she urged. 'Who knows? I may be able to help. There's nothing goes on in and around the entertainment business that I don't get to hear about.'

Could she be of assistance? Although Will's body was responding to her, his mind was still razor-sharp. He hardly knew her, had only met her that one time in Cornwall, but they had struck up an instant rapport, two wily contenders in the battle of life. Bored with the cocktail party, and losing sight of Julia, he hadn't hesitated when she'd invited him to her room. Both of them knew what they wanted - raw, uncomplicated sex, but if more than that developed, then all well and good.

'She's always fancied her chances as a model,' he repeated, unable to stop himself from reaching out and fondling her nipples. They reminded him of rosebuds in the snow.

Theona looked sceptical. 'Oh yes?' she said. 'Are you sure there's nothing else behind it? If there is, I may be able to help.'

He could feel himself melting into the bath water. He wanted to be that single shining bubble on her right nipple. Nothing else was important. She was stunning, her skin a suntanned joy to behold, her hair, her eyes, everything about her making her the most desirable of women. 'Um, how come you were singing at the party?' he prevaricated.

'Vincent asked me to. I managed to squeeze the gig into my schedule.'

'Vincent Gabor?' he said. 'You know him?'

'Oh yes, we go way back,' she confirmed.

'How come?'

Theona shifted position, getting to her knees, one thigh clasping each side of his belly. She rose from the water like a naiad, her body glistening, her nipples crimping. She braced her hands on his shoulders as he lay back against the bath. His upwardly mobile cock nudged her entrance. She lowered her hips, and her pussy lips parted. Will felt her slide down on his cock, engulfing him.

She giggled and moved in a circular motion, her inner walls clasping his erection. 'I'm filled with bathwater, and you,' she purred. Then she stilled, resting her weight on his lower belly and looking down into his eyes. 'You want to know how I know Vincent? It's a long story, babe. Let's get more comfortable.'

With that she released him, his cock slipping out of her as she stood up and climbed out of the tub. Hot on the trail of clues, as well as her cunt, Will followed. She ran ahead of him, her feet leaving damp imprints in the deep pile carpeting. The bedroom was as sybaritic as the rest of the suite and when he reached it, Theona was already installed on the regency four-poster bed. It had fluted columns, a tester drawn up into a central rose, with red and white striped drapes hanging from it. Gilded plaster ostrich feathers sprang from the top of each post.

Theona patted the space beside her and Will stretched his still-wet body on the duvet. She leaned over him, her hair dripping on his chest. She tangled her fingers in the matted hair coating his pectorals, and scratched his nipples with her nails. Will could feel himself going quietly crazy under these ministrations. He had to have her. There were no ifs or buts. But it seemed she wanted to play games, tormenting him into a fever of desire.

'Theona,' he gasped. 'Straddle me as you did in the bath.'

She chuckled deep in her throat and placed her fingers over his lips. He opened his mouth and sucked them in, tasting soap, and pretending he was slurping at her delta. 'Not yet,' she teased. 'I thought you wanted to hear about Vincent and me?'

He sighed and resigned himself to waiting for her. 'I do,' he said.

'Well then, listen up and listen good,' she ordered, her body pressed into his side, his hand roving her breasts and dipping down to her pussy. 'I met him when I was struggling to get a singing career together. I wanted to sing opera, would you believe? My parents had both been classical musicians and, if there'd been enough money, they would have sent me to Italy to be trained. Unfortunately, there wasn't. Dad died and mother soldiered on, though never recovering from his loss. They fought like cat and dog, professionally jealous of one another, but she couldn't live without him. You've heard of people dying of a broken heart?' Will nodded. 'Well, that's what happened to her.'

She sounded sad, her guard - that feisty front with which she faced her public - lowered. Will wanted to pet her, to draw her head down to his shoulder and simply hold her like a friend, silently offering his support. But even under the stress of that moment, his cock remained engorged.

'I'm sorry,' he said, for want of better words.

'That's okay,' she said with a sniff. 'I'm not about to bore you with details of my early life, simply to say that I met Vincent around this time. He became like a surrogate father, although I was twenty. He suggested he might send me to singing teachers and use his influence to help me enter contests, but I rather think it was too late for me by then. Besides, he wasn't sincere. He saw he could make money out of me in other ways.'

Will stroked her back soothingly. 'I can't imagine him doing anything without a motive,' he said.

'Too true,' she agreed, and stroked a hand over his belly, finding and grasping his cock. 'He let me sing all right, but it was in the *Merrymen Club*. He owns it.'

'Does he?' Will said thoughtfully, though his concentration was wavering as she played a sensual tune on his eager instrument. 'But that's a sleazy strip joint, isn't it?'

'Oh yes, a very sleazy strip joint. He won't admit his involvement in it, but he's the boss. You can get anything there; women, male prostitutes, drugs.'

'So I've heard. And did you ever have to do anything but sing?' Unable to resist, he stroked her breasts and, lifting his head from the pillow, licked the stone-hard nipples.

97

'He wanted me to, suggested that I entertain some of his clients with more than a song. By that time I was completely under his influence. He'd taught me the language of the whip, how to enjoy pain and through it, to obtain the heights of pleasure. He was my master, my lord, my mentor. He obsessed me, and I was in love for the very first time. I didn't want to disobey him, but a steely core inside me insisted that I could do better for myself.'

'You were very brave; he's a formidable man, by the sound of it,' Will said, almost losing his erection as he thought of Julia, who was even now in Gabor's hands. He wanted to get her out of the man's clutches without further delay, but knew he'd have to be patient. 'What did you do?'

'By that time I was in with the members of the band. They were an ambitious bunch, using the club as a steppingstone to higher things. They liked my singing and wanted me to go on tour with them. Their agent was a pushy sort of a guy, and I knew they were going to do well.'

Theona stopped talking for a moment and dreamily closed her eyes, her breasts rising as she breathed deeply and enjoyed his caresses. She mounted him and began a slow, sensual circling movement, her inner muscles embracing his penis. It was as if she didn't want to talk any more just then, but simply enjoy the uniting of their flesh. Will, too, was finding it hard to do other than respond to her smooth, rhythmic ride. He was close. He placed his hand between their pubic bones, finding her open labia and rubbing the protruding clitoris. Whoever had taught her about love, and he assumed it to be Vincent Gabor, he owed him one. Theona was a magnificent mistress.

But to get the ultimate joy he had to know more, his conscience troubling him. Julia could be in danger. 'So, did you run off with the band?' he croaked.

'Hmm... what?' It was as if she was blind and deaf to anything other than the sensations pouring through her body. 'Oh, yes, I left all right, after a monumental showdown with Vincent. I'd never realised how tyrannical and ruthless he was. In the end I had to run away, literally, fearing for my freedom. He was quite capable of holding me by force. Fortunately the band was booked for a tour of the States, so I was well out of his reach, though not entirely safe. He has contacts all over the world.'

'But you're safe from him now?'

'I'm rich and famous. My manager arranges security. There are always bodyguards about.'

'Even now?' Will glanced around uncomfortably, but his fingers did not stop their slippery massage on her bud.

'There's one outside the door and another on the balcony,' she said with a chuckle, rocking her hips against him. 'Vincent knows this and he's being friendly, at the moment. He thinks I'm no threat to him, and I'm not, unless he bugs me.'

Plucking and teasing, he worked her sex-lips between his fingers, and then gripped her and rolled on the bed till she was beneath him, his cock still buried within her. There was more information to be gained from her, but Will's need was overriding all else. They could talk after they'd orgasmed, when his dick no longer controlled his brain. He moved out of her and fastened his mouth to hers, kissing her passionately, then he nibbled at her throat, her breasts and nipples, moving steadily lower, pausing at her navel, then down to her sex. He raised her to his mouth, lapping at her succulent flesh. He felt the pulse between her legs and nipped gently at her clit. She started to convulse, and gave a cry as she came. He replaced his tongue with a finger, and poised himself between her thighs, entering her with one sure stroke.

Everything was wiped from his mind. Like a thing possessed he felt her tight wet walls gripping him and he spiralled over the edge in frenzy. He erupted into her, and then collapsed onto her body.

'Cigarette?' he said, a little later when, recovered, they sat propped up by satin pillows, side by side like a couple of longstanding.

'Please.'

He lit up for her. 'How cliché,' he said, smiling.

'Cliché or no, there's nothing quite like a nicotine hit after bonking,' she said, holding the cigarette he'd lit for her, then drawing deeply on it. 'Now, let's get back to Julia. Is she still a virgin?'

'No,' Will said, an arm about her satin-smooth shoulders.

'Who took it from her? Was it Vincent?'

'Uhuh,' he replied, and scowled at the thought.

'I see. And now what? You'd better tell me the whole story, Will. I'd like to help her if she's in any kind of trouble.'

Oh, what the hell, he thought, and gave her an outline of events. When he'd finished, she didn't answer at once, but eventually said, 'That sounds like Vincent. And as for Marty, he's nothing more than a conceited jerk. Clever in his own way, but utterly amoral. You want to find out more? I can get you into Vincent's office, and Marty's atelier.'

'You can? How?'

'I have the password to Abbey Reach. Don't forget, Vincent trusted me once. And, when I left him, he was stupid enough to overlook my knowledge of his ventures. He's corrupt, and would sell his own grandmother for sixpence. I'd like to see him brought to justice. You should get Julia out of there before any real harm is done to her. I expect she's infatuated with him, which is how it usually starts, but then it can turn nasty, as I know to my cost.'

'Thank you, Theona,' Will said, and lifting her hand in his, raised it to his lips. 'You're okay, you know that?'

'I try,' she said, and smiled.

If he hadn't known her to be a tough lady who gave the press a hard time and was reputed to drive a very hard bargain, Will could have sworn that she blushed.

Chapter 10

The pub was seedy, a meeting place for down-and-outs, shady dealers and informers. Will wondered how Theona came to know of such a dive, but it wasn't prudent to ask questions.

They had left the *Majestic Hotel* after she'd made a phone call. 'Don't bring your camera,' she had advised, and changed into jeans and a sweater, a denim jacket slung round her shoulders. Dark glasses obscured her eyes, and her giveaway hair was stuffed into a baseball cap.

They'd jumped into a taxi, accompanied by one person only, the bodyguard called Roy. He looked villainous enough to pass without notice where they were heading. Once they'd entered the dingy portals of the *Hat and Feather*, he melded into the background, but Will was aware of him and glad of his presence. Unlike the *Flying Goose*, this place lacked any suggestion of bonhomie. The landlord stood behind the bar, a massive individual with fists like sledgehammers. He eyed the strangers suspiciously.

'Two pints of bitter,' Will said, at Theona's prompting.

'Ain't seen you around before,' the landlord rumbled, deep in his beer belly. 'New to the district, are you?' He hauled on the china headed pump, and soon the glasses of frothy brew stood on the bar.

'We're looking for Pete,' Theona said frankly, and even the landlord wilted under her authoritarian mien. 'Tell him we're here.'

'Who shall I say is asking?'

'Never mind who. Just do it.'

'He's in the back bar.' The landlord obviously thought better of pursuing it further, and jerked his broad thumb towards the rear.

Will carried the drinks. The inner bar was even more sleazy, situated near the toilets. Every time the door opened a smell of stale urine and damp wafted through. A jukebox thumped out sixties tunes, and Theona made straight for a table in a dingy corner. 'Hello, Pete,' she said, and sat down.

A pair of watery blue eyes looked across at her, and then slid to Will. 'Who's this geezer?' Pete asked, his voice gritty.

'A friend,' Theona replied, and then added, 'What are you drinking?'

'A pint will do,' he said ungraciously.

Will went back to get one, but he didn't delay, keen to know what Theona was saying to this unprepossessing character. He was skinny and gaunt and dirty. The bloated flesh of an alcoholic had obscured good facial bone structure. Where in hell's name had Theona come across him?

He found out as he put the pint on the table. 'How're you doing now?' Theona was saying. 'Are you drumming anywhere? *Jesus*, what a waste of talent! You've lost the plot, man. Too many joints, too much Charlie up the nose, too much smack and booze.'

She was scolding Pete like a concerned mother, and he stared down sheepishly at the drink-ringed table surface. 'I know, sorry, Theona,' he mumbled feebly. 'Couldn't keep it together. And once you'd replaced me with Johnny Carr, that was it.'

'Don't try and shift the blame. It's you who're the addict. No one else. I even paid for you to go to that rehab centre, but you ran away after a week.'

'I know, I know,' he sighed, reaching for the beer. 'I'm a hopeless ungrateful shit.'

'A waste of space, more like,' she said severely. 'Johnny's good, but no one can drum like you. You could have been up there with the boys and me. But no, you'd rather stick a needle in your arm. I could say you're an arsehole, but even arseholes are useful. You're good for nothing.'

'I'm right down there, Theona. I've no money, no proper place to live, in a squat with others like me.'

'And you're willing to do anything for a fix? I won't enable you to do that, but I will help you any other way I can. But I do expect something in return.'

'Like what?' he asked cautiously, hovering between defiance and hope.

'Here's the deal. You've worked for Vincent Gabor since you split from the band, haven't you?'

Over the rim of his beer glass Pete's eyes shifted to Will and then back to Theona. Then he lowered it to the table and gazed at it for a few moments. 'Yes,' he said shiftily. He had emptied his glass and was sitting there sniffing and rubbing his nose with his hand.

'What sort of work?' Theona pressed.

'Oh, this and that,' he said vaguely.

'He's into drug smuggling, isn't he?'

Again, those bloodshot eyes darted around, looking anywhere but at her. 'He might be,' he vouchsafed.

'Oh, come on, don't give me that crap,' she hissed, careful that no one should overhear their conversation. 'He's got deals going in South America, hasn't he? He's in league with the cocaine barons. He was when I was with him, and I don't imagine he's changed his ways.'

'I can't tell you anything.' Pete was sweating and looking very agitated. 'I daren't. He'll have me killed stone dead.'

'Stoned dead, more like it,' she commented dryly. 'Okay, so I give you enough money to split, and to make sure you leave the country. I'll buy you a one-way ticket. Go to LA. I've got mates there who'll sort you out.'

'What kind of mates?' In his paranoid state, he distrusted everyone.

'Friends who care. They'll help you to kick the drug habit, including booze. Do it, Pete. It's your last chance. If you carry on this way you're going to end up dead in a gutter somewhere.'

'I need money now,' he said ungraciously. 'I'm meeting my dealer in half an hour.'

'Talk first,' she said, and drew a wad of bank notes from her breast pocket, waving it in front of him.

'Vincent will do me in,' he quavered.

'He won't find out. You can get out of England now, tonight. I'll get one of my heavies to escort you to Heathrow.'

Will, sitting in silence and listening to her, felt nothing but admiration. She was strong and dominating. His balls clenched and his cock lifted. He'd had her two hours ago, yet lusted to do it again.

'I need another drink first,' grunted Pete.

At the bar Will rubbed shoulders with Roy. They didn't speak. Ye gods, Will thought, was he taking part in a James Bond movie, or what?

'It's not only cocaine, there's the Middle East connection as well,' he heard Pete saying when he got back.

'Guns?' Arlene responded crisply. 'I can believe it.'

'And he launders the money through his interests in the fashion industry.'

'You're sure of this? I suspected it when I was with him, but proof is needed.'

'Get into his office. It'll be on the computer.'

'With a password no one knows.'

'I know it,' Pete sniggered, showing stained teeth as for once he looked pleased with himself. 'I'm into computer hacking.'

She threw him a questioning look, and Will shared her disbelief that a junkie like Pete could possibly keep it together long enough to get into complicated systems.

'Right,' she said. 'You give me the password and that'll be worth a further thousand pounds.'

His eyes narrowed in that wreck of a face. 'Two grand,' he said.

'Fifteen hundred pounds,' she haggled.

'Make it seventeen and we've got a deal.'

They shook hands across the beer puddles on the table. 'My bloke will stay with you and see that you catch the plane,' she said. 'Now, what's the password?'

He leaned nearer and whispered in her ear. Then, on the pretence of going to the toilet, she paused and had a quick and quiet word with Roy. 'Ring for Ken,' she whispered.

They left the pub separately and met up in a back alley. Will was more and more convinced that he was taking part in a spy film. Ken duly arrived and Theona handed him the money.

'But it's mine,' Pete protested, looking grieved. 'What about my dealer?'

'He or she will make a fruitless journey,' Theona snapped. 'D'you think I'm going to part with my hard-earned cash and have you give it to scum like that? Oh no. Ken will hand it over when he's seen you safely to the departure gate.'

'But that means I'll have to be straight.' Pete was almost weeping. He made a pathetic, slouching, squalid sight. 'You've no idea what it's like. I'll never survive it.'

'There's plenty of duty-free booze on the flight,' Theona tried to reassure him, understanding his fears. 'You'll be just fine. And I'll phone and make sure there's someone to meet you at the other end.'

As she climbed into the back of a taxi with Will, she murmured to him, 'My friends are Buddhists. He couldn't be in better hands. They'll straighten him out.

Poor old Pete, he was an ace drummer. Maybe he'll be so again, one day.'

'And the password is?' Will asked, more concerned about getting Julia out of the clutches of Gabor than for the welfare of a washed-up musician.

'Wouldn't you like to know?' she teased.

As soon as Roy had shut the car door on them and taken his place in front beside the driver, Theona, under the cover of the darkness in the back of the cab, unzipped her jeans, grabbed Will's hand and pressed it into the gap, and his fingers encountered the soft damp silk of her panties. He didn't need to be asked twice, pushing the gusset aside and finding her swollen sex-lips and clit. The cab purred through late night London, Roy and the taxi driver separated from them by a perspex panel. Theona wriggled down a little, working her pelvis against Will's middle digit, then reaching out and tracing his thickened penis through his trousers.

He decided to torment her for keeping him in the dark. 'I don't think I'll bring you off,' he said, his tongue lapping the rim of her ear, and he part removed his hand from her pussy.

'Damn you...' she groaned. 'Why not?'

'You don't trust me enough to tell me the password, so why should I bother to treat you to an orgasm?'

'Oh, pooh... don't be like that. You know I'd have told you sooner or later.' She seized him by the wrist and rubbed herself against his hand. 'Have it, then, but don't let anyone else know. It's *Incagold*. No space between. All one word.'

'My lips are sealed,' he promised, and massaged her briskly.

A few moments later, after she had come quietly, clinging to him, she whispered huskily close to his mouth, 'You know, there's nothing like a bit of sharp dealing to rouse the libido...'

Arlene grabbed the phone on the bedside table. 'Yes? Who is it? D'you know what the bloody time is?'

'It's me - Will,' she heard him say.

'Where the hell are you? What's happening?' She was so agitated she pushed away Eugene's hand, which had snaked around to cradle her pubis. 'You woke me up, you bastard, and I'd only just got off to sleep. Hell, I've been crying ever since I got back from that fashion fiasco.'

'This is important. I'm at the *Majestic* with Theona Blue.'

'You what?' She could feel curiosity seeping through her anger and pain. Eugene, curled against her back, spoon-fashion, continued to fondle her bush, and she couldn't help easing her buttocks towards him. His dick was erect, yet again.

'I've spent the evening with Theona Blue. It's been most enlightening. She knows Vincent Gabor, or rather, did know him. I think we've got a lead on him. We've got to talk about this. Where's Julia?'

'I don't know. She hadn't come in by the time we went to bed.'

'We?'

'Eugene and me, if it's any of your business.'

103

'Look, I'll be here all night, at the *Majestic*. This is my number,' and he reeled off a sequence of digits belonging to his mobile.

'I think I already have it somewhere, but hang on, let me take it down again,' Arlene said, fumbling for her notepad and pen, always kept handy in case she got inspired in the night or wanted to jot down her dreams.

'Call me when she arrives,' he went on. 'It's important, Arlene. She may be in danger.'

He rang off and, swearing, she flung back the duvet and climbed out of bed. Eugene, his soot-dark eyes heavy with sleep, said, 'Who was that? What's rattled your cage, babe?'

'It was Will,' she said grumpily. 'It's all right for some; seems he's knocking off Theona Blue. I was hoping Julia was with him, but it seems she's still at Abbey Reach. I hope she's all right.' She frowned and padded to the door, her slender spine part covered by her tangled mane.

'Come back to bed,' Eugene urged, and lifted his side of the cover to display a penis that was impressively full and stiff.

Upset though she was, still wanting to emasculate Marty Blake, her body responded to the sight. Eugene was a gem. He had taken her home and treated her tenderly, listened to her ranting and held her while she gave vent to a storm of angry, frustrated tears. She was growing fond of him, and this in itself scared her. Caring meant commitment, and she'd had her fingers burnt before.

But that cock! It seemed to beckon, luring her with promises of fulfilment. She enjoyed women and vibrators, but there was nothing quite like a healthy, upright penis. Especially if it belonged to a thoroughly nice man, like Eugene.

'You did well at the show,' Marty Blake said, sitting on the side of Vincent Gabor's spectacular bed, helping himself to coffee and eyeing Julia speculatively.

'The show or the party?' she asked sleepily.

'Both,' he said, with a lop-sided grin. 'You made a stunning bride.'

'I enjoyed it,' she said, moving her bottom carefully. It seemed to be on fire, scored by the marks of the riding crop with which Vincent had chastised her prior to her penetration by Lopez's out-sized dick. But it had been worth it. When the party was over, Vincent had taken her to this splendid room and there, amidst silk sheets, she had known the greatest pleasure as he satisfied, then took her.

Now the maid had brought her breakfast on a tray, but hardly had she time to explore the buttered toast and marmalade, orange juice and steaming coffee pot, before Marty Blake came in without a by-your-leave.

'I shall use you again,' he said. 'Kevin's coming along in a while to fix up a photo shoot. You'd be free to come to Bermuda at a moment's notice? That's where we'll be filming next summer's range.'

'Why, yes, I suppose so.' Julia's mind was working overtime, brushing away the languor of a sexy night. She wasn't sure what steps to take next, needing direction from Arlene and Will.

'That's great,' Blake said, putting down his cup and sliding closer to her. 'I can see that we're going to make a first-class team. I've not forgotten the fun we had at lunchtime not so long ago. Let's do it again, now.' He unzipped quickly and got out his cock. 'Suck that,' he ordered.

A refusal would have risked incurring the spiteful man's wrath and raised suspicions.

He shifted position, lying on his back, fully clothed except for his naked spear pointing upwards from his flies. Though it cost her in pain from her tender weals, Julia leaned over him, cupped his balls in one hand and gripped the base of his cock with the other. He groaned as she slowly rubbed it, and his helm reared up, shining wetly.

Julia lowered her head till her face was level with his prick, then she opened her mouth and slid down over the glans, working her tongue round it in little, exciting sweeps.

He dug his fingers into her hair, and she remembered Gus, the first man she had ever tasted in this way. This spurred her to greater efforts, and she sank down till his tip was at the back of her throat, then she drew out again till it rested on her lips. In and out, the ebb and flow of feeling rippling down his shaft.

She temporarily forgot that he was the fiend Arlene accused of stealing her designs, and that she was supposed to be helping her and nailing him. The touch and taste of him, the scent of his skin, seduced her. Vincent had left her early, left her still turned on when she had hoped he would be there, but Marty Blake would do instead. Her mind and emotions said no, but her wanton body said yes.

'Don't stop,' he grated, his nails abrading her scalp.

She glanced up, and was overwhelmed with excitement to see the expression on his face. He looked like a saint undergoing martyrdom. She had the power to do this to him. She felt omnipotent, the earth goddess incarnate. Let him and Vincent be two unprincipled schemers; at that moment she didn't care. She could be selfish too, deliberately pushing thoughts of Arlene from her mind.

Then the door opened, and she glanced round to see Kevin mincing across the carpet. His thin face was flushed, his eyes outraged. 'Marty, I've been looking all over for you!' he cried, halting by the bed. 'As for you, bitch,' he added, and if looks could have killed she'd have been dead. 'Haven't you got enough men sniffing round you without wanting him, too? I call that greedy!'

'Get out of here,' Blake said, unfazed by being discovered on the point of ejaculation.

'I won't,' Kevin stated, uncharacteristically defiant. 'Tell *her* to go away, if anyone. I thought we were going to discuss photos with her, and this didn't include ones of her slurping on your todger.'

Julia slipped away from Blake, swinging her legs over the edge of the mattress as far from Kevin as she could. 'It's all right,' she said, spreading her hands placatingly. 'I don't want to be taking up anyone's space. You're welcome to him, Kevin. Take him, with my blessing.' And she knew that what she was saying was how she truly felt. Her brain was no longer between her legs. She wanted out of there, eager to get away from the creeps and talk things over with her fellow conspirators.

'Get into Blake's studio,' Arlene said, pacing the sitting room in a state of great agitation.

'And how am I supposed to do that?' Julia asked, feeling guilty because only that morning she had been sucking his cock, when Arlene obviously wanted to cut it off.

'I don't know,' Arlene snapped, on the edge. 'Use your ingenuity.'

'Can't you profess an exaggerated admiration of his work?' Will suggested. 'Cajole him into letting you try on the *Queen of the Night* outfit, and express a burning desire to see the sketches from which it was designed. Dammit, you're a female, aren't you? Up to all sorts of wiles?' Although his words were caustic, they lacked any real bite when he addressed them to Julia.

'I'll try,' she promised. She sipped her cup of milky tea and was suddenly weary of the investigation, which had turned out to be so different from what she had expected.

'Denise is waiting for a result,' Will reminded.

'All right, I'll tackle Blake,' she said, trying to keep the stress from her voice. It was all getting too much.

'You better had,' Arlene retorted, then added a grim rider, 'It's Gabor we want to nail as much as Blake. What he's done is child's play compared to Gabor's heinous crimes. He's dealing in drugs and arms and laundering the loot through his other businesses, chief of which is the clothing industry, including sponsoring Blake.'

'That's evil,' Julia murmured, and her feelings of shame and guilt multiplied. She didn't know much about high finance, politics or illegal trafficking, and found it hard to relate such a charismatic man with trade in arms abroad, and the importation of drugs known to do insuperable harm to the unfortunates hooked on them.

'He is evil,' Will agreed. 'I didn't realise how bad until I'd started to become involved in this latest carry on.'

'And you say we're being helped by Theona Blue?' Julia asked, with a puzzled frown. She remembered the singer vividly.

'That's right. We've got a way into Gabor's private computer system. She's offered to get into Abbey Reach with the aid of her passkey and have a poke about on his PC.'

Julia's eyes roamed the familiar room with its old but now fashionable furniture and knick-knacks. Aunt Mary had never thrown anything away, and the relics of bygone eras occupied places on the mantelpiece, the tops of cupboards, and the glass-fronted shelves on either side of the marble fireplace. There were Royal Doulton figurines of garlanded cupids; shepherds and shepherdesses; spooky slender hands formed of white porcelain, moulded from those of the deceased; intricate silk flowers under glass domes, and a conservatory with wicker chairs, aspidistras and cacti.

It was a monstrous white elephant, but Julia loved it and never wanted to sell up and move. She had modernised the kitchen and had a TV installed in the sitting room, along with a video machine and her sound system. The ancient piano with its carved frame and candleholders positioned each side of the music-rest, stood against one wall. It was all part of her childhood. Aunt Mary had endeavoured to keep the place up to standard, and Julia, its present custodian, struggled to find the money to do the same. She couldn't bear the thought of it being sold for redevelopment. Sentiment apart, it was her one and only investment.

All this talk of plots and counterplots, of breaking into offices and hacking into computers seemed foreign to her. Aunt Mary wouldn't have had any truck with it. Times had changed drastically. She hadn't been dead for more than five years, but if she returned she'd find this new century filled with attitudes, mores and manners of which she would heartily disapprove.

'You'll do it?' Arlene asked hopefully. 'Find my sketches, if he hasn't already destroyed them?'

'We'll sort out Vincent Gabor, and then, if we find there's any truth in his shady dealings, get the police in to investigate,' Will confirmed, and put his arm about Julia's shoulders in a warm, comforting way to encourage her.

'Okay,' she agreed, though reluctantly. 'I'm going to Blake's apartment this afternoon. Kevin Dean will be there. I'm to be photographed; a trial run for a session in Bermuda.'

'Don't look so woeful,' Will said, giving her a hug. 'You won't have to go, of course. With a bit of luck they'll soon be exposed. Then you can write your piece for Denise and come back to the magazine.'

'Yes,' she answered pensively, wondering if this was really what she wanted; modelling was certainly more glamorous than working for the press.

The atelier was filled with light, as an artist's studio should be, but totally deserted. The sewing machines were shrouded in dustsheets, the chairs ranged neatly in front of them, the pattern-cutting table free of fabric, the dressmaker's dummies naked and forlorn looking.

'You expressed the desire to see where it all happens,' Marty Blake said, a hand under Julia's elbow.

'Where is everyone?' She was surprised by its emptiness, for this was a weekday.

'On holiday,' he replied, examining his territory, making certain that all was in apple-pie order, obsessive when it came to his beloved work.

'You closed it down for a few days?' Julia kept her remark casual, though she was thinking what a grand opportunity this might be for a spot of espionage.

'I always do after a show. They've slaved away for me to get it all ready in time. They're a loyal crew, and they deserve a break.'

'And this is where you store your sketches and patterns?' she asked, noting the big cupboards, the angled drawing boards.

'Some of them,' he confirmed. 'Others, if they're very new and precious, I keep

107

in my apartment.' He chuckled a little. 'I suppose I'm paranoid really, for the whole building is linked to a security system second to none. No one is likely to break in.

'Come along, let's go - Kevin will be waiting and he's already wildly jealous of you,' and he smiled and gazed with evident relish at her nipples, the outline of which could be seen through her T-shirt. 'He jumps on the wrong bus, whereas I ride on both. Don't look so confused; he's a gay submissive and I'm a bi-sexual dom.'

Kevin was in the apartment's lounge, fiddling with his camera. He glanced up, his eyes sharp as a bird of prey's as Julia and Blake entered. 'About time,' he said reprovingly. 'I've been here over an hour.'

'Set up outside,' Blake retorted, ignoring Kevin's sulky remark. 'The weather's sunny and we want to see what Julia looks like in the open air.' He flung a small bundle, which she caught. 'Put that on,' he instructed.

'Where can I change?' She didn't want to undress in front of Kevin, knowing he'd endeavour to find fault with her figure.

'Use my bedroom along the corridor,' Blake, halfway through the glass door to the patio, said over his shoulder.

She opened several doors. Three were guestrooms with no sign of personal effects. There were two showers and a study, all superbly decorated, and then she found what must be Blake's room, the best, largest and most lavishly furnished, with it's own bathroom. Unfortunately now was not the moment to search for Arlene's drawings, though instinct told her he would have hidden them there. She stripped quickly, laying her clothes across the wide bed, and watching herself in the pier-glass as she stepped into the minute gold bikini bottom and then attached the matching triangles over her breasts. The cups were a shade too small, and she filled them to capacity. She adjusted the halter neck, which was made of thin chains and decorated with beads, and fastened the ties centre back.

A filmy silk sari in a contrasting material came with the skimpy outfit, and she draped it round her, then barefooted, padded her way out to the patio. She moved silently, pausing when she reached the screening shrubbery growing profusely over a trellis. She was about to make her presence known when a sound arrested her, a moan, a sigh. Holding her breath, she peered through a small gap in the honeysuckle.

Kevin was leaning across the wrought iron table situated beneath a large striped sunshade. His shorts were down round his knees, his T-shirt pushed up, his bare hindquarters lifted. Marty Blake, as handsome as a Greek god, was just raising his arm. In his hand was a belt, coiled up, turning into a lash. He brought it down savagely across Kevin's white buttocks and Julia repressed a gasp, her own posterior burning in sympathy.

Kevin winced, his arms outspread as he gripped the edge of the table. 'That was for daring to interfere this morning,' Blake snarled. 'If I fancy Julia, then I'll have her. Understand?'

'Yes, I apologise,' Kevin bleated, and reached down for his groin, groping for

108

his penis. 'Forgive me.'

Blake lashed him again. 'Don't touch that till I give my permission,' he said coldly.

'All right, I won't... will you rub it for me?'

'Oh, I'll do more than that.' Blake opened his jeans and his cock sprang out. He fondled it and, taking a bottle of sun-oil from the table, laved his tool lavishly in the slippery lotion and then spread Kevin's legs and worked three greasy fingers into his anus.

Julia was flabbergasted. She had never seen two men at it before, knowing she should withdraw till they had finished, but so fascinated that she couldn't move. For some reason the sight, instead of repulsing, was making her horny. She touched her nipples, and they were rock-hard, firmly pronounced within the thin gold cups. Her clitoris throbbed and she slid two fingers into the bikini briefs, combing through her soft pubes. She rubbed, parted her sex-wings, and toyed with the rapidly swelling nubbin. All the while she never took her eyes from the scene being enacted in the roof garden.

Blake oiled his palm and slid it round till he encompassed Kevin's dick. The long, stiff, pale-skinned organ jerked as he rubbed it, and Kevin gasped in rapture. Taking his own cock in his other hand, Blake slid on a condom and then, standing between Kevin's thighs, fed his erection into his well-prepared arsehole. Julia, speeding up the friction on her clit, saw him move, slowly at first, then faster.

'I'm going to come in you now, and then take off the johnny and do it again, all over your face,' Blake growled, his hips pumping rapidly.

'Yes, yes, do it!' Kevin urged, clinging to the table, his cock jumping in Blake's hand. 'That's just how I like it!'

'High, hot and a hell of a lot!' Blake chanted.

Shockwaves of sensation were gathering in Julia's groin. Her clit was fully roused, her labial wings engorged. She was climbing to the peak, blood racing, heart pounding. She could hear both men panting like Olympic runners. By now she had joined in the contest of who would come first. Then Kevin cried out and shot a jet of creamy semen into Blake's fist.

Julia was there, riding the crest of the wave, feeling her whole being convulsing. Perspiration dampened her fringe as the final spasm passed. Then she saw Blake rake across Kevin's back with his fingernails, saw the trail of red marks, and saw him arch. His ragged breathing stopped for a second. He grunted, thrust once, twice, thrice, and climaxed.

The scene righted itself; a peaceful, sweet-smelling garden once more, filled with the sound of birds singing and the bubbling of the jacuzzi in its little glass-roofed house. Julia took her fingers out of her bikini bottom. The gusset was soaking wet.

Lust appeased, the men pulled apart. Blake did up his jeans and Kevin hoisted his shorts. Neither said a word. Both lit up a cigarette, and Julia stepped under the flowery arch, the sari knotted round her waist.

'Ah, there you are,' Blake said, cool as a cucumber. 'Did you enjoy our display of homosexuality?'

She could feel herself going bright red. 'How did you know?'

'Darling, it was obvious. I saw the foliage moving. Did you come as you watched us?' Before she could answer, he pulled her close, parted the sari and shoved a possessive hand tight between her thighs. 'A dead giveaway,' he crowed. 'You're very wet.'

'Dirty bitch,' muttered Kevin, then linked his arm with Blake's. 'But we don't care, do we?'

Blake freed himself coldly with a shrug. 'Have you set up the tripod?' he snapped.

He was most professional as the afternoon progressed. Kevin shot Julia from all angles, sedate shots, compared to George's; her bra top was kept firmly in place, as was the minuscule tanga. The sun burned down fiercely, and she applied Blake's lotion, her body gleaming with an oily sheen.

Kevin bitched throughout. 'God, but she's awkward,' he complained. 'She doesn't have a clue how to pose.'

'She did all right for George,' Blake countered, sitting in the sun, shirt off, browning his legs in the tiniest of shorts.

'That's as maybe,' Kevin huffed. 'But she's bloody unprofessional. A novice, my dear. A rank amateur.'

The more he criticised, the more she found herself floundering. It had been almost better to do open crotch shots for that slimy little toe-rag, George.

'I think we've got enough,' Blake said at last. 'Fetch me a large gin and tonic, Julia. Plenty of ice, mind.'

Rather offended by his offhand manner, she stalked into the kitchen, found the drinks, raided the fridge for ice-cubes and returned. This time she didn't stop when she found Kevin kneeling in front of Blake, whose cock was raring to go again. Neither of them took any notice of her as she placed the glass on the table. Kevin bent forward and licked the dew from Blake's glans. He placed his hands on Blake's hips to steady himself, the cock disappeared into his mouth, and moved his head up and down.

What better time than now, she thought, when they were so absorbed? She retraced her steps through the lounge, along the hall and into Blake's bedroom.

First she changed into her skirt and T-shirt and slipped on her sandals, for she knew she might have to make a quick exit. Ready to flee at a second's notice, she began her search.

The wardrobe yielded nothing, neither did the tallboy. Then she saw the desk, a valuable Napoleonic piece, the top covered in bottle-green leather and edged with brass filigree. There were two stacks of drawers on each side and a large central one. Julia tried it. It wasn't locked. Marty Blake must have been so convinced that no one would break in, she thought.

It slid open. Inside were several drawing-pads. These revealed nothing but rough sketches that he must be working on. Then, right at the bottom, she found a folder. She lifted it out and spread it open on the desktop. She recognised Arlene's style and the *Queen of the Night* gown. Her signature at the lower right hand corner further confirmed this. There were others, too, garments that Blake had kept under wraps until the moment of the show. These also bore Arlene's signature.

Got him! Julia wanted to shout aloud with glee, but instead she closed the drawer, rushed to the bed, picked up her tote bag and stuffed the drawings inside.

'And where do you think you're going with those?' said Kevin, from the open doorway.

Julia pulled up sharply and gasped. Now she was in trouble. 'I... I'm off home,' she faltered feebly, wondering how long he had been standing there, watching her. 'We've finished here, haven't we?'

'What's that in your bag?' he said slowly, a predator tormenting its prey.

'Um, nothing... th-the usual stuff... make-up, my chequebook and credit card... you know.' This was awful, Julia's worst nightmare realised.

'Let's have a look,' Kevin said, and snatched it from her. He spilled the contents on the bed and grabbed the sketches. 'Marty will be interested to see these,' he added heavily, and hauled her along to the lounge.

'I've just caught your golden girl poking around in the desk,' Kevin announced. 'She's got the sketches, Marty. You know, those you stole from Arlene Murphy.'

Marty Blake rose from the white leather settee. His brows swooped down in the blackest scowl Julia had ever seen on a man's face. 'What's all this?' And he glared at the drawings Kevin had shoved into his hands.

She stood there shaking. 'They don't belong to you,' she quavered. 'I wanted to return them to their rightful owner.'

'I told you she wasn't genuine, didn't I, Marty?' Kevin beamed triumphantly. 'Model, my arse! Ask her what she's really doing here?'

'I don't have to answer that,' she said, spine straight, shoulders back, chin held defiantly high. 'I'm leaving now, and I'll thank you to let me take those with me.'

'You're not going anywhere.' Marty Blake's voice was heavy with brooding menace. It sent icy shivers down her spine. 'We'll see what Vincent has to say about all this.'

She glanced at the door, made a dash for it, but was hauled back by Kevin, who was surprisingly strong under his weedy exterior. He held her tight, his nails gouging her spitefully.

'Come over here right away, Vincent,' Blake said into his mobile. 'We've a spy in the camp.'

Chapter 11

Vincent Gabor listened in silence to Marty Blake's litany of complaints, and Julia stood before them like a prisoner in the dock. She was so frightened she couldn't function properly.

'So, Julia, what do you have to say for yourself?' Gabor asked at long last, his dark eyes expressionless, his face set.

'Nothing,' she blurted out.

'Why were you taking the sketches?' he persisted, with the grim patience of an inquisitor.

'I-I-I don't know,' she stammered, aware that it was useless. He was too shrewd to believe any cock-and-bull story she might try to concoct.

He rose, looming over her. 'I want the truth, Julia. Don't even attempt to lie. Tell me, you are acquainted with Arlene Murphy?'

'Possibly. I may have met her once or twice... in the pub, or at a club. I can't remember.'

'You can't remember?' His hands were clenched threateningly at his sides, but she could feel excitement gnawing through the fear. Was he about to hit her?

'No... that is...'

'I've made some calls, Mr Gabor,' Kevin cut in eagerly. 'And the jungle drums report that Julia and Arlene live at the same address.'

'Ah, so you have been lying to me,' Vincent Gabor said, more in sorrow than anger. 'Dear me, Julia, you're a very silly and naughty girl.'

'I only wanted to help her,' she burst out. 'She was so upset at the loss of her designs...'

'And you thought you could worm your way in here, nose around and find out things that would get me into trouble,' Blake spat venomously.

'It wasn't fair; you have so much and she struggles so hard and has so little.' By now Julia had lost the will to lie. It didn't much matter. Something unpleasant was going to happen to her anyway, no matter what she did or said.

'This is intolerable,' Blake cursed. 'She's got to be punished, and if you don't do it, Vincent, then I will.'

The sleek black limousine snaked through the traffic. Julia could look out of the darkened windows, but no one could see in. She was seated in the back, with Vincent Gabor on one side of her and Marty Blake on the other. Kevin occupied the front passenger seat and a uniformed chauffeur was driving. An ironic touch, she thought, considering his employer's intentions towards her, though she could only guess as to what these might be.

She had been frogmarched to the parking lot. Gabor kept his hand round her arm, preventing any attempt to escape. They had removed her mobile from her bag, and she was thankful she'd had the forethought to erase any incriminating numbers; Denise's, Will's and Arlene's. She could only pray they might get worried if they couldn't get in touch with her. There was one small ray of hope: her abductors obviously thought she was after the sketches, nothing more. Neither suspected she was involved with the press, or that Theona Blue was working to expose Gabor's involvement with contraband.

She recognised the route. The car was heading towards Hazel House, and she rummaged through her memory bank to recall if she had given Will the address. She had, but how long would it be before he put two and two together and came up with the right answer? She might be held prisoner for days. It was useless trying to convince herself that she had been removed there for any other reason.

She was Vincent Gabor's captive.

The limousine swung between electronically controlled gates, rolled across the gravel, and braked outside the house. Grace was the first person Julia saw as she climbed out. Tall and gaunt as ever, she spiked her with her gimlet eyes and took over from Gabor. Julia's wrists were drawn behind her back and manacled. With her hands bound and her shoulders back, her thrusting breasts looked like a sacrificial offering. Grace eyed them and licked her lips, and then conducted her up the stone steps and under the portal.

'Take her to the cellar,' Gabor barked. 'Prepare her. We'll be with you shortly.'

It was cool down there after the heat outside, as dimly lit and sinister as Julia remembered. What would they do first? Hang her from the crosspiece? Her imagination painted lurid pictures and her flesh crawled, but she was unwittingly aroused, a hungry ache in her epicentre.

Grace marched her across the stone floor and sat her on a high-backed wooden chair fitted with chains, to which the handcuffs were attached. This forced her to keep her spine straight. She stared at the door, waiting for Vincent. Grace stood at her side in the attitude of a warder. Julia dared not speak to her, feeling that they were both taking part in a strange, sexual ritual. The area between her legs was moist, and she wriggled slightly, bearing down so the central ridge in the seat pressed into her sensitive labia.

Vincent Gabor materialised. He was carrying a small cane, no more than eighteen inches in length. He swished it against his palm as he stood in front of Julia. 'You need severe correction,' he said. 'If there's one thing that offends me, it's disloyalty.'

'I was being loyal to Arlene,' she croaked, her throat suddenly dry.

'I'm speaking of loyalty to me,' he continued, his handsome face hard, as if chiselled from granite. 'You're very lovely, my dear, and I've grown fond of you. It grieves me to think that you were about to betray Marty, and in doing so, betraying me.'

He grabbed the neck of her T-shirt, tearing it away. Her breasts rose above the tatters, lifted high by her lace-trimmed bra cups. He smiled sombrely, and bent to suck each in turn.

When he left her the material formed two dark wet circles over her pronounced nipples. Julia's breath shortened, the exquisite sensation caused by his lips shooting straight down to her clitoris. Then she gasped fearfully as her mind associated the cane with her breasts. She felt it for a split second before he actually hit her. The first blow across those tender globes raised a raging heat and broke the terrible tension of anticipation. She glanced down at the smooth upper slopes, seeing a red stripe forming on the tanned flesh.

'Stand up,' Gabor demanded.

Grace unhitched the chains and Julia got to her feet, though it was awkward with her arms strained behind her. Her breasts smarted intolerably.

Gabor smiled a cruel smile. 'I think it's time she was pierced, don't you, Marty?' he said.

'And shaved,' added Kevin, almost hopping with delight at the prospect of his rival's torment.

'And plugged,' Blake said spitefully. 'Didn't you say her arsehole was tight? Grace should be given the job of stretching it, using her wicked collection of dildos. That'll make the bitch squirm.'

'Exactly,' Gabor agreed, and he drew the cane across the tops of Julia's thighs, worked it under the hem of her short skirt and dragged the tip between her legs. 'But first, she needs to learn what it means to be punished for her misdemeanours. Julia, bend over the trestle.'

She hesitated, but Grace pushed her towards a bench normally associated with supporting wood when being sawn. With a hand on Julia's bottom, Grace thrust her over the top, which had been modified with padding. She then spread Julia's wrists and ankles and chained them to eye screw bolts, so that she was firmly anchored to the contraption's legs.

'It's too tight,' Julia whined, and Grace slackened the restraints a trifle. Then the cool air caressed Julia's rear as her skirt was raised and tucked up. She winced at the feel of cold steel touching her opened sex as her panties were sliced across and pushed up to join her skirt. The trestle pressed against her tender breasts, the cuffs cut into her skin, and she needed to pass water, her bladder irritated by nerves. What was it called? The relief of fear.

She was coping better than on former occasions, having had practise in the art of submission. Yet when the cane rapped across her bare, rounded hinds, she knew she'd never become blasé about it. He did it again, harder this time. She screamed, bucked and wet herself. Another blow followed, and then another, until Vincent Gabor had laid on six more. Each one was an agonising, exhilarating experience. Her bottom was bathed in fire, and her pelvis pushed against the trestle as she sought pressure on her clit. Her nipples rubbed on the padding, and she wanted Vincent with a raw, passionate hunger.

The last stroke brought tears to her eyes and she shrieked, unable to endure more, needing a break. Yet she didn't want mercy. If Vincent had suddenly softened, she would have been cast into a wasteland of confusion. A blinding flash of insight revealed that she wanted him to be cruel and despicable, mastering her, making her his slave.

She heard the cane clatter as he threw it down, then felt smooth trouser fabric and hot flesh as he pushed between her legs, his covered thighs nudging hers further apart, his cock positioned to penetrate her. He thrust firmly and planted it inside. Julia jerked with the force of it, waves of pleasure mingling with the hot wash of pain as he chaffed her stripes with each inward stroke. She felt him lodged all the way in, but though her vaginal walls responded, he was ignoring that most important piece of sexual equipment - her clitoris.

'Please, Mr Gabor, rub me,' she begged, shameless in her extremity.

'Not this time,' he panted, and finished the act selfishly, concerned with nothing but his own climax.

'Let me,' Marty Blake said, his voice husky.

'Be my guest,' Vincent answered with a smile, withdrawing from Julia's glistening sex.

No, no! She wanted to protest, hating the treacherous Blake, but she felt him there, taking Vincent's place, felt the slippery slide of his latex covered cock possessing her. It took him longer to reach his apogee. Kevin had already satisfied him twice that afternoon, and now he pumped and panted, threshed and rocked, till he finally came, groaning and leaning his weight on Julia's welted buttocks.

Vincent Gabor was waiting with ill-concealed impatience, hardly giving Blake time to recover before commanding, 'Right, get off her. Unchain her, Grace.'

Grace snapped open the ankle and wrist cuffs and Julia started to rise, every movement causing her anguish. She ached so badly that her legs trembled and she almost fell. Vincent caught her, and deliberately tore one of her bra straps. The cup drooped, baring her breast. She instinctively put up a hand to protect her modesty, but he slapped it away.

'Why?' she whispered, cringing from him.

'You look so tarty with your clothing torn and your breast exposed. I want to see you like that, and to proclaim to all that you're a dirty whore.' He jerked at her skirt and she heard it rip. He chuckled, and continued, 'You'll keep this on, but no doubt it will be in tatters by the time my men have finished using you.'

'You'll look like a slag,' Kevin said bitchily. 'A right slapper.'

'They aren't gentlemen, by any means,' Blake added spitefully. 'Big boys, all of them, and uncouth in the extreme. You won't know what's hit you.'

'The trouble is, she'll probably enjoy it,' said Kevin.

'What d'you mean?' she demanded, her eyes so full of tears she could hardly make out those mocking, leering faces. 'What are you going to do with me?'

'Well, we can't let you go, can we?' Gabor replied. 'You know too much. Can't have you sounding off about Marty's little peccadilloes.'

'My friends will search for me,' she said.

He laughed again. 'Oh? And who might they be? Arlene, perhaps?'

'Arlene and Eugene, yes.' She clung steadfastly to this thought.

'They won't find you. I shall let it be known that I've sent you on ahead to Bermuda. I might just do that, but first you must undergo more training.' He turned to Grace, issued an order, then said, 'Lie on the couch, Julia.'

'I can't. I'm too sore.'

'Do it!'

She staggered over to where a bench stood. Covered in brown leather, it resembled a doctor's examination couch. She eased herself onto it, groaning as she did so. It was impossible to get comfortable on her back, so she propped herself up on one elbow, making a feeble attempt to cover her naked lower regions with her skirt.

'He said to lie flat,' Grace said, knocking her supporting arm from under her. The skirt rode up, displaying her pussy. 'We'll have to shave you there,' she said.

A man appeared from the shadows. He had a military shaven haircut, tattoos and the build associated with weightlifters. A spiked collar circled his stout neck, and bands of studded leather passed across his wide chest and clipped to the belt round his waist. He wore tight leather shorts, but his genitals were bare.

They were bound by thin straps drawn tight, lifting his balls and keeping his cock in a permanent state of erection. A smooth onyx ring pierced his foreskin, and this too was attached to the belt by a chain. She recognised him as one of Gabor's henchmen, had seen him lurking around Abbey Reach, along with others. All strapping men, casually dressed but with the air of soldiers in mufti.

He carried a small plastic bowl and a tray of implements. He set them down on a table drawn close then went off again, returning shortly with a jug of hot water. He took up a cutthroat razor and opened it. Julia heard the vigorous sound made by the blade as he honed it on a leather strop. She wanted to press her thighs tightly together, to put her hand over her bush and prevent this further rape of her privacy. Once, it seemed a lifetime ago, Roberta had talked of shaving her, and now she wished it had been done then.

Grace leaned over and spread Julia's legs. She struggled and managed to fight her off, but Grace was strong and quickly subdued her. To Julia's horror and embarrassment, the man positioned himself on a stool placed at the foot of the couch. He adjusted a reading lamp, directing the beam directly between her thighs. Her lower lips unfurled, revealing the pink slit between, and in spite of herself, she experienced that telltale tingling in her clit that betrayed her inner arousal.

'Get on with it, Jason,' Grace said, striking him across the shoulders.

He flinched and looked at Julia, and she read sympathy in his eyes. Big man though he was, maybe once a paratrooper, he was also a slave, and so was she - a slave of her own passions. She trusted him, longed to confide in him, needing a friend most desperately in that fraught moment. But she said nothing, just met his gaze mutely. He worked the shaving brush in the basin's soapy suds, and then wet her hair-fringed lips with warm water. The shaving brush tickled as he stroked it over her mons. It was a stimulating feeling, and her nubbin began to swell. She closed her eyes, relaxed and opened her legs further, inviting Jason to trail the brush over her clitoris. But he didn't, carefully avoiding contact with it. He had his orders and dared not disobey.

Peeping from beneath lowered lids, Julia saw that Gabor and Blake were watching. Jason picked up the razor and held her sex lips together with one hand while he let the blade glide over her hairy triangle. He shaved her with sure sweeps till her mound was as smooth and bald as an egg. It felt cold, stinging slightly, and she opened her eyes and craned her neck to look. So pink, so naked; she'd not seen it like that since puberty.

Dew seeped from Jason's glans, but he didn't touch her, simply washing the razor off, removing the blonde floss and soap from the glistening steel. He then eased her down on the couch till her legs dangled over the edge. Her arousal intensified as she lifted her legs, one at a time, so he could snick off stray hairs that curled round her perineum.

'All done,' he said, his lips curving in a quirky smile.

He bathed her labia and dabbed her dry, then dusted it with talcum powder. She fought the urge to drag him down and kiss him till they were both senseless. She longed to feel his tongue in her mouth, his hand on her breasts, his thumb bringing bliss to her clitoris.

But it was Vincent Gabor who ran a hand over her satin-soft pubis, smiling. 'That looks so sweet,' he said, and then probed the bud that crowned her delta, the sensation acute, almost bringing on her crisis.

'And the nipple piercing?' Kevin asked, absentmindedly twisting the rings in his own.

'That, too,' Vincent promised, and signalled to Jason.

'No...' Julia cried, sitting up, her bruises forgotten.

'But yes,' he insisted. 'Look on it as a fashion accessory. Many use piercing these days, but for you it will be my mark; a constant reminder that you belong to me.'

Grace's arms snaked around her. The back of the bench was raised and Julia's wrists and legs tethered to it. The last remnants of her tattered T-shirt were hauled off and her bra removed. She felt the astringent sting of disinfectant as Grace applied it, after carefully washing her nipples with a pad of cotton wool.

'Do her navel too, while you're about it,' Gabor said, regarding the preparations coolly.

Part of Julia wanted to run away, but deep inside her smouldered a dark ember of desire. She had secretly considered having her bellybutton pierced, and had poured over pictures of women with rings through their nipples, labia and clitoris, wondering what it would feel like. The write-ups suggested that they enhanced sexual sensations - especially the one through the clit. But she would have come to this in her own good time, maybe. Now she was being forced. Vincent had made up her mind for her.

There was no escape. Grace held her still and Jason loomed with an instrument similar to that which had pierced her ears long ago. She had been frightened then, but this was as nothing compared to the terror that now made her tremble. Grace held Julia's right breast steady and, so swiftly that she hardly felt it, Jason pierced her nipple and inserted a gold guard ring. There was a minimal loss of blood, Grace bathed it away, and the disinfectant stung.

'Nice,' Vincent said, nodding his approval.

'She didn't scream - you're being too soft with her, Jason,' Kevin whined.

'Shut up,' Vincent growled. 'Do the other one.'

After what seemed like an eternity her ordeal was over, both nipples ringed, and her navel too. At first these wounds were numb but, as the shock wore off, they began to throb. Tears streaked her cheeks and she crawled wearily from the couch, dreading what further torments lay in store for her. Grace made her put on her bra and the remnants of her top, the fabric rubbing against her sore teats, while her skirt and what was left of her knickers added to the pain in her navel.

She still harboured the faint hope that she would be locked in one of the guestrooms, but to her dismay, she saw Jason and Grace manoeuvring a cage into position. It was small and on wheels, similar to the kind once used by circuses to contain wild animals.

'Get in,' said Grace.

'This is a joke, surely?' Julia said, her voice rising in desperate appeal.

'No joke; a means of correction,' Vincent Gabor answered.

Julia glanced round wildly, but each face wore an implacable expression 'I won't go in there,' she insisted. 'It's too claustrophobic. I can't stand confinement.'

Kevin and Marty Blake gripped her arms and dragged her towards it. She stumbled on the low step, cracked her shin, and was then catapulted into the musty interior. The gate clanged behind her and the padlock shut with a snap.

'Good night, and sweet dreams,' mocked Blake.

'Have you seen Julia?' Will said, arriving unannounced in Arlene's workshop.

She was on her knees, working on a made-to-measure garment draped on a dummy and looked up, mumbling through the pins held between her lips. 'No, I thought she was with you.'

'I haven't heard from her for two days. Not since she went to Marty Blake's studio,' he said, and searched his pockets fruitlessly for his cigarettes.

Arlene straightened up, removed the dressmaker's pins, returned them to their crimson velvet cushion and reached for her own pack. 'Have one of mine. Shit, this isn't good news. Have you tried phoning Abbey Reach?'

'I didn't; I'm not supposed to know her. But I did get Denise to do it, with the excuse that she wanted to interview Julia after her success at the fashion show. She was told that Miss Jones was away on a shoot.'

'D'you believe that?' To give her hands something to do while her thoughts whirled, Arlene made for the kettle and jar of instant coffee. 'Sugar?' she asked, while her imagination dreamed up images of Julia being enslaved, used, turned into Gabor's whore - or worse still - seriously hurt if she'd been caught snooping.

'Two,' Will answered absently, then added, as if his thoughts were on the same track, 'Supposing she fouled up, and they've kidnapped her?'

'That's pretty farfetched, isn't it?' she said. 'I can't believe that.'

He frowned, and ran a hand through his untidy hair. He looked crumpled and worried. 'Would you have believed a year ago that Marty Blake would rob you?' he said sharply. 'I'd have dismissed it as crap, and so would you.'

'You're right. So, where do we go from here?' Arlene asked, making a space on the table for her cup, and fishing for an ashtray among the debris - snippets of fabric, reels of cotton, scissors, scraps of paper covered in rough sketches - but underneath these practical actions, she was running around screaming, panic-stricken for her friend's safety.

'We could try Hazel House, or Blake's apartment. Denise has Julia's notes. She's been scrupulous about keeping the magazine informed of her actions and whereabouts.'

'But there's been no communication?'

'Not over the past forty-eight hours.'

'I'll give Eugene a bell. He'll be up for it. He can ferret around, maybe make a trip out to Hazel House. Don't worry. He's cool.'

'Someone may recognise him from the show.'

'I doubt it. They were all too busy wanking their own egos.'

'If she doesn't turn up, then I'll get hold of Theona. She's gigging up north till tomorrow.'

'Then you'll hack into Gabor's system?'

'There won't be any alternative; we've just *got* to find her.' Will's brown eyes registered deep concern, and Arlene realised he really did care for Julia. She was lucky to have someone so devoted. In many ways, he was like Eugene.

'Maybe I'd help you, if you were nice to me,' Jason said, letting Julia out of the cage and walking her up and down, a lead attached to the collar that encased her throat. It was part of his job to see that she was exercised. He had been entrusted with her care, and took his duties seriously. He brought her food, loosened her manacles so she could eat, and emptied the slop-bucket provided as a toilet. He also changed the pile of hay that was her bed.

'What d'you mean, *nice?*' Julia asked, though she already guessed the answer. 'And what day is it? What's the time?'

The hours dragged dreadfully when she was alone down there in the gloom. Grace came in twice a day to check on the rings in Julia's nipples and navel. They were healing well. There had been no sign of Gabor, but Grace had been unable to resist taking advantage of Julia's helplessness. Keeping her chained, she had entered the cage on the first day, and slipped Ben Wa balls into Julia's sex. Then, getting Jason to assist her, she greased a large black dildo and worked it into Julia's bottom.

'You'll wear these till I come again tomorrow,' she had said and, before departing, stood in front of her, lifted her grey skirt and wanked herself to a noisy climax.

Julia had been unable to dislodge the foreign bodies inserted into her body. Every time she moved she was aware of the balls stirring in her vagina, and tormented by the enormous plug in her arse. Next day, Grace took it out long enough for Julia to relieve her bowels, watching as she did so, and then inserted an even larger one.

Yet this constant reminder of her sexual area had another effect; it made Julia randy, but her hands were fastened in such a way that she couldn't touch herself to masturbate. When she wanted to pee she had to stand astride the bucket and let her water flow, and she longed for the removal of the objects that stimulated and stretched her, and longed above all, for a bath.

'It's Sunday, and,' Jason glanced at the watch strapped round his thick wrist, 'three in the afternoon.' He pressed closer to her, no longer in bondage gear, but wearing jeans and a sweatshirt. His cock and balls seemed even more prominent, though covered. They bulged against his flies, and despite her sorry predicament Julia's fingers itched to curl around that promising package.

'Did you mean it when you said you could help me?' she asked sweetly, and didn't move away.

'Sure,' he confirmed, and one of his large hands closed on her bare breast.

'In what way?' There was no question of pushing him off. She couldn't

119

anyway, given the shortage of chain linking her wrists. 'Could you get a message to my friends?'

'Maybe.' He planted a wet kiss on her lips.

'If I give you a phone number, will you ring it?' she asked, breaking the kiss for a moment.

'I'll try, but I've got to be careful. They'll slit a man's throat as soon as look at him.'

'Mr Gabor?' She could still hardly credit him with being a murderer.

'Not himself, but he'll pay others to do it. He wasn't always a businessman. In his early days he was a mercenary. Spent time engaged in warfare in South America, the Middle East, and trouble spots on the Russian border, anywhere he could get rich pickings. He's no stranger to violent death, that's for sure.'

He said this so matter-of-factly that she went cold. Jason had become brainwashed into accepting this as the norm. The army had started it, and employment by Vincent Gabor had completed the job. Yet he was a sensitive brute. He probably sent his mother a card on her birthday, maybe even flowers.

So Julia took a chance on him, reeling off Will's mobile number. 'Slow down,' Jason said, and fished in his jeans, pulling out a stub of a pencil and a crumpled till receipt. 'Say again?'

She repeated it and he printed the numbers, slowly, like a six-year-old. Then he folded the paper and tucked it into his hip pocket, grinning, anticipating his reward. He slackened her manacles and she moved her hand over his bulge. It grew bigger. When she unzipped him his serpent leapt through the gap. She had seen it in bondage, but now, freed from restraint, it displayed its majestic length and generous girth. Fascinated, her clitoris a hot kernel of desire, she took it in her hand. Her fingers didn't meet round it. Jason groaned and moved it through her palm, leaving a sticky trail.

His hands rested on her shoulders and she felt their steely pressure, obediently sinking to her knees. His crotch was on a level with her mouth now, and she breathed in his body warmth, the musky scent of male genitalia, which no amount of showering entirely erased. Her nose brushed against the tight scrub of pubic curls and she lapped at the long, brown-skinned stem of the cock that reared upwards to his belly. His strawberry-coloured helm gleamed with the emission which tasty salty on her tongue.

The tip alone distended her lips and filled her mouth and palate so that she had difficulty in sucking him. Its taste and texture were wonderful, and she wanted him to frig her, but he was too engrossed in his own fast approaching climax. She felt his cock's urgent tension, and achieved a result far sooner than she expected. He groaned like a wild beast and she felt the power of his discharge rushing along his shaft. He bucked, growled, and his semen filled her mouth and bespattered her face and, when she recoiled, volleyed over her throat and breasts.

'Oh, oh... that was *wicked*,' he panted, laughing in a hoarse vibrato.

At that moment the vault seemed to explode. Vincent Gabor burst in, followed by a gang of men wearing sleeveless green string vests, khaki trousers and hobnailed boots. They were young, tanned and muscular, their tops straining over powerful chests, their bare tattooed arms bulging. Grace was with them, also dressed in camouflage, as butch as the rest of them.

Jason tried to cover up, but not before Gabor had spotted his still large, though rapidly shrinking cock. 'You've been keeping her in training, have you?' he bellowed, and Jason abandoned her, trying to melt into the shadows.

Gabor seized Julia by the hair, jerking her head back so that she was forced to look up at him. Her face and breasts glistened with Jason's creamy spunk. 'You like a bit of rough?' he asked, and then went on without awaiting her reply. 'Then you shall have it, darling. I can be as rough as you like, and so can my men.' He was dressed like them, though a sweatband confined his hair. He looked scruffy and muddy and stank of fresh sweat. He could have been the leader of a band of mercenaries, and for some reason she found it incredibly sexy.

He handled her crudely, feeling between her legs. 'How wet you are,' he goaded. 'Grace tells me you've not been allowed to come since she introduced you to her little toys. I think the boys and me can do something about that. We've just completed some intense training, so we're hyped up and looking for a way to release our energies.'

Grace moved to his side and crudely pulled on the string attached to the Ben Wa balls, and they left Julia's wet sex with a sucking sound. The anal plug was also removed, but before she had time to appreciate the relief, a blindfold was slipped over her eyes and firmly tied, tangling with her hair and plunging her into darkness. She was guided across the stone flags, hearing the clump of heavy boots, the whispered comments. Hands were all over her, dipping between her thighs, fingering her clit and then her nipples. Someone was hauling her along by the leash. The collar tightened round her throat and she was forced to move faster.

Her knees encountered the edge of the couch and she was pushed down onto it, disoriented by sightlessness, though her remaining senses had become super-sharp. Her chained hands were free momentarily, and then the cuffs were fastened to ringbolts, as she lay there spread-eagled.

Someone lifted a leg over her head, straddling her face so that a penis dangled close to her face. She could feel its warmth and smell its potent scent as he trailed the tip over her forehead, lips and nose, leaving a wet smear in its wake. It was an alien smell - one of Gabor's hellions, not the man himself. She was certain she would have recognised his personal odour anywhere. He moved off and another cock nuzzled insistently against her lips. She opened them, taking it into her mouth. Two others stood on either side of her and thrust their pricks into her hands. All three plunged and pumped, and they came almost simultaneously, Julia bearing the brunt of their eruptions, almost gagging as she swallowed that which filled her mouth. The three men left her abruptly, their place taken by one person only.

Fingers were opening her, probing vagina and anus and rubbing her clit. The tingle started in the depths of her womb. She was coming, rising, soaring, not caring who or even what was giving her such bliss. Blindness added to the euphoria; her senses centred on the fulcrum of her pleasure. She climaxed, screaming. A man spread her thighs, shoved a hand under the small of her back and lifted her to him, then thrust into her, deep and long and strong. She guessed by the size, shape and the way he did it, that Vincent Gabor possessed her. It was him! She could tell by the odour of spice that clung to his hair.

He unbound her legs and had her lift them so that her feet were on his shoulders. He withdrew from her, smoothed the tip of his cock up and down between her rear entrance and her sex, and then his huge helm dilated her anus with awful force. The plug had done a lot to make her more receptive, but even so it was chicken feed compared to this mighty violation.

'V-Vincent,' she gasped. 'Is that you?' She wanted verbal confirmation that it wasn't some ex-squaddie spearing her on the end of his rod.

He didn't answer, but she was pretty sure it was. It was hardly likely that he'd relinquish his mastery over her and let his troopers plough either of the furrows he'd already made his own. He decided who had her and who didn't. As he had already said, if she pleased those whom he selected, then she pleased him. Obviously his henchmen weren't in the running. They could take her, but only orally or through having her masturbate them. He wasn't sharing her with them totally.

She felt his hands at the back of her head and the painful tug on her hair as he whipped away the blindfold. Then she looked up into his glinting dark eyes. 'Are you happy now that you know it's me, my Julia?' he whispered, in that fascinating foreign accent that always turned her knees to water.

'Yes, Mr Gabor,' she murmured.

'Good, then you shall roll over and present your bottom to me,' and with the deftness of a magician, he released her manacles.

His soldiers were watching the show, cocks in hand, already wanking themselves to further climaxes. She caught sight of Jason in the shadows and wondered if he'd keep his side of the bargain and phone Will. Grace was staring at Vincent as if he was a god to be worshipped, one hand down the front of her army issue trousers.

Gabor eased Julia to her knees, her buttocks lifted high, her breasts pressed into the surface, shoulders too, her head to one side, cheek encountering the padding. Vincent was kneeling behind her. She felt his cock pulsing against her anus again. He reached beneath her, working his fingers past her vulva, wetting them in her juice, and then withdrawing before she had time to arch against them. He spread the copious fluid around her forbidden hole, and then entered it.

The force of it made her want to scream, but she kept silent, rocking against him, relaxing her muscles to make it easier for herself. It didn't hurt so much that way. The butt plugs had helped. Now she was stretched enough to take all of him. Her stripes were eased, too, for he was kneeling upright, his hands gripping her hips, holding her steady as he moved inside her rectum and the fear of his invasion suddenly subsided. Her resistance gave way to desire.

His arm came round her and he found her sex, drawing the lubrication up to her clitoris and squeezing it. She cried out, orgasm rioting through her. He grunted, pleased with her reaction, then pressed in deeper, his groin welded to her rear. He rode her fiercely, pinching and slapping, and these little stings and hurts were pleasurable, making her melt into him. He was frenzied now, and the sounds he made were blissful to her ears. She knew he was reaching ecstasy. She felt the heat of his spunk as it flooded into the condom, and she trembled as if she had just had another orgasm herself.

She had expected he might relent, invite her upstairs to cleanse herself and then treat her well, as he had done in the past. He moved away from her and she turned over and sat up, looking at him expectantly.

He must have seen the entreaty in her eyes, but turned his back on her deliberately. 'Get her back in the cage, Grace,' he barked crisply.

Then he strode out, leaving her staring at his uncaring back through tear-filled eyes.

Will took the phone call. It was from someone who wouldn't give his name. 'Julia Jones is at Hazel House. Take care if you go there. You may put her in greater danger.' That was all the stranger said before hanging up.

Will was for leaping into action, but Arlene advised caution. 'Wait till Theona returns,' she said. 'We need ammunition to use against him. If all I hear about him is true, then he's as cunning as a fox. You won't catch him easily, or rob him of his prey. Julia, in this case.'

'At least we know where she is.'

'Then why did someone at Abbey Reach tell you she'd gone abroad? And what did the caller mean about her being in danger?' Arlene poured them two stiff whiskeys: this was time for the hard stuff, not caffeine.

'I don't know,' Will replied, gloomy again. 'I think I'd better drive out there.'

Julia's presence seemed to be in every corner of the house. At any moment Arlene expected to see her come bouncing in, chattering animatedly about a man, a news lead, clothes, the latest trends. It was all too quiet without the bubbly girl around.

'I've done this to her,' she said, on the brink of cracking up. 'I've put her in danger.'

'Don't blame yourself,' he said. 'If anyone's at fault it's me. I was only thinking of the story it would make for *Hi Life*.'

'Why don't you ring Hazel House?' she suggested. 'Just ask to be put through to her. That's an innocent enough request, surely?'

'You do it,' he said. 'The number's ex-directory, but Julia gave it to me,' and he handed her his address book.

She dialled the sequence and nodded to him. 'It's ringing.' Then a woman answered, and Arlene adopted a Home Counties drawl, controlling her Irish lilt. 'Hello,' she started. 'I wonder if I could speak to Julia Jones, please?'

'She's not here,' the woman snapped, her voice cold.

'Oh? I understood she was staying there,' Arlene persisted.

'She's away. Gone off on a modelling job in the West Indies.'

'Well, can you give me the name and number of her hotel there? This is really rather important. A family matter, you see.'

'Can't help you. Don't ring here again.' And with that the woman slammed down the receiver.

Will was already out of his chair and making for the door. 'That's it,' he said, 'I'm going out there.'

'Will, don't!' Arlene cried, but there was no stopping him.

Chapter 12

'Come on, you, out of that cage,' Grace commanded, striding into the cellar. Her army gear had been replaced with a black leather suit, cut like a man's. 'You're being moved.'

As far as Julia could judge, two days had passed since she'd been subjected to the lust of Vincent's men before he re-established possession of her. She rose stiffly, brushing off wisps of straw that clung to her dirty clothing. She could see Jason waiting at the foot of the wooden steps. He'd still been demanding sexual favours for agreeing to phone Will, and told her he'd done so, but she couldn't be sure he was telling the truth.

'Am I to be set free?' she quavered, tears never far away these days.

Grace gave a harsh bark of laughter. 'You should be so lucky,' she said, making certain that the chains were firmly attached to Julia's handcuffs. 'No, someone was apprehended in the garden... two men on separate occasions, as a matter of fact. They were both caught by the guards, roughed up a bit, and sent on their way. Nosy, they were, asking about you. Mr Gabor didn't like it, didn't like it at all. He's a very private person when it comes to his personal life.'

'Where are you taking me?' Julia cried as she was pushed down the steps. 'You can't keep me a prisoner forever. This is ridiculous.'

Jason got hold of the leash and tugged it. She felt as if she was being throttled by the collar, so she stood still, head bowed.

She wished she was braver; Arlene would have fought, bit and scratched, kneed Grace in the crotch and made a bid for freedom, but Julia was still timid, and her experiences since she'd been in the cellar had subdued her. She longed to ask for a description of the intruders. Could it have been Will or Eugene? If so, then Jason must have kept his promise.

'Mr Gabor has several hideouts,' Grace informed her. 'No one will find you where you're being taken.'

'But, why me?' Julia pleaded, desperately playing for time, trying in vain to put off the frightening prospect of being removed, far away from her friends. 'What have I done to hurt you all, apart from know about Marty Blake's dirty work—?'

Grace slapped her hard across the face, stunning the poor girl and silencing her in an instant. 'Shut up!' she snarled. 'You ask too many questions.'

Julia was marched to the elevator, whisked up to the ground floor, out through the deserted kitchens and across the cobbled yard. The buildings that had once been stables now housed cars. A gleaming bottle-green Range Rover stood there and Julia was bundled into the back of it. Grace climbed in beside her and tidied her up, placing a fleece around her. She tugged a comb through Julia's matted curls and wiped her tear-streaked face with a cleansing tissue.

'This is for the benefit of passing cars or curious pedestrians, or even policemen, heaven forbid!' she said acidly, and changed her leather jacket for a weatherproof cagoule and tied a scarf around her head. 'They'll think we're a happy family off to the country. I should have borrowed a spaniel from somewhere to complete the picture.'

Julia stared, drinking in the scene. It was wonderful to see the sky again, and the blessed, blessed daylight. How awful to be a prisoner serving a life-sentence, she thought; even though she was in such dire straits, at least there was a possibility of escape, slim though it may seem. She was hungry for the everyday sight of people, cars, and the pulsing life all around as Jason drove from Highgate and headed out to the country.

When they stopped at a service station she was conducted to a waiting van, put in the back and blindfolded. Grace stayed with her, though there were four men and the driver, and Julia recognised them as some of Vincent's hell raisers, before the scarf was tightened around her eyes.

It was stuffy in there, and the vehicle lacked the Range Rover's suspension. Seated on a slatted bench, Julia couldn't steady herself against its jolting. She felt hands groping, heard heavy breathing and inhaled sweat. It wasn't Grace, though she sat to Julia's right. This was an undeniably masculine odour.

'Can we do it?' she heard a gruff voice ask. 'Can we touch her?'

'He's given orders that she's not to be penetrated, but apart from that, yes, use her,' Grace replied.

Deprived of tactile contact and sight, Julia stayed still while fingers pushed her thighs apart and slithered across her shaven pubis. The hair was sprouting again, forming an itchy stubble which she couldn't even scratch. She needed the attentions of Jason and his razor, and welcomed the alien hands that now relieved the irritation. A man was kneeling between her thighs on the van floor, probing and investigating. Fingertips felt slippery, moistened by the juice trickling from her vulva. Her clitoris responded, a traitor when it came to being offered pleasure unlimited.

More fingers found her nipples, rolling and pinching them, a hotline of yearning darting down to her swelling labia and gravid bud. She moaned as the feeling intensified, resting her head against the back of the seat. A mouth took the place of the busy fingers, and her unseen lover was licking her avenue, then fastening his lips on her clit, sucking it strongly, drawing it from its cowl. Another person straddled her, squeezing her breasts together to form a channel for his cock. As she started to peak, awash with intense lust that insisted on being satisfied, so he rubbed his weapon up and down between her breasts and then showered her throat and cleavage with hot, cloying semen.

Others took the place of the first men, and throughout the long drive she experienced climax after climax, and heard Grace coming, too; she was always vocal when her crisis was upon her. She may have preferred her own gender, but was never one to look a gift horse in the mouth. And there was sex aplenty in the van that afternoon. Even the driver stopped at one point, and there was an argument as he insisted on changing places with one of the already sated bodyguards, refusing to be denied his share.

When they at last reached their destination Julia was helped out, exhausted by frequent orgasms.

She could smell the sea, hear its hiss and the cries of seagulls dipping and swaying in their constant search for food. After being confined in the stuffy van for so long she inhaled deeply the fresh sea air, gratefully filling her lungs. The blindfold was removed, and she blinked and focused her eyes. Though the light was fading it was still bright enough to disorient her. She stood near a jetty. One end led to the water, the other to a boathouse and this, in turn, was part of an unkempt garden. She glimpsed chimney pots through the trees and, as she was led forward up a winding path, the frontage of a large tumbledown mansion came into view.

The wind gusted from the sea, and the place had a remote and menacing air. She had no idea which part of the coast this was. There were no signposts, and there wasn't a name on the gate, only a large, battered, lop-sided piece of wood printed with the words: KEEP OUT. PRIVATE PROPERTY.

'Where are we?' she asked, walking behind Grace, guarded by men on either side.

'Never you mind.'

'What are you going to do with me?'

'You'll see, all in good time.'

Anyone would think she was a political prisoner or something, she fretted. And where were Gabor and Blake?

The windows of the house were boarded up or shuttered, and the front door creaked as Jason pushed it open. Julia stared at him, but he wouldn't meet her eyes. If ever a man looked guilty and ill at ease, it was he. They had orders to kill her, she was becoming convinced, and went cold from head to foot. She didn't want to die. This couldn't be real. She would wake at any moment and find herself in her own bed at home, and this would all have been part of a horrible nightmare.

She was escorted across a baronial hall with holes in the floorboards and a trapped bird fluttering somewhere high among the rafters, having entered through one of the broken windowpanes. The poor thing was like her, she thought sadly, a blanket of gloom engulfing her.

A monumental staircase loomed ahead. It looked as if it needed scaling ladders to climb it. There was dust and cobwebs everywhere, and the scattered bones of small rodents. Owls and bats no doubt inhabited its upper regions.

A doorway yawned, leading into blackness. A blast of cold air rushed up as Julia was led down treacherous, winding stone steps. She was so glad that no one had taken the fleece from her. It just might help her survive in whatever hole they flung her.

The darkness gave way to a faint glow that grew stronger as they reached the bottom. It was a cellar, perhaps, or maybe a torture chamber left over from a much earlier time when this place had belonged to a feudal lord. She saw cells with iron bars; braziers and rusted implements the use of which didn't bear dwelling on; a whipping post; a rack and, by an alcove in one of the moist, moss patched walls, stood Vincent Gabor, with a whip braced between his hands.

'Oh, you're here!' she cried, misplaced relief making her voice break into sobs. 'I'm so glad to see you!'

He smiled sardonically. 'How sweet,' he said. 'It's heart-warming to be so popular.'

'I hoped you'd be here,' she babbled. 'Why have I been moved? Why won't you let me go?'

'Could I survive without my Julia?' he questioned darkly, and moved closer, the many-tailed whip slapping against the side of his trousers. 'I never let go of anything that belongs to me,' he went on, and inserted the silver butt of the whip between her legs, crudely twisting it into her sex. 'Oh, Julia, you've been having orgasms, haven't you? I can smell it, and look how wet this has become.'

He withdrew the handle and held it in front of her face. The silver was smeared with her juice. It had even run down and stained the lash. Her cheeks burned, and so did her buttocks. 'Your men... they took advantage of me on the j-journey,' she faltered.

'Did they indeed? And you couldn't stop yourself from coming, is that it? You say you're devoted to me, yet any common soldier can bring you to bliss.' He flicked the whip across her breasts. The fleece tangled in it and he shook if off, sending it flying across the cellar.

Now she shivered, the cold draping around her naked torso like a wintry mist. 'But, why here?' she asked plaintively. 'Why do you continue to punish me?'

'People have been to Hazel House, prying and asking to see you. How did they know I owned it? What have you been telling Arlene Murphy and your friends?'

'N-nothing,' she stammered, limp with fear but still inexplicably aroused as she read the merciless fury in his eyes.

'Then why won't they accept the story that you've gone to Bermuda?'

'I don't know.'

'You've been very foolish, my dear,' he murmured, bending to kiss her on the lips. 'I could have given you everything. I still could, but I want your promise that you'll never reveal anything you see here.'

'I'm yours, Mr Gabor,' she whispered, strangely enough, almost meaning it, yet using her reporter's instinct to try and bleed him of information without him being aware. 'I'm happy to serve you.'

'This place is a repository,' he said, with an expansive gesture that encompassed the cellar, the mansion, the grounds and the boathouse. 'Here I take delivery of goods from abroad, if they can't be immediately shipped to my depot at Abbey Reach. Here, too, I dispatch them to foreign buyers. Sometimes it's prudent to keep my operations away from London. If the customs and excise officials have been on the knock and it's too risky to send my lorries on the ferries going to the continent, I'll do shipments from here until the trouble dies down. There are two fast cruisers moored in the cove. It rather depends on the delicate nature of the cargo.'

The bottom seemed to drop out of Julia's world. She had hoped against all hope that what Arlene had told her about him was untrue. But now she could no longer deceive herself: Vincent Gabor was a dyed-in-the-wool villain, a greedy man who cared nothing for the lives that were ruined by the illegal use of drugs, or the people maimed and killed by the arms he supplied to any country or military organisation prepared to buy them.

It was as if she had been rudely awakened from a hypnotic trance. But, just for now, she had to go along with it, or risk her life, for she no longer had any doubt that if she crossed him, he'd be as ruthless with her as he was with everyone else.

'How clever of you,' she breathed, pretending vast admiration. 'So no one knows about this house?'

'No one,' he said, with that arrogance she still found exciting. 'I bought it ostensibly as a business venture. Told the estate agent I was going to open a hotel. I pay the council tax, run my own generator, use cell phones instead of land lines and no one interferes.'

'Why are you telling me this now?' Keep him talking, she thought, even though she'd never be able to prove a thing.

'Because I believe you would rather die than see me come to harm. You say you're mine, and I'm sure it's true. Wherever I go, sweet Julia, you shall be with me.

'I've arranged a welcome for you,' he continued, and pushed her towards the solid wall of the alcove. Ringbolts had been anchored to the stone. He replaced the shackles with ropes around her wrists, then made her stand at the base, her arms strung up so high that they almost lifted her feet from the cold floor.

With Grace's help he secured the spreaders that forced her legs wide and fastened her ankles to iron rings. With her face and body pressed to the chilly stone, she was strapped tightly across the thighs to keep her in position. She knew she was being prepared for a severe dose of punishment, but also knew that any form of resistance was futile.

A draught wafted across her spine, making her shiver. She was naked to the waist, but this wasn't enough for Vincent Gabor. He took a knife to her skirt and the scrap of silk that had once been her panties. Both were cut away, and cold fingers of air crept impudently between her thighs, exploring her denuded mons and tantalising the hard gem of her clitoris.

The whip descended and left a trail of fire. Her bottom burned with the heat of the leather biting into her flesh, not one strand, but nine. They were like fiery sparks, and then turned into the patter of driving tropical rain. He struck her a second time, and she was lured into the pain, aroused by it, and so was he. She knew without looking that seeing her suffer was turning him on and giving him an erection.

He would mark her, she was sure, yet thought of the thrill she would get from turning round in front of her mirror and seeing her striped backside. Then she'd become wet between the legs as she remembered him pushing his cock into her vagina or anus, so excited that she'd have to play with herself. But that was in the future; now there was the reality of the whip.

'Ah...' she cried, agonised, taking blow after blow till the endorphins kicked in and she entered a state bordering on oblivion, aware of the sounds of the lash landing on her body, aware of the searing pain, but distantly, as if it was happening to someone else.

Her muscles relaxed. She didn't thresh any more, too limp and dazed to even cry. He stopped beating her and undid the ropes. There were indents on her wrists and ankles. She swayed and almost fell.

He pushed her to her place at his feet, and she bent low until she could put her lips to his instep. She clung to his legs, feeling the smoothness of the material under her hands and rising higher, till she could mouth the long line of his cock pressing upwards towards his waistband. He thrust his pelvis towards her, and she rubbed harder, sensing his need to ejaculate very soon.

She expected him to do it there, in front of the bodyguards and Grace, but with that mercurial change of mood that was a part of his enigmatic personality, he suddenly swept her up and strode towards the steps. He moved as easily as if she weighed no more than thistledown, reaching the hall and running lightly up the staircase. The second floor was as gloomy and magnificent as the hall; there were dusty portraits in chipped gilt frames, moth-eaten rugs, tattered hangings, suits of rusted armour, a fine headquarters indeed for a swashbuckling pirate king like him.

He kicked open a door, crossed a dusty floor and deposited her in the midst of an antique bed. More dust rose from the embroidered quilt with its tarnished gold stump-work. Kneeling over her, he pulled his sweater off over his head and, hands akimbo, smiled down.

'This is the master bedchamber. This is where I sleep - not often, but occasionally. I like to think of the men who robbed their brides of their virginity, or seduced housemaids or even pageboys, in this great monster of a bed. I haven't brought a woman here before. Count yourself privileged, my dear. First, I shall fuck you. Then you'll dress up for me. I found a number of old garments left behind in the wardrobe. Imprisonment won't be so bad, Julia. Come, confess that you're enjoying it and want me to go on. Say it, Julia... say, "I want you to use me, master. I am your slave".'

Julia's back was burning and she longed for him to apply some of his special lotion, and her sex was burning and she longed to have him bring her relief and peace. 'Yes, master,' she said, mesmerised by the glinting, enlarged pupils of his dark eyes. 'Use me as you will. I belong to you...'

It was as easy as taking candy from a baby, Theona thought, letting herself in the main entrance of Abbey Reach, using the code that opened the majority of

129

its doors. Vincent Gabor may be a smart cookie, but he was no match for her. If she'd have been him and fallen out with her, there was no way she'd have kept the same pass code. No sir, she'd have had it all changed, and hang the expense. But, like many a tycoon before him, he had a mean streak and often spoiled the ship for a hap'orth of tar, as her old granny used to say.

The light was on in the cubbyhole usually occupied by a security man. She could hear a sports commentator on a TV channel, and a glance in showed the uniformed guard glued to a football match on the screen. She had been prepared to seduce him, if need be, but he was obviously in love with the 'beautiful game', probably preferring it to sex any day.

She flitted across the foyer and decided against using the lift. Gabor's office was on the third floor, and she climbed the stairs, thanking her lucky stars that she worked out every day, Gus keeping her body in trim and watching her food and alcohol intake like a hawk.

It was spooky there, the winding staircase, the vastness and silence of the building. It was brightly lit everywhere, and she found the office of Hunter's Moon without any trouble. This was the name of a chain of hotels of which Gabor was president. Which meant that he sat in on board meetings and took a hefty slice of the profits. All very innocent, and he kept the taxman happy, but she knew there was much more behind it.

She navigated the rooms and reached his locked office. She used the key-card again, and opened it easily.

Now for the computer.

In her days of working for him, when she had been infatuated like Julia was, he carelessly made her privy to many secrets. She recalled how she sat on his knee while he punched in files, although at that time she had been more concerned in wriggling her fanny against his cock, than in observing what was happening online.

But Pete had given her the password, and she winged a prayer to LA. Damn Vincent Gabor, she thought savagely. Damn him; her friend could have been dead because of the stuff he smuggled.

Controlling her anger, she calmly booted up one of the machines and searched through the files. This showed her nothing vital, merely linked to business accounts pertaining to Hunter's Moon. She had noticed another standing on Gabor's desk, a high-powered personal computer. This seemed promising, so she opened up the system and found that most of the files were protected by a password. She logged on under *Incagold*. It worked and she began to investigate the secret documents, and her pulse quickened as she found everything she needed; records of monetary transactions, dates, times, and destinations, Swiss bank accounts and offshore accounts and the means by which he laundered the money. There was enough evidence to send him down for fifteen years or more. His contacts were all there, men with names like Juan Lopez and Ali ben Hamal, and Russian ones, too - Anatolii Pashenka, Sacha Rurik and suchlike.

'You've been careless, dear Vincent,' she chided him quietly. 'This is what comes of having too high an opinion of yourself and your abilities. You've landed everyone up shit creek without a paddle.'

Now she clicked the mouse and opened another file. It listed the locations, phone numbers, e-mail addresses and residential districts of every property he owned in England. There was one strong possibility, and the more she scrolled and read about it, the more convinced she became that this was where Julia was being held.

It was a manor house called Wylde Court, situated in a remote corner of the Suffolk coast. It sounded perfect for a hideaway; ancient, rundown, of little interest to local authorities, and right on the edge of the sea. What could be better for smugglers, and as a handy prison for a kidnap victim? Theona had a gut feeling about it.

She'd had the forethought to bring a packet of floppy discs with her, and it was a matter of seconds to begin downloading all the information. Every one of her suspicions had now been confirmed and she knew she had to tell Will, then go to the police.

Will would want to go rushing off like a knight-errant to save Julia, and Theona realised she'd have a hard job stopping him. But if the police knew, then they'd send a posse after him. Rather like an old-style western, she mused, and then sobered immediately when she remembered that this was for real and Julia was at risk.

The computer buzzed and clicked and took its time. She glanced around nervously, and then caught sight of herself in the darkened plate glass window. She was dressed entirely in black - black trousers, black anorak, a black balaclava. What, she thought suddenly, was she doing there? She should be off gigging and entertaining the masses, not prating about playing at being a private eye.

The download complete, she slipped the last disc out of the slot and tucked it into her pocket. Then as silently and swiftly as she had arrived, she left Abbey Reach.

'Is that Marty? It is? Good, this is Arlene Murphy.' The phone was tucked under her chin, her fingers coiled nervously in her black, Irish tinker hair, as she liked to call it. 'No, don't hang up,' she added quickly, instinctively putting her free hand up as if to halt someone. 'I want to apologise for the fracas at your last collection. I was wrong to kick up such a fuss. I see that now, and I'd like us to meet and talk about it. After all...' she purred in her most seductive tones, 'we got on rather well at the Cloth Show, didn't we? I was *very* impressed. Everything I've heard about you was true...'

She judged him to a nicety, smiling as she heard him fish in his most charming, conceited tones. 'And what have you heard, Arlene?'

'Rumour had it that you're *seriously* well hung... and now I know...'

There was a silence for a moment, and Arlene wondered if she'd somehow messed up, but then he went on. 'Tell me more.'

'Well, you obviously remember our little *tete-a-tete* in the storeroom?'

'I do indeed.' His voice had thickened and she wondered if he was stroking his cock through his trousers, even as they spoke.

'Shall we meet, then? I could do with your advice about my work. Who knows, we could even indulge in a repeat performance? Would you like me to come to yours, or would you rather come to mine?'

He hesitated. Her call had obviously thrown him. Perhaps he was feeling guilty about Julia? Not for long, she thought. Will was already en route to Wylde Court and the police had been informed.

'Let me deal with Blake,' she had begged Theona during the meeting when they read the printout of Vincent Gabor's chicanery. 'It doesn't seem that he knew what was going on, being too concerned about his own fame and fortune. Keep his name out of it and please, let me have him. He owes me one.'

'Well, if you're sure,' Theona had said doubtfully.

'Quite sure,' Arlene insisted, a calculating look of intent in her eyes.

'Must you?' Eugene asked, looking troubled. She knew him to be jealous, but nothing would shift her from her purpose.

'I must,' she said, slipping her arms around his neck. 'It's a matter of honour.'

'What are you up to?' Will wanted to know, though he was abstracted, already planning his Suffolk rescue operation.

'You'll see,' Arlene said, tapping the side of her nose mysteriously.

Now Marty Blake and she agreed that she should go to his apartment later that day. He seemed eager, intrigued, and she felt a hot itch within her when she recalled his spectacular good looks, his lean body, long legs and dark wavy hair. And she had only slightly exaggerated his development in the genital area; he had a most impressive cock.

His warehouse home was impressive, too. So this is one of the perks of being a famous dress designer, she thought, strolling through the wide hall and into the lounge with its polished teak floor and stylish chrome furniture upholstered in black leather. The few ornaments were the original works of well-known sculptors, as were the surreal paintings on the original brick walls. It breathed money, fame and fortune, and Arlene intended to have all three.

Blake led her outside. The garden was beautiful, filled with greenery, sunshine and birdsong. Though made safe by high wire fencing draped in flowering climbers, she found it hard to remember that they were several floors up, and that every ounce of earth, each plant and shrub, even the water feature had been placed there artificially, not by nature.

'Would you like a drink?' he asked, but she hadn't come there to exchange pleasantries over gin and tonics.

'I'd rather you showed me your bedroom,' she answered frankly, giving him an impish glance with her green eyes. She had practised this look, and found few men could resist.

'Didn't you want to talk about your work?' he said, but was already moving back inside. She could see the shape of his hardening cock within his baggy white cotton trousers.

Her nipples peaked and her clitoris thrummed. There was no denying that she still fancied him, unprincipled bastard though he was. She was fond of Eugene, might even make a go of it with him, but weren't the bad boys always the most exciting?

When they reached his bedroom her anger was still simmering dangerously, but she moved close and slipped her arms around him. His response was immediate, though he looked cautious. 'So, are you still accusing me of stealing your designs?' he asked.

'Oh, let's not talk about that,' she murmured seductively, and reached up to kiss him. It was as pleasant as she remembered; firm lips and an active tongue.

She could feel his cock, vertical against his belly, the stem pressing through her flimsy cotton frock. She had dressed herself for seduction - his, more than hers. His hand delved beneath the skirt, lifting it high and caressing her bare thigh and then her bottom crease. She started and raised her hips towards him as his fingers edged round the tiny tanga which barely covered her mons, then wormed their way between her dark bush and landed unerringly on her clitoris. Lust poured through her, making it hard to remember her purpose there.

She raised a leg and hooked it round his thigh, wriggling against the large bulge tenting his trousers. He responded by gyrating his pelvis, his hand going to her breasts, tweaking the nipples through the fine fabric, but even then his trade impinged as he said, 'This is cotton voile, isn't it? Did you make it?'

'Yes, and yes,' she replied, ready to yell with frustration as he continued that delicious manipulation.

Still holding her, he led her towards his bed. She felt the edge of the mattress against the backs of her knees. But she didn't intend to fall across it, legs wide, arms embracing him while he fucked her. Oh no, she had other plans for Mr Marty Blake.

'Lie down,' she commanded dominantly.

His eyes widened. 'What?'

'I said, lie down,' she repeated, implementing her words with a sharp rap across his tight muscled arse. The delicious feel of it was almost her undoing, but she hung on in there. 'You enjoy dishing it out, don't you? Well, how about if we experiment a little. I'll be tops to begin with and you'll be bottom.'

His face cleared, and he grinned boyishly. She tried to ignore the brilliant charm of him. 'Okay,' he said. 'I'm game if you are. Do we have a safe word?'

'Yes,' she said, testing him. 'Let's use *Incagold?*'

He looked genuinely surprised, and not in the least guilty. 'That's an odd one, but yes, I agree, though I'll bet you say it before I do.'

'You first,' she said, with a determination that stopped any argument.

Soon she had him where she wanted him, naked and spread on the bed, his arms and legs spread and tethered to the posts with silk scarves and belts she had found in the chest-of-drawers, and the glorious sight of him almost swayed her from her intentions. His body was so beautifully proportioned; wide shoulders and a muscular chest, a flat belly, a nest of dark curls and that magnificent cock rising stiffly upwards, his balls in their taut sac resting on the sheet between his thighs. He had an all-year-round tan, his skin contrasting with the snowy whiteness of the pillows.

She had retained one of the leather belts and suddenly brought it down with full force across his thighs.

'Bitch!' he yelped, his cock jerking, crimson marks forming on his sinewy flesh.

'Now, now, that's not the way to address Mistress Murphy,' she reproved and, just to remind him of her power, she flicked his helm with the belt. Pearly dew oozed from the single eye, and he groaned through gritted teeth.

She knew she was right. This wasn't the first time his passion had been roused through pain. Her control was slipping; she wanted to yield to temptation and have him penetrate her. First though, there were other things she must do.

Standing where he could see everything but was unable to touch, she undressed slowly and languidly. First her button-through dress, then her icing sugar-pink bra, though she took this off with the tantalising, cynical skill of a professional stripper using men's lusts to support herself and her dependants. She paused then, retaining her panties and high-heeled shoes. This had the desired effect on him and he writhed on the bed like a landed fish. He tugged at his bonds, swore at and cursed her. She smiled, enjoying seeing him roped there, helpless. It was unusual; he was always so confident and full of himself.

'I wonder what your fan club would make of you now?' she remarked. 'That American woman, Mrs Hooper-Jones. I thought she was going to have an orgasm when she spoke of you.'

Hooking her thumbs in the ties each side of her tanga, she partially pulled them down, giving him a glimpse of her crisp pubic hair. Then, disappointing him, she turned her back and shimmied towards the tallboy to find her supposition was correct. Inside one of the drawers was an array of sex-toys, almost as comprehensive as her own. She took them out, one by one. There were oriental eggs for anal or vaginal insertion, a mock plastic vagina, penis rings to delay orgasm, and several lifelike vibrators.

'By all the saints, Mr Blake,' she drawled. 'What a collection! It's nearly as large as mine.'

She stood close to the bed and dropped her panties, then placed one foot up on a chair, giving Blake an uninterrupted view of her cleft. She played the tip of the vibrator round her salmon pink inner lips and stroked it over the puckered anal mouth. Then she switched it on and held it against her clitoris. She gasped, coming in a rush, and Blake groaned with longing.

Returning from the blissful realms of orgasm, she snatched up the belt and belaboured him furiously. Stripes marred him from thighs to belly to chest. She even lashed him once across the veined length of his cock. He squealed, but didn't use the safe word.

'Climb on me, ride me, mistress,' he begged, and Arlene took up position astride his genitals, lowering herself and allowing the tip of his glans to brush over her wet quim, teasing him. 'Where is Julia?' she demanded.

'Wh-who?' he stammered unconvincingly.

'Julia!' she hissed viciously, reaching down and squeezed his testicles.

'I don't know!' he bleated, capitulating instantly. 'I promise you. She was at

Hazel House, but he's moved her.'

'Gabor, you mean?'

'Yes, that's right.' He was panting heavily with alarm and sweat glistened on his chest.

'And all this fuss because of my designs?'

'As far as I know,' he admitted. 'He's a dark horse and keeps his business affairs to himself.'

Arlene reached for the vibrator and wetted it at her delta, then trailed it over his body. She held the buzzing end to one of his nipples and he almost wept. 'God, you're a witch!' he wailed pathetically, increasing her contempt for him. 'What is it you want from me?'

'I need to find Julia.' She passed the vibrator across his scrotum, paused, holding him with a challenging stare, and then pressed it inexorably into his arse.

He jerked like a puppet on a string, his back arching off the bed. 'I've told you everything,' he wailed, his cock weeping milky tears.

The sight of it was too much for Arlene, and she was pretty certain he was speaking the truth; that he knew no more. She was confident Will was about to save Julia, and she could no longer deny herself, so keeping the dildo in place with one hand, she impaled herself on Marty Blake, writhing up and down, feeling the glorious sensation of his huge organ within her and the spreading vibrations from the thing embedded in his rear.

He came almost at once, and Julia only a few seconds later.

She sat back on his thighs with a sigh, her head slumped forward as she savoured the last spasms of her delicious orgasm.

'Take out the vibrator,' he panted, his chest heaving. 'I've had enough. I can't take any more.'

'And the safe word is...?'

'*Incagold*,' he breathed.

She'd beaten him on every issue and was empowered by the good feeling this evoked. But before she withdrew the sex-toy, she said, 'I want you to show me your atelier.'

'Anything, anything,' he panted, his cock stiffening again under the continual stimulation of the buzzing plastic deep in his bottom.

'And you'll take me into partnership,' she pressed. 'Do you agree?'

'Yes, I agree - now please turn that thing off!'

'Only if you promise not to rescind.'

'I do, I do. Arlene, mistress, don't torment me any more.'

Arlene swung a leg over him, reached down and flicked the switch, then pulled the dildo from within his rectum. 'Marty,' she said, smiling down at him and starting to unfasten his bonds. 'I think I can say that you've been well and truly shafted...

'Now, it's time to show me your studio. I need to see which part I'll take over for my own use.'

'Sir!' Grace shouted, hammering on the door of the master chamber. 'Mr Gabor, we've caught an intruder!'

Julia was already awake, her mind in a ferment. She sat up sharply as Gabor got out of bed and slipped into his trousers, sweater and sneakers. 'Bring him here,' he called, and then turned on Julia. 'Is this your doing? If it is you'll be sorry. Now stay where you are.'

Within a minute several of the guards crashed though the door, hauling Will in and then throwing him down at Gabor's feet. Grace had a revolver trained on him, and Jason stood in the background, looking uncomfortable.

'Julia, are you all right?' Will said, ignoring his captors and looking at her.

'Yes, but I want to go home, Will,' she said, her chin trembling with emotion at the sight of his familiar, ruggedly handsome face.

'I know—' he began, but was silenced by a vicious blow to the face, delivered by a hefty guard.

'How did you manage to track me down here?' Gabor raged. 'No one knows about Wylde Court. You may be a member of the press, but this smacks of something more. Internal espionage. Someone's been hacking into my computer. Who? Tell me. You'd better comply, or suffer intensely. My men are expert torturers and I'm determined to tear the truth out of you.'

'Do your worst,' Will said defiantly. 'You have no right to keep Julia here against her will.'

'Against her will?' Gabor echoed scornfully. 'I think not. You should have seen her performance last night. She couldn't get enough of me. Get out of bed, Julia, and let this cretin judge for himself if I'm speaking the truth or not.'

She obeyed, fearful for Will's well being, knowing that Gabor was capable of anything. She had dressed up as ordered, and it was like taking part in a fantastic play where everything was upside down and nothing like real life. She suspected that Gabor had laced her wine with an aphrodisiac, for it had seemed that she became the characters he demanded; the eighteenth century courtesan in powdered wing and hooped skirt; the blowsy Edwardian whore in a bustle, corsets, feather boa and wide-brimmed hat; the chambermaid in pink stays, black woollen stockings and cambric knickers with a wide slit in the crotch.

She was still wearing the latter, having fallen into an exhausted sleep without undressing again. The corset was laced very tightly, her breasts bulging over the top, displaying her pierced nipples. Long pink suspenders were clipped to the tops of her stockings that showed mid-thigh where her drawers ended. Somehow, during their sexual excesses, these had been torn, and the gusset, far from covering her, exposed her treasures, denuded mound and all. She stood there with her head down, cringing because Will would see it all and doubt her loyalty.

'Oh Julia,' he said dismally.

'Will, it's not what it seems,' she insisted desperately, daring to meet his eyes. 'I've been kept here by force. Please Will, take me home.'

'You're not going anywhere, my dear,' Gabor said icily. 'And neither is he. I'm afraid your friend has foolishly put himself in an untenable position. I can't possibly let him go, and shall give orders for his demise. As for you? A sojourn in one of my foreign establishments will suffice - for the time being.'

'You won't get away with it,' Will warned, and Julia's heart bled as she saw his bruised eye and cut lip.

'Won't I?' Gabor sneered, and Grace handed him his riding crop. 'Bend over, sweet Julia.'

Oh, Julia was mortified, not wanting Will to witness such things. But Gabor pulled down her knickers and had her present her buttocks so that no one could miss seeing the perfect globes, marked with last night's whipping.

She gasped and could hardly maintain her subservient pose as the crop struck, welting her already bruised bottom. He laid them on cruelly and precisely, forming a vivid criss-crossed ladder over the fleshy area. Then he flung the crop at Grace and pointed at Will. 'Beat him if you want, then lock him up! I'm sick of the sight of him already. I'm hungry, and I want my breakfast!'

Julia cried when Will was hustled away. 'Please say you won't harm him,' she begged.

Gabor bit into a slice of toast from the tray of steaming food and eyed her with scorn. 'Why should I not?' he provoked. 'He's a busybody who should have kept out of my affairs. He'll get what's due to him.'

Carrying his coffee cup, he paced to the window that overlooked the front. One of the shutters was open a crack. Julia saw him stiffen, and then he spun round, slammed the cup on the table, and grabbed her by the arm.

'What is it?' she shouted.

'Police cars.'

He snatched up his jacket, barked a crisp order into his mobile, and then dragged her towards the fireplace. He pressed a carved rose and an aperture swung open, emitting a dark odour. Without giving her time to think he shoved her in and switched on a flashlight. Steps and more steps, dripping walls and a passage that led into further blackness.

'W-where are we going?' she managed to shriek.

'To freedom,' he said. 'A helicopter is waiting for us in a field at the back.'

'Us?' She was too shocked to think straight.

'Of course. You're coming with me, Julia. To France, and then Rio. I have friends who will help me.'

'But—'

'No buts - I've decided. I could leave you down here to rot where nobody would ever find you, but I want you too much.'

There was no answer to this, but everything within her was rebelling. His grip on her was unbreakable, but when they broke cover, climbing up into the daylight and arriving at a small mock Greek temple, she fought with renewed vigour.

'No!' she cried. 'Let me go. I don't want to go with you!'

Just then Grace appeared from the trees, dressed for action in her combat gear, a gun in her hand. In the distance Julia could see the helicopter, its blades rotating rapidly. Then Gabor was running towards it and she couldn't get away, dragged along behind him.

'Leave her, sir!' Grace shouted, above the increasing rhythmic beat of the blades and the mini storm they stirred up. 'She's holding us up!' Then Julia felt a stunning blow as Grace hit her. The field spun and she collapsed on the grass. She heard the sharp staccato of shots, saw Grace firing behind her as she ran, saw men chasing her then stopping as she fired repeatedly. Then Gabor was in the chopper, holding out a hand to Grace. She jumped aboard. The aircraft began to lift, and still Grace fired from the open cockpit.

Julia saw Will fall and, screaming his name, scrambled to her feet and ran towards him as the helicopter rose and disappeared into the clouds.

'What a story!' Denise exclaimed, as they sat round Will's bed. 'And thank goodness you're all right.'

'That's another of my nine lives gone,' he joked, but he was ashen-faced. One of Grace's bullets had winged him in the shoulder. Surgery had been necessary, and the police had taken him to the nearest hospital. After surgery, an ambulance shipped him to a private clinic in London, courtesy of *Hi Life*.

'They'll have a hard job catching him, even through Interpol,' Eugene said, his fingers linked with Arlene's. 'No one will talk. All his people profess his innocence, but we know different. He'll hardly suffer, either. His empire will go on, supplying him with money.'

'He'll make a mistake one day,' said Will, and reached across the coverlet to stroke Julia's arm. 'The undercover agents won't give up.'

Julia was so proud of him, and proud that everyone could see how much he cared for her. He would recover quickly and then she'd take him home to recuperate. She lingered by his bed when the others had gone, and he patted the mattress beside him. 'Come here,' he said.

'What is it, Will?'

'I've never made love to you,' he said, and he was smiling. 'Hop in beside me.'

'I can't,' she said, blushing. 'What about the nurses? Anyway, you've got a bad shoulder.'

'I'll manage,' he chuckled. 'I'm not talking full-blown coitus here, but I'd love to hold you for a while.'

The idea was most tempting and she slid under the sheet. He kissed her lingeringly, then wrinkled up her miniskirt, found her panties and eased them aside. She came in seconds, clinging to him with her arms around his neck. 'Oh, Will... Will...' she murmured against his throat.

'And when I leave here, which should be tomorrow, I'll expect you to return the favour,' he said huskily.

'Of course I will,' she promised, and then wriggled off the bed. 'I'll come and fetch you as soon as the doctors give you the all clear.'

She drove home in a reflective mood. The magazine had promoted her. Arlene was getting on well with Marty and had retrieved her designs. She was planning to move in with Eugene, so there would be plenty of room in Julia's house if Will needed to be looked after for a while. She liked him a lot, but wasn't ready for a commitment.

She and Denise had been discussing plans for Julia's next assignment. The world was opening up before her and she anticipated more adventures looming on the horizon where she could satisfy her endless quest for excitement. She thought of Vincent Gabor, and as she waited at a set of traffic lights, she instinctively slipped a hand down between her thighs and touched her damp panties. He had been so dangerous, so sexy, and so compelling. For some reason, just to think of him made her chest tighten with excitement. Who could say whether they would ever meet again, but she sincerely hoped so. Perhaps without realising it he had taught her so much, turning her from a naive junior reporter into a young woman who knew what she wanted - and how to get it.

Also by Roxane Beaufort and available to order
as paperbacks at AMAZON
Devil's Paradise
Fate's Victim
Foxy Lady
Forever Chained
Memoirs of a Courtesan
Rebel Girl
Savage Bonds
Schooling Sylvia
Stranger in Venice
Strictly Discipline